Screams began to sound within the Reliance audience, and she finally noticed the war waging above the Dome. Soldiers fell left and right, their blasters and pulse guns no match for the airborne ships and their firepower.

One of the smaller salvage ships in the group, more heavily armored than the others, broke away from the fracas and aimed a laser at the Dome. The beam collided with the structure's projector, blowing it to smithereens. The hardlight projection around them flickered before disappearing completely.

They were free.

Shots fired around her from both sides, but Finn only had eyes for the chancellor. He stood near his seat, surrounded by a large group of soldiers protecting him. He yelled orders at them above the fray and darted panicked eyes around the arena.

Finn tightened her grip on the dagger and walked in his direction. She ignored the lasers and blasts firing all around her, waiting for the chancellor to spot her. A stray shot pierced her shoulder, but Finn barely flinched. She barely even felt it.

"Finn!"

She turned to see a small pod had landed several feet away, and found Conrad staring at her. His dreads were tied away from his face and his jaw was set with anger. His blue eyes scanned first the bloody dagger in her hand, then the blood and carnage covering her face and upper body. She watched, impassive, as his familiar azure gaze widened with horror.

DISOBEDIENCE

Also by Kaitlyn Andersen

Reliance

DISOBEDIENCE

Book Two of the
Reliance Trilogy

Kaitlyn Andersen

Heliosphere®
BOOKS
San Diego

DISOBEDIENCE
Book Two of the Reliance Trilogy
Heliosphere Books®

Copyright © 2021 by Kaitlyn Andersen
Published by arrangement with the author.

Library of Congress Cataloging-in-Publication Data

Names: Andersen, Kaitlyn, 1986- author.
Title: Disobedience / Kaitlyn Andersen.

Description: San Diego : Heliosphere Books, [2021] | Series: The Reliance
trilogy ; book 2 | Summary: "Finn No Last Name has fled her crewmates aboard
Independence, after discovering that she'd been betrayed by the person she
trusted most. Now on her own, she searches for other hybrids like her, with
powers she can only imagine. That search brings her to Enyo, a Sirian warrior
who has been a captive of the Reliance for years. Finally free, she is more than
eager to join Finn on her mission to locate and free more hybrids. But that
search brings her back to Independence, whether she likes it or not. And back
to Conrad whom she is starting to realize has feelings for her she can't quite
fathom. And to Iliana, her long-lost sister, whose breach of trust left Finn feeling
even more alone than she had when she thought Iliana dead. With Enyo and
AJ in tow, Finn goes on a mission to locate and free other hybrids, only to find
herself caught up in the twisted games held in the Dome, the Reliance's coliseum.
What had been an undercover operation has now become a true battle between
life and death, in front of an audience of thousands"-- Provided by publisher.

Identifiers: LCCN 2020057216 (print) | LCCN 2020057217
(ebook) | ISBN 9781937868741 (trade paperback) | ISBN
9781937868826 (epub) | ISBN 9781937868833 (kindle edition)

Subjects: GSAFD: Science fiction.

Classification: LCC PS3601.N436 D57 2021 (print) |
LCC PS3601.N436 (ebook) | DDC 813/.6--dc23

LC record available at https://lccn.loc.gov/2020057216
LC ebook record available at https://lccn.loc.gov/2020057217

ISBN-13: 978-1-937868-74-1 (trade paperback)
ISBN-13: 978-1-937868-82-6 (EPUB)
ISBN-13: 978-1-937868-83-3 (Kindle)

Cover design by chrisodesign.com

Sky image by Neida Karate via Unsplash; Man image by Dallas Wade via Unsplash;
City image by 3000a via Shutterstock; Planets image by Algol via Shutterstock

Heliosphere Books are published by Endpapers Press,
a division of Author Coach, LLC.

Heliosphere Books is a registered trademark of Author Coach, LLC.

For Jack, the slayer of all my dragons.

ONE

Finn No Last Name stepped out of the shadowed alcove shielding her from view. With her red velvet cape covering her dark auburn waves, elbow-length gloves, and copper-colored, high-collared silk shirt, she blended seamlessly with the other citizens of the Reliance.

The population on Arcturus nearly exceeded 4.7 billion. In their midst, she floated by like a drop of water in a vast sea. After spending endless cycles too terrified to return to the Inner Rings, Finn now found it more than a little exhilarating to discover how utterly invisible she was.

She wondered what Grim would say if he could see her now.

Grim, who had raised her from feral child with no memories to competent thief. The giant Khaleerian who had served as her mentor and closest ally for countless cycles was a complete stranger to her now.

Not just a stranger . . . the Luminary.

Only a month ago, he'd sent her on a farce of a mission to retrieve a stolen Khaleerian locket. All too eager to please him, Finn had left behind the Mud Pit—the only home she'd ever known—to pursue an upper-caste courtesan.

An upper-caste courtesan who had turned out to be Finn's long-lost older sister, Iliana.

An older sister she hadn't been too keen to see again.

With that jolt of a reminder of her past, Finn's memories had come flooding back and, in a matter of days, she'd wound up changing the course of her very existence.

What I wouldn't give for a time machine, she mused darkly.

Her pursuit of Iliana had led her to Captain Shane Montgomery and *Independence*, a ship full to bursting with alien/human half-breeds, each one sporting their own unique set of special abilities.

The *blended*, as Shane Montgomery called them, were considered persona non grata by the Reliance and their Arcturian forefathers, who had spent the better part of the last century peddling negative propaganda and hunting the half-breeds to the point of extinction.

Naturally, Finn was more than a little surprised to find a ship full of them.

The blended.

Finn grimaced at Shane's flowery word for the persecuted race. She supposed it was better than half-breed, but she couldn't bring herself to use it with any real frequency. She preferred a more scientific approach . . . hybrids.

In a matter of days, Shane and his hybrid crew had flipped Finn's world on its head. One of the many lies they had told during her brief stay on *Independence* came undone when she realized the job they were pulling for a Farthers middle-man, the Toad, was really just their cover for stealing a list of the hybrids being held in Reliance captivity.

Worst of all, they had committed this theft for their almighty leader—the enigmatic Luminary—whose identity they had sworn to protect.

But the crew hadn't been finished turning Finn's life upside down. Not only was the Reliance holding groups of hybrids captive—rather than executing them as their propaganda would have the worlds believe—Finn and her sister, Iliana, were also hybrids themselves.

Thanks to their alien mother, both women could steal the memories of others with a mere touch.

When the mysterious Luminary and orchestrator of chaos had turned out to be none other than Grim, Finn had swallowed about as much betrayal as she could take, stealing an escape pod and leaving *Independence* and its crew of liars in the dust.

As Finn made her way past sweeping glass skyscrapers and countless holojectors flashing images of smiling socialites and streets lined in gold, her eyes remained focused on the planet's two tallest towers and the giant Arcturian eye nestled between their peaks.

The headquarters for Arcturus's hand-selected, cream-of-the-crop council was nearly impenetrable. Trying to break through its security to rescue the hybrid inside would be considered a suicide mission by even the most capable of thieves.

A heaviness settled in Finn's chest, sadness spreading from its center.

Two hybrids were imprisoned on Arcturus: One in James Jessup's sprawling countryside manor, the other within the heavily guarded confines of the Council Headquarters' domed building.

Finn would only make it off this planet with one.

It wasn't so much that she feared death. The strange sense of resolve she'd found on the Mud Pit's streets after fleeing *Independence* so many weeks ago made such worries seem inconsequential.

However, the cold fact remained, Finn couldn't help anyone if she was dead.

Now, the time had come to face the hard truth she'd been avoiding. The truth she'd known the moment she realized one of the captive hybrids was imprisoned within those impassable walls.

I can still save one.

She repeated the sentence over and over in her mind, rubbing away the ache just below her sternum as she continued down the busy street, all the while taking care to avoid eye contact with the upper-caste passersby as she went.

More heavily guarded than any other Inner Rings planet, Arcturus was populated by the most important, influential members of the Reliance upper caste and Finn planned to steal a hybrid right out from under their haughty noses.

Maybe her newfound detachment wasn't purpose.

Maybe it was insanity.

When she'd found James Jessup, the puritanical leader of the Union of the Planets' largest house of Arcturian worship, her first day on planet, it had only taken one look for all thoughts of indecision to flee her mind.

She had watched him for days as he'd casually strolled between the four Houses of Arcturian Disciples wearing his unassuming burgundy robes, surrounded by half a dozen Reliance soldiers serving as his personal guard. A golden ring with a ruby centerpiece and a tattoo of an eye marking the center of his forehead were his only adornments.

People stopped him on the streets everywhere he went to request blessings and prayers on their behalf. He always obliged, his carefully masked features the picture of tranquility. Some of the more dramatic members of the upper castes cried freely when his ringed hand rested atop their heads and his eyes closed in prayers of benediction.

His humble demeanor only made Finn loathe him more, because she knew something the rest of them didn't: Jessup held a hybrid captive somewhere on planet.

A hybrid she intended to find. She would not leave Arcturus until she had robbed him of his prized possession.

It would have been easy to lose him in the ever-changing tide of red and gold, as the upper crust of the Reliance hustled and bustled between glass-plated skyscrapers. She'd noticed from her trips to Inner Rings planets that the Arcturians and their Reliance followers had an overzealous admiration of the ancient Romans of Earth. Finn had spent enough time pouring over Grim's contraband books to recognize the obvious homage in everything from mosaics and fountains to the purely aesthetic aqueducts feeding water to the synthetic gardens.

The way the upper-caste citizens carelessly meandered through their sprawling metropolis, spending the gold the lower castes broke their backs for, nearly penetrated Finn's wall of calculated dispassion.

She kept to the shadows, never letting Jessup stray too far from her line of sight. Each day, when the three suns of Arcturus rose, she followed and she watched, learning his routes and routines.

The longer she followed, the more she witnessed.

Each day Arcturus's masses held countless public feasts and extravagant buffets with enough food to feed the entirety of the Outer Rings making up the Farthers for a whole cycle. Each meal was heralded first by a prayer to the Gods, then to the Arcturians. Small statues of their alien forefathers—complete with golden skin and ruby red eyes—adorned each table. As it turned out, the upper castes prayed to the Gods and the forefathers in equal measure.

Seeing their sickening idolization of the golden prigs up close and with such brutal relentlessness had threatened to tip Finn over the edge.

On the Mud Pit, she'd worried that a life of peace stood out of her reach because of all that her time on Shane Montgomery's ship had revealed. Now, she knew it without a doubt: Finn would never be able to block out the images of the things she'd seen here.

No matter how hard she tried.

A body slammed into her . . . hard, distracting her from her thoughts, and she caught herself before the force sent her to the ground. Strong hands grasped Finn's gloved arms above the elbows, steadying her.

She glanced up at the senior-ranking officer from Jessup's Reliance guard, his barrel chest bursting the seams of his deep red jacket.

She pretended to blush, slipping a hand into the pocket of her burgundy trousers.

He barely gave Finn's bashful act a cursory glance, before letting her go and moving away with a stern, "Pardon me, madam."

"I am terribly sorry, Major."

With a curt nod at her apology, he moved off to join the other guards surrounding James Jessup as he made his way through the crowds of the admiring masses. Finn trailed them at a safe distance, pretending to be one of his marveling followers.

On and on he walked, the crowds thinning the farther away from the city center he went. Gradually, she separated herself, ducking into the shadows and pausing around corners. Soon, the guards reached a sleek, convertible golden pod with the top rolled back, a thick glass dome protecting the opening, and affixed to four outdated rubber wheels, giving it the appearance of an oversized Roman chariot.

This particular transport stretched long enough to fit ten men inside comfortably. The soldiers hastily ushered Jessup in.

Once they'd gotten their precious cargo settled, the major called out an order to the six synthetic horses attached to the strange chariot-pod hybrid by an assortment of rainbow-colored wires.

The pod was more than capable of operating on its own, but Finn had learned that Jessup—like so many other members of the Reliance—leaned toward the flamboyantly unnecessary when it came to their methods of travel. Red eyes flickered open and iron hooves began to shift as their inner mechanics whirred to life.

Trailing behind the giant beasts as they sped off into the distance, Finn jogged at a brisk pace. Together, they traversed five kilometers of rocky terrain, the steady rhythm keeping Finn at a healthy distance. After the fourth kilometer, she finally began to feel winded, but urged her tired legs to keep stride, knowing they would soon reach their destination.

Moments later, the chariot stopped. Finn slowed her steps, breaking through a grouping of synthetic cherry trees just in time to watch the horses pass through massive iron gates. Moving with silent steps past rows and rows of blooming hedges, her eyes tracked Jessup as his guards led him past the towering stone walls surrounding his four-story manor.

Everything looked calm . . . as it had the last two times she'd followed him home.

Finn reached into the pocket of her trousers and fingered the ID chip she'd swiped from the major.

Tonight, Jessup would regret his callous arrogance.

TWO

As darkness fell, Finn remained crouched behind the same bush, sizing up every inch of Jessup's forbidding manor. The manufactured, sickly-sweet scent of synthetic blossoms filled her nostrils and she struggled not to sneeze at the effect. The moons were distant tonight and darkness shadowed the property, making Jessup's pristine home stand out amidst the obscurity.

Several thick, white pillars supported the building's massive structure.

Perfect for masking her approach.

Finn slid the cloak from her shoulders and folded it up tightly, tucking it into one of the zippered compartments on her belt. She tightened the auburn ponytail at the top of her crown. Clutching the ID chip in a gloved palm, she hunched down low and ran for the gates, jumping, weaving, and zigzagging as she went.

Thanks to her previous visits to observe the manor and its security, she had managed to make it there without tripping any of the motion sensor spheres strategically floating within the foliage of nearby trees.

The chip glided easily into the security console attached to the gates, flashing green before she heard the groan of iron as they opened wide. She stepped inside but remained on the outer perimeter of the property, as close to the stone walls as her body would allow.

Two guards patrolled Jessup's gardens on the south side of the estate, their voices carrying to her as they joked with one another.

Letting the shadows hide her, Finn waited for them to pass, then resumed her routine of dodging, weaving, and bobbing as she avoided more motion sensors spread throughout the grounds.

Under a veil of passing clouds that dimmed the light of Arcturus's three moons, she sprinted the final six meters to the servants' entrance around the side of the house, using the chip to once again gain entry.

Quiet greeted her inside.

The shadow of a servant passed by the kitchens and Finn ducked behind the cover of a glittering gold-dusted countertop to watch the woman pass.

The servant's uniform of burgundy pants and copper top perfectly matched Finn's, making the need to hide a moot one. She'd learned from the last few days of surveying Jessup's manor that he had an abundance of servants attending to his every need. The fact that they were all required to wear the same monotonous (by Arcturian standards, anyway) garb, day in and day out, only made Finn's infiltration that much easier.

The manor's layout flashed in her mind like a virtual map—a trick she'd only recently learned to attribute to her hybrid genetics.

Through direct contact, Finn had the power to see and share the memories of others, imprint maps and layouts, and a host of other things she'd yet to learn. The extent of her abilities remained a mystery. She knew they came from her mother, but she'd decided it was better to ignore thoughts related to her mother, her hybrid status, and how she'd found out about it. Those thoughts only led to more painful ones, ones that involved Finn's sister . . . and other people she was better off forgetting.

Following her instincts, and with images of the layout flashing behind her lids, Finn made her way down a narrow hallway to the cellar. The red door that greeted her screamed restricted access, just as she'd expected.

She pulled the stolen ID chip out once again and took a breath, then ran it over the scanner just above the door's handle. The light above the small box flashed green and the lock clicked.

Finn paused. It just figured she'd end up with a half-Sirian for her first rescue attempt. In her limited experience with the race—which included a recent run-in at a Reliance ball—she knew Sirians to be vicious, aggressive, and more like feral canines than reasoning, logical adults. It was the reason they made such perfect soldiers for the Reliance Guard.

Taking one last cautious look around, she hauled open the door as quietly as possible and slipped inside. The darkness that greeted her within the cellar was eerily silent as she descended the stone staircase, her breathing and soft footsteps the only sounds to be heard.

As she made her way down, she began to see the outline of a large cage taking up most of the cellar's limited space, its bars running from floor to ceiling. At the sight, Finn fought back a wave of foreboding.

Reaching the bottom, she approached it with caution. Surprise furrowed Finn's brow. For all her expectations, she certainly wasn't prepared for the sight that greeted her, or for the very female body lying prone on the cage's floor.

The half-Sirian lay on her stomach next to a pool of what Finn assumed was her own vomit. Given her position facedown on the ground, it was hard to see much of her, other than the unique cascade of thick caramel, blonde, and red waves of hair shrouding her face from sight.

Worried now for the female's condition, Finn ran the ID chip over the scanner mounted to the cage's door and, as soon as it unlocked, pulled the heavy bars open with as much silent haste as she could manage. She moved with quiet steps, anxious to make sure the female still breathed. Finn's hands made it to within an inch of her before the sounds of clanking at the Sirian's feet froze her on the spot.

Suddenly, the much taller and more muscular hybrid was up and in her space. The female's surprisingly strong forearm pushed into Finn's neck, pinning her against the wall. A pair of clear, tawny eyes filled with hatred looked into hers.

"Come to gawk and look your fill?"

The lilt in her throaty voice was certainly a surprise, but Finn's eyes couldn't help but remain focused on the rows of tiny, pointed fangs filling the female's mouth. She could almost have passed for a human were it not for those razor-sharp incisors.

Finn realized, belatedly and with no small amount of surprise, that the Sirian was quite pretty . . . especially with that long multicolored hair.

A layer of short, tan fur covered her lean body and face, but she lacked the characteristic pointed ears, long snout, and bushy tail one might see on a full-blooded Sirian.

Now that she'd stood, Finn had a clear, unabashed view of her curves; the ragged shirt and shorts she wore barely doing the job of covering her body. She tracked the direction of Finn's gaze and her eyes narrowed in calculation. With a stare exempt of shame or embarrassment, she moved her free hand up to Finn's face. Five black claws began to lengthen and grow, only stopping when they made contact with Finn's pale cheek.

That's new. She'd never seen a Sirian do *that* before.

"Or perhaps you've come to *touch*," the hybrid growled, pulling Finn from her thoughts.

Glancing over to the barred door she'd left open, Finn listened intently for the sound of approaching bootsteps. When only silence greeted her, she turned back to the Sirian. She held the female's stare as she threw an arm up and over the fur-covered forearm at her neck.

Using the momentum, Finn's elbow slammed down hard. The Sirian stumbled, lost her footing, and flew backward; her chains tangled around her four-toed feet as she began to fall.

Finn's gloved hand shot out and caught the falling woman by the arm. Ignoring the Sirian's ferocious growl, she hauled the large female against the barred cage in a hold almost identical to the one Finn had just been in.

A feral snarl slipped past her full lips, her unsheathed claws grasping Finn's gloved forearm hard enough to draw blood. Her glinting eyes watched closely for signs of pain, but Finn kept her face neutral, despite the burning and the growing bloodstain on her sleeve.

Finn forced a grim smile through the pain. "Actually, I'm here to rescue you."

She saw surprise flash in the yellow depths of the hybrid's eyes—far too intelligent for any regular Sirian—before they hardened once again with anger.

"You're strong, but it won't save you." She peeled back her lips in a horrifying mockery of a smile. "I am a champion . . . the greatest *N'Goza* in my tribe. Were I not reduced to *this*"—she snapped her jaws so close to Finn's face, it was an effort not to flinch—"I would bring this manor and everyone in it to their knees."

Her powerful body began to thrash, but Finn didn't ease the pressure. Instead, she removed the ID chip from her pocket and held it up for the Sirian to see.

"I'm going to hold you to that. At the rate we're going, the whole manor should be down here shortly." Narrowed eyes snapped to Finn's, something like hope warring with the pain and fury in them. Finn met her stare unflinchingly. "I meant what I said. I'm here to rescue you, but the longer you fight me, the more you risk our chances of getting caught."

She took the female's silence as a positive sign she wouldn't lose a finger or some other valuable extremity to those claws and fangs. Finn released the pressure against her neck and knelt before the Sirian, examining the chains around her ankles. The skin beneath looked raw and ragged, and Finn sucked in a breath at the familiar sight.

"If you don't have the stomach for something so trivial," the hybrid mused, "I can't wait to see how you intend to pull off this rescue attempt."

Biting back a growl of her own, Finn glared at the Sirian and mumbled under her breath.

"I should've rescued the other hybrid, I'm sure *he* would've been more gracious."

The Sirian's body stilled and the air around her pulsed with looming danger.

"What other hybrid?"

Finn reached into the holster at her ankle and removed a small, handheld plasma gun courtesy of the Mud Pit's black market.

"We don't have time for this," Finn murmured. "Once I get you out of here, we can talk all about the other hybrids being held prisoner. Right now, we need to get to the pod I have waiting to take you far away from here. Now, hold still."

The Sirian's eyes widened and then narrowed into frightening slits. With steady hands, Finn aimed the plasma gun and burned through the locks at the hybrid's feet. They released and fell to the floor with a loud clank.

When the Sirian remained motionless, Finn looked up to find her staring, her face devoid of the bitter rage that had filled it moments before.

It made her look painfully young.

When she finally spoke, her voice was hoarse.

"You really intend to free me?"

Finn rolled her eyes and stood up.

"That's what I've been saying, isn't it?"

"Even though I could very well kill you as soon as the chains are removed?"

Finn smiled wide and gave the plasma gun a pointed look.

"You can give it your best shot, but I think I can take you."

Her claws lengthened once again—a full inch this time— but not before Finn caught the smile in her unique eyes.

She set to work on the wrists, keeping up a steady dialogue as she did in a bid to distract the female.

"So, what should I call you?"

"Are we to make small talk then, *N'Goza*?"

N'Goza? There was that strange word again. Finn shot her a confused shrug.

"Sorry, my Sirian's a little rusty."

The hybrid had the audacity to click her tongue in vexation.

"I suppose the closest translation to your tongue would be *warrior*."

Finn presumed she should be flattered, but it didn't stop her from rolling her eyes.

The chains around the Sirian's wrists came crashing to the ground and Finn heard a sigh of relief the female couldn't quite hide. Finn holstered the plasma gun and pulled the cloak from where she'd tucked it into her belt. She moved to wrap it around the hybrid, but before she got close, the Sirian hissed and crouched into a defensive position against the wall. Finn eyed her carefully, showing her with slow, deliberate movements what she intended to do. The Sirian continued to glare but didn't shrink away. Once covered, she wrapped her arms around herself and huffed.

"My name is Enyo."

"How old are you, Enyo?"

"I was fourteen when they took me from my home. I have no way of telling time here. I used to carve marks in the walls, but I stopped long ago."

She looked to be about nineteen or twenty, but the hardness in her eyes made her seem older. Finn motioned with both hands for her to pull the hood of the cloak up and over her head. She did, and Finn found her willingness to cooperate both surprising and pleasing. The cloak covered her from scalp to feet, shadowing her face and most of that unique mane of alternating shades.

"Are you ready to get out of here?" she asked Enyo with a wink.

The woman bared her fangs and nodded.

"If you want to make it out of here alive, I need you to follow me and do everything I say," Finn told her with authority.

Enyo's eyes burned with rage at the command, but she didn't object. It would seem this Sirian was the type of warrior who didn't enjoy taking orders but could do so when necessary.

Thank the Gods for that.

Finn took the lead, creeping through the barred doors of the stone cell. Enyo followed, equally silent, and Finn smiled to herself, already impressed with the female's stealth. They moved in time together, their silent steps mirroring each other until they reached the top of the stairs.

Lifting her shirt, Finn pulled out a compact, short-handled blade from where she'd strapped it to her stomach. Enyo raised a multihued brow, but didn't comment, her claws elongating even farther until each hand became like its own set of black-tipped blades.

Finn wondered at the Sirian's strange control over her claws; it must have been a uniquely *hybrid* perk. Finn raised a finger to her lips, giving Enyo the signal to remain silent, and proceeded to open the door a fraction at a time. She stuck her head out and peeked around. Once she saw the coast was clear, she motioned for Enyo to follow.

They crept together through the kitchen, slowly making their way to the exit. She sensed the moment Enyo's steps slowed and turned back to find her staring in awe at the opulence of Jessup's manor, from gold-dusted countertops, tile, doorframes, and crystal chandeliers, to red satin drapes adorning the windows. Fury sparked in her eyes once again. Finn's stomach dropped, and she moved to get into Enyo's space, her nose barely reaching the Sirian's chin.

"You don't like what you see? You want to do something about it?" Enyo's tawny eyes shot fire down at Finn as she continued to speak. "The only way you're going make that happen is if we get the hell out of here."

The hybrid inhaled a deep breath, her eyes small slits and her jaw clenched, but she gave a tight nod. Finn figured it was the most acknowledgement she was going to get. Suppressing a relieved sigh, she turned her back on the Sirian and directed her to the servant's entrance leading outside.

They'd just made it past the second set of motion sensors—albeit much more slowly with the Sirian in tow—taking as much time as their racing heartbeats would allow so Enyo could mirror Finn's movements, when a voice stopped them in their tracks.

"You there. What do you two think you're doing?"

Finn turned, stepping in front of Enyo as a beam of light emanating from the comm device around the wrist of a patrolling Reliance soldier washed over them. Fortunately, he was far enough away that he missed Enyo's hiss of aggression, but he was closing in fast. Finn slipped the knife up her sleeve and threw her hand over her eyes to stem the brightness.

"My sister is sick, sir," she called to the soldier, distress lacing her tone. "She needs a doctor."

The soldier's steps slowed, most likely worried about exposing himself to whatever disease her "sister" was carrying. His arm moved and it looked like he might be reaching for his comm. It was hard to tell with the light hitting her square in the face, but she couldn't risk him calling more soldiers to their location. Letting the knife drop into her hand, Finn pulled back with her wrist and released, watching as the blade sailed across the distance and sank into the soldier's comm device.

She moved to run at him but froze, shocked as Enyo loped on all fours straight for the man, her movements faster than Finn could track. She'd removed her cloak, her long hair in all its shades now in full view. The soldier seemed transfixed, wide-eyed as he watched her lithe body make its way toward him with the smooth, precise movements of a predator.

When she reached him, there was a blur of movement, and then Enyo was on top of him, those deadly knifelike claws slashing into his throat and chest with a sickening gurgle. The man didn't even have time to scream.

Claws receded and finished with her kill, Enyo strolled back to Finn's side, wiping the blood and gore from her hands and body with the discarded cloak.

"Are we leaving, *N'Goza?*" she asked, as though they were discussing the weather.

Finn finally snapped out of her stupor enough to fume, "What was that? We don't kill people unless we have to."

The Sirian had the temerity to laugh.

"I do."

Finn did her best to ignore the fingertips still partially caked in the soldier's blood. Her eyes narrowed on Enyo and she took a threatening step forward.

"Not anymore. You're part of *my* crew now. We do things my way, and my way is . . . *we don't kill people unless absolutely necessary.*"

Enyo regarded her impassively for a moment before responding.

"Did you truly expect to secure our freedom without a few meager fatalities?"

Lights went on around the first floor, the activity making Finn's skin prickle.

"We don't have time to argue about it. If you're coming with me, you need to promise me you will exercise a little control and you *will* follow my rules. Understood?"

A war waged behind the Sirian's eyes. After a beat, she seemed to come to a decision. "Get me out of here and I will not *kill* anyone until we've had a chance to speak on this further."

Finn puffed out a groan at the carefully placed emphasis and all it implied, imagining Enyo leaving a slew of maimed and moaning soldiers in her wake. Finally, she gave the Sirian a sharp nod. She figured a win was win, even if it was only half of one.

THREE
_____

O nce they'd sprinted the two kilometers to the rendezvous
point, Finn all but shoved Enyo into the awaiting luxury
pod. Nova, a Mud Pit doxie before she chose to join Finn
on her mission, sat behind the controls, her back to them as
one scarred, bony leg dangled over the side of a flight chair and
she gnawed on a hunk of fresh bread. Without even bothering
to turn around, she tossed the veiled hat from her head to the
ground and called, "Can I change yet? These clothes are itchy."

Finn had forced her to wear the ostentatious hat with a veil
and a long-sleeved garnet dress with a tulle hoop skirt and
high collar, just in case any wandering soldiers decided to
have a look inside and question her. The doxie had squawked
like an Inner Rings meadow bird when she put them on,
much more at home in something a little less *constraining*.

"Not yet," Finn called. "Did we have any visitors?"

"Nope, I was actually starting to get lonely." Nova finally
turned, her cheeks filled with the bite she'd just taken. She
nearly choked when her wide eyes caught sight of Enyo.
"Holy Gods," she whispered.

Finn shot a warning glare at Nova and the crumbs falling from
her mouth in a cascade, but she was too busy gawking at the Sirian
to notice. An unholy rumble began to emit from Enyo's chest at
all the attention. Nova's eyes shot even wider at the sound and
she finally looked to Finn, swallowing her bread with a loud gulp.

"Nova, this is Enyo. She'll be joining our crew." Finn
turned to the Sirian. "Enyo, this is Nova. She's been instrumental in your rescue, so play nice."

Enyo examined Nova from top to toe; taking a few extra moments to linger on the doxie's newly revealed crater pox scars and lanky brown hair, her wary gaze clearly finding the woman wanting.

"How was *she* instrumental in my rescue?"

"*She* is going to fly us out of here . . . without crashing. Right, Nova?"

Nova blinked at Finn's question and offered them both a wobbly smile. "I'm getting much better," she told the Sirian breathlessly. And she was, considering she now only managed to crash into something thirty-five percent of the time as opposed to the whopping eighty-five percent when they'd first purchased the pod. Turning back to Finn, she flashed a smirk. "We'll get out of here as soon as we settle the small matter of my payment."

Of course. She'd almost forgotten in all the excitement.

Finn moved from the cockpit to the connecting bedroom within the depths of the designer pod. It was built to make long trips as comfortable as possible for the upper castes and had three rooms connecting to the cockpit as well as two bathrooms. The layout was more like a small ship than a pod, but by Reliance standards, Finn supposed it wasn't nearly spacious enough to earn that title.

Finn headed for the lockbox she kept inside the false bottom of her dresser and grabbed the key she wore around her neck to unlock it. Pulling out two gold coins from her dwindling stash, she returned and flicked them at Nova. The doxie caught one coin in each hand and shoved them inside the top of her dress.

"All right then, ladies," Nova exclaimed. "Let's get out of here."

Finn felt and ignored the Sirian's eyes burning meteor-sized holes into the back of her skull. When they broke orbit, Enyo finally interrupted the silence.

"You have to pay your crew for their loyalty?'

Finn snorted and shot the Sirian an amused smirk.

"I was a little short on time and crew." She turned fully and her smirk became a hard stare. "I kind of had to put things together in a pinch. See, I had this Sirian hybrid I was trying to rescue from a life of imprisonment."

Something flashed in Enyo's eyes and her shoulders sagged infinitesimally.

"You have granted me my freedom and for that I am grateful, but I still don't understand your intentions."

Finn's chest warmed a little at the show of humility from the Sirian. Her hesitance to trust was something they could all easily understand.

Finn called over to Nova where she sat at the controls of the pod.

"Are you good to handle the Reliance checkpoint on your own? I think it's time Enyo and I talked."

The doxie waved a dismissive hand, her brows puckered in concentration.

"All good here, boss lady."

"Reliance checkpoint? How are we to make it past that?"

Finn caught the edge of panic in Enyo's voice and turned to find the female's chest heaving with alarm. She rushed to sooth the hybrid.

"It's fine. This pod is registered to a Reliance aristocrat; the daughter of an heiress sold it to keep a nasty Faze habit secret. No questions asked. We won't raise any alarms when they scan us." She forced Enyo's eyes to meet hers, voice steady as she whispered, "Trust me."

They'd paid a small fortune—half of Finn's earnings as a Farthers thief—just for the guarantee the ostentatious pod would get them safely through the Inner Rings.

Some of the panic seemed to subside.

"I think you are right, *N'Goza*. We should talk."

Finn nodded, leading her through the cockpit and into the big bedroom. She waited for the Sirian to choose a spot to sit, watching with quiet curiosity as she ended up in the plush, highbacked chair next to the room's white-marble vanity;

giving her the advantage of having her back against a wall while her darting eyes scanned the room for threats.

Finn took a seat on the bed, carefully crooking a knee and resting her arm on top of it in a casual, nonthreatening pose.

She barely had time to open her mouth wide enough for a mud-fly to sneak through before the hybrid launched in. Her back ramrod straight, Enyo's angry eyes shone with defiance.

"I do not regret killing that soldier."

"Good for you," Finn remarked, keeping her tone light. "Do you want something to eat?" She motioned starboard, eyeing the places where the girl's rags clung to her ribs. "I'm pretty sure Nova keeps a stash of sweets in the spare room."

Enyo's eyes narrowed in confusion before she seemed to shake herself free of it.

"I am not so easily distracted. Did you truly believe you could steal me from Jessup's home without any casualties?"

"I really hadn't thought about it," Finn fibbed. "But I do know that keeping the Reliance off our tails is going to be a hell of a lot harder if you keep leaving a trail of dead bodies behind for them to follow."

Enyo's multihued brows furrowed, considering Finn's words for a moment before abruptly changing the subject.

"Tell me about the others who are imprisoned like me."

Great, another stubborn hybrid, Finn thought, sighing.

"I recently came across a list of hybrids being held in captivity by the Reliance. Most of them are spread out pretty evenly throughout the Inner Rings, from Aquarii to Cartan." She couldn't be sure, but Finn suspected the Sirian had stopped breathing. "I've spent the last few weeks putting together a rescue."

"How did you come to be in possession of such a list?" Enyo asked on a barely perceptible inhale.

"That's a long story," Finn hedged. Met with the newfound loaded silence, she rubbed her temples and relented. "I worked with a crew a while back. We pulled a job on Cartan.

It turns out we were there to steal the list from an upper-caste senator."

"And you double-crossed your crew?" Enyo clicked her tongue, the censure in the sound causing Finn to grit her teeth.

"*No,*" she bit out, her voice going hard as memories threatened to overwhelm her. "*They* double-crossed *me.*"

The Sirian released a breath and nodded in understanding.

"So, you took it for yourself."

"More like memorized it," Finn corrected. "At least some of it anyway."

"And what of the rest of it?"

"When the time comes, I'll get my hands on the original list." Enyo's eyes shot wide, but Finn continued before she could interrupt. "I won't need it for long. All it'll take is a touch . . . I think." Finn shrugged her shoulders. "Just one of the many new and fun hybrid abilities I'm learning about."

"*You* are a half-breed?" Enyo seemed to choke on the question.

"*Hybrid,*" she corrected. "*Half-Teslan.*" Finn stretched the tension of the day from her shoulders and regarded Enyo with a half smile. "You don't have to look so shocked."

"And your . . . *pilot?*" Finn chose to ignore the way she gagged on the word.

"She's an Altaran doxie, not a hybrid."

"I noticed the scars." Enyo said, as though she expected the answer, her gaze far away and lost to whatever thoughts swirled behind those intelligent yet dangerous eyes.

Finally, Finn took pity on her. Rising, she made her way back to the dresser and removed a sealed box of fragrantly spiced crackers. She threw them to Enyo before taking her seat back on the bed.

"You really should eat something."

The Sirian eyed the box like a coiled serpent, before the telltale rumbling in her stomach gave her away. She tore the box open, the heady scent of Inner Ring herbs and spices filling the room.

In response, her stomach grumbled louder, like a cry of despair begging to be answered. Finn hid her smile as the hybrid devoured a dozen of the crumbling morsels before pausing to take a breath. Speaking around a mouthful, she finally said, "What will your former crew do with the list?"

"I don't know. I ran before I could find out, but I intend to free the other hybrids before it becomes relevant."

Enyo nodded at the wisdom in her plan—at least that's what Finn assumed—before swallowing.

"You said there was another like me on Arcturus. What are they doing to him?"

Something cold squeezed the back of Finn's neck and refused to let go.

"Probably the same thing they are doing to all the hybrids. The same thing they did to you."

Something dark and so painful it actually hurt Finn to see it shadowed Enyo's face as her eyes sparked with anger.

"Then we must go back and save him," she hissed.

"It's not that easy. He's in the planet's house of worship. The place is impenetrable."

Some of the anger deflated from her body as she regarded Finn seriously.

"Why are they doing this to us?"

Finn nudged the crackers in her direction, encouraging her to eat more (as though anyone could have an appetite after what she'd been through). Surprising her, Enyo obeyed, operating on autopilot as she waited for an answer.

"I don't know," Finn whispered, eyes gleaming with her hatred. "I think because they can."

The Sirian paused her assault on the crackers to meet Finn's gaze with a hard stare of her own.

"I do not like leaving another behind."

Finally, something we can agree on.

"I don't like it either, but we don't have much of a choice." Finn leaned forward so the weight of her words could truly sink in. "At least not until there are more of us." She paused long enough to watch as the glitter of anticipation began to fill Enyo's eyes, slowly spreading and erasing the lines of fatigue from her face. Finn recognized it immediately. "Does this mean you'll be joining me?"

Enyo's full lips lifted, curling above the sharp row of her fangs in a frightening mockery of a smile.

"I would not miss it, *N'Goza*."

"Good. Let's discuss my rules."

FOUR

Finn sat awake in the dead of the night, her body perched and alert in a flight chair at the pod's helm while Enyo and Nova slept soundly in the spare rooms. She ran her hands nervously through the long auburn waves that now fell past her shoulders. Sleep had never come easily back on the Mud Pit, but nowadays it was a luxury Finn could no longer afford. Her mind was too busy plotting, always planning for the next step and the next three steps after that.

It hadn't been easy getting Enyo to come around to Finn's way of thinking when it came to not killing the enemies they encountered on their journey.

The hybrid was somewhat of a legend on her home planet of Siri. The tribe of native Sirian warriors there worshipped her hybrid abilities as Gods-like. Whereas most hybrids were raised in hiding and taught to fear their heritage, Enyo had grown up believing she was *special*.

A fact which only made it more difficult for Finn to convince the tenacious woman that her right to revenge after cycles of torture and imprisonment at the upper-caste's hands would have to wait in favor of a grander plan.

Though Enyo's unpredictable claws itched for retribution, it seemed Finn's first assessment of the Sirian had been correct. Her strange yellow eyes housed a unique intelligence within their depths, and after what seemed like hours of arguing, the hybrid finally agreed to try things Finn's way; even going so far as to defer to her leadership "for now."

Finn took the win, but those words, *for now*, and the casual way the Sirian had delivered them, plagued her mind, joining the thousands of others that played repeatedly like a holojector stuck on loop. It didn't help matters that they all seemed to assail her in the low, gruff timbre of Grim's unmistakable voice. They bombarded her in echoing decibels too loud to ignore.

Is this solitude everything you dreamed it would be, Dhala?

Every decision counts. Every move carries a consequence.

What will happen to the hybrids if you get yourself killed? It only takes one mistake.

Even worse, what if you get them *killed?*

There is no shame in admitting this mission is far too big for one such as you.

"Shut up," she moaned.

Finn dropped her head to the pod's console, forcing herself to inhale slowly through her nose. All the while she cursed Grim for embedding himself so thoroughly in her head. All those cycles side-by-side under his tutelage had exacted its toll.

Unlike so many other unpleasant memories from her past, Grim, it seemed, would not be so easily erased.

Finn let out an agonized sigh and returned her attention to the endless chasm of space outside. What if she couldn't do this by herself? What if imaginary Grim was right? Every decision she made carried the weight of one hundred sacks of mud tied to her waist and dragging her down below the surface.

If she made just one wrong move, someone was going to pay the price . . . with their life.

On that depressing thought, Finn doubled over in agony, a tiny moan slipping through her lips. As usual, the pain came so suddenly, she was completely taken off guard. It always seemed to happen this way, late in the night as she tried to outrun her insomnia, her squadron of worries marching in formation close behind.

Another spasm hit just below the center of her chest, in the exact place where the cursed *Independence* had impaled her with a jagged shard of its metal during a high-speed chase with the Toad and his meteorhead bodyguards, sending shockwaves throughout her body. Finn gasped, struggling for air as she pulled herself up.

Blindly using her hands for purchase, Finn put her weight against the console and forced herself into a standing position. She made it there just before the next wave of suffering hit.

Lifting her shirt and forcing air into her lungs through the pain, she examined the old wound for signs of any new trauma. As was the case every time this happened, she found nothing but smooth, unblemished skin where Isis, *Independence*'s resident Aquariian, had healed her all those weeks ago.

Releasing her shirt, Finn grimaced at the pale, sweat-soaked reflection staring back at her in the domed window above the pod's controls.

What had Isis done to her?

She'd considered herself lucky to have survived her brush with death, grateful to the Aquariian healer for using her strange gifts to mend the undoubtedly fatal wound. Now, Finn wasn't so sure.

Each night, the pain worsened. Surely, she couldn't survive much more of it. Whatever the Aquariian had done under the guise of "healing" needed to be undone before it was too late.

Exhausted, Finn's head fell into her hands. They barely had enough strength to hold her weight.

Returning to Isis meant returning to *Independence* and with that ship came a whole host of people and things Finn had no desire to revisit . . . Grim . . . Iliana . . . Conrad. Finn groaned as another stabbing pain hit her like a double tap to the gut. Had this been Isis's intention all along?

What if whatever she'd done to Finn was intended to keep her close, causing blinding agony whenever she dared venture too far?

"*Finn?*"

The voice, as melodious and comforting as it was unwanted in that moment, filled Finn's head.

"Not now, Tiri," she groaned against her fingers.

"Finn? What's happening? You're in pain. Are you hurt?"

She closed her eyes, trying not to think about how difficult it was becoming to breathe, and focused on the darkness behind her lids.

"Your timing sucks, kid," she informed Tiri on a wince.

Her little friend had never stopped trying to find Finn—most likely at the behest of Grim and the rest of *Independence*'s crew—using her hybrid abilities to pop into Finn's mind at the most inopportune of times.

Finn had taken to recording the instances, curious at their sporadic nature. At first, she'd refused to speak to Tiri, worried that the tiniest error in judgment would get her and Nova caught.

From what she could deduce, the girl could only enter her mind when close by, which meant *Independence* and her crew were within a sixth of an AU of their travel pod even now. She fought the panic, reminding herself that as gifted as Tiri was, she was still having difficulty locating Finn.

There'd been a few close calls, with Finn and Nova sighting *Independence* as she'd orbited the Inner Rings outside of Arcturus mere days ago, but Finn quickly learned that by focusing her mind, she could keep Tiri from reading her thoughts. She had even stopped sleeping in long stretches, fearing the vulnerable state of her subconscious in slumber might reveal something.

As it turned out, Tiri seemed resigned to their ongoing game of cat and mouse—though the little imp did let her frustration be known every time they spoke—so long as Finn continued to check in and stay safe.

"Finn, did you hear me? Where are you hurt?"

Her body responded to the worry in the little girl's voice, the pain slowly receding as she focused on answering.

"Ask Isis. She's the one who did it."

Finn could almost see the child's nose scrunched up in confusion as she said, *"That doesn't make any sense. Tell me where you are right now. You need help."*

Keeping her eyes closed, she tried to raise her head, but the muscles in her neck gave out beneath the weight.

"You know the rules, kid. I can't do that. So how about a story instead?" Finn dutifully ignored Tiri's protests, everything around her disappearing as her body became dead weight. Her voice took on a distant, slurred quality as she said, *"Did I ever tell you the one about the Goslan and the Aquariian?"*

It was the last thing she heard herself say before unconsciousness took her and the already dark world around her went black.

FIVE

"**D**id I ever tell you the story of the Goslan and the Aquariian?" Grim asks the question on an exhale, pivoting to counter Finn's attack and slashing his bokken in an upward arc until the long rubber blade collides with her stomach. His dark horns shine in the light and his red skin ripples over his heavily muscled seven-foot frame. Quirking a brow, he flashes pointy teeth and says, "Focus, Dhala."

Finn rubs the throbbing sting from her abdomen and groans, "How can I focus if you keep asking me questions?"

"Do you think your opponent will politely face you in silence so that you may gather your concentration?"

Grim punctuates the sarcastic question with another strike, distracting her defenses long enough to sweep her legs out from under her. She lands on the floor of his office with a loud "Oomph."

Blowing the stray hairs out of her eyes, she waits for her body to remember how to breathe.

She knows she is lucky. At fifteen cycles, she has already learned basic self-defense, a skill most girls on the Mud Pit never get the chance to acquire. Grim is taking a vested interest in her learning and her future. With his tutelage, she could be a great fighter someday; maybe even as great as Grim himself, though she doubts it.

With his size and strength, combined with his unique training in the old-Earthen techniques of fighting—so different from that of the typical berserker style Khaleerians tended to prefer—he is nearly impossible to beat.

But she is learning, and every day she grows stronger.

It is something she finds herself thinking of constantly—a welcome reminder of the reward for all the pains and hard work.

"All right then, Grim," she rasps, rising to her feet. "Tell me about the Goslan and the Aquariian."

His fangs gleam in the candlelight as he smiles at her, his big body falling into a battle stance.

"One day," he begins, circling her with his bokken raised, "an Aquariian priestess came across an injured Goslan amidst her precious plants. Several of his tentacles had been torn from his body and without healing, he would soon die."

Finn focuses on his movements, her eyes watching his feet as one moves forward followed by the other. She begins to counter his steps, moving back and around until they are at a standstill.

"Don't tell me she healed the Goslan?" She can't help asking the question, as Goslans are renowned for two things: an abundance of deadly tentacles packing enough punch to squeeze the bones from a Khaleerian, and their incredibly impulsive natures.

Grim lunges forward, striking with his bokken, but Finn is watching his shoulders and sees the attack coming. She counters with her own bokken and their weapons meet in the middle with a loud thwack. He nods his approval.

"Don't forget, Dhala, it is in the nature of an Aquariian to help those in need. She brought the Goslan back to her temple, healing him just enough each day to keep him alive."

"Why didn't she heal him all at once?"

"The Goslan sought sanctuary within the walls of her garden temple. The Aquariian was good-hearted but she was not stupid. She hoped that by the time the Goslan was fully healed, he would have grown to love the temple as she did, making a betrayal impossible."

She almost misses it, but Finn catches the intent behind Grim's eyes a second before his massive leg shoots out. She dives out of the way just in time, crouching low and winking at her mentor. They both know had her timing been a second later, he would have flattened her again.

"Let me guess, when he was fully healed, he killed the Aquariian for her troubles," she muses sarcastically.

"No," Grim barks, charging Finn at full speed. She barely has time to register his attack before he slides low, gliding across the floor on his knees as his weapon sweeps her legs out from under her. It really isn't fair that a giant of his mass can move with such remarkable speed and grace. He looms over her prone form, holding his sword at her throat. "While she slept, he robbed her sacred temple, stealing her people's most holy possessions. She awoke to find her gardens screaming at his attempted escape."

Finn hangs on his words, curious now to know what became of them both.

"Go on then," she prods. "What did she do?"

"She found him before he could flee and she let the plants take him. Slowly, over a period of weeks, they fed on him until he became a part of their garden, no longer resembling anything close to the creature he'd once been."

Finn gulps before she catches herself, narrowing her eyes on her mentor.

"So, what? Is this another lesson on naïveté? Don't trust Goslans?"

Grim finally pulls the bokken from her throat, offering her his hand. He isn't offended or surprised when she doesn't take it.

"No," he rumbles, watching her stand. "The lesson is, never underestimate the depths of an Aquariian's rage."

Finn came into awareness slowly, the last dregs of her memory clinging to the edges of her consciousness like a hangover. Before even allowing herself to open her eyes, she took inventory of her body. Wiggling all ten toes and fingers, she winced as her slow inhale of breath exacerbated the aches and pains left over from whatever "episode" had plagued her the night before.

Never underestimate the depths of an Aquariian's rage.

Grim's warning reverberated throughout her head. Perhaps she should've paid closer attention to his lesson. She didn't know what the ship's resident healer had done to her all those weeks ago; but if last night was any indication, whatever it was couldn't be good.

Finn's body tensed as she remembered her brief contact with Tiri the night before. She'd never lost consciousness while still connected to the little girl. What if she'd somehow given away their pod's location?

She forced her heavy eyelids open, blinking away the last remnants of sleep as she struggled to get her body to do something other than just lie there. Her mind became so focused on the task, it took a few moments before her surroundings came into focus and she realized she was no longer on the flight deck of her pod.

Don't panic, she ordered herself, taking in the familiar white walls and steel desk below a domed window that provided a spectacular view of the vast spacescape outside. Her heart disobeyed, pounding against the confines of her chest as the rest of her senses screamed in recognition.

The conversant hum of *Independence*'s mechanics was impossible to mistake. She'd recognize it amidst a fleet of thousands.

As though with a will of its own, Finn's body shot up in bed, her frantic eyes searching the room she knew so well yet hoped to never see again. Her heart sank like a stone before immediately lodging itself in her throat.

Isis, in all her statuesque glory, sat calmly at the foot of the bed, silver eyes watching Finn with casual interest. Her blue lips parted in a half smile.

"Welcome back, Finn."

Finn assessed the Aquariian she had once considered a friend from the top of her bald, iridescent blue head to the graceful blue hands resting atop her knees. All the while, Grim's lesson rang in her head.

"Shit."

SIX

At Finn's muttered expletive, Isis's smile widened.

"The ship has been painfully dull without you, my child." The Aquariian's silver eyes grew serious as she regarded her. She set a new pair of black gloves on the bed next to Finn's hands. "We have missed you."

"Oh you have?" Finn bit back a groan of leftover soreness as she forced herself to sit up. "You've got a funny way of showing it."

She dutifully ignored the way Isis's head tilted in genuine surprise at the thinly veiled accusation.

"We were worried. Tiri said you were hurt. We couldn't just leave you out on your own."

Finn scoffed, subtly testing the strength in the muscles of her arms and legs.

"You wouldn't happen to know anything about my *injury*, would you?"

"Whatever do you mean?"

She couldn't help but be impressed. Isis was putting on quite the show. Her glittering skin wrinkled above her eyes and her lips parted in confusion.

"Just tell me what you did to me, Isis," Finn bit out in frustration. "I know you put something inside of me when you healed me . . . something to cause unbearable pain when I get too far away. It's pretty devious actually. I didn't know you had it in you. Well, you've got me back where you want me now, so you can take it the hell out."

The Aquariian's eyes shot comically wide.

"You think *I* did this to you?"

Finn paused, her breaths stalling in her lungs as she forced out a whisper.

"Didn't you?"

The genuine affront clouding Isis's face made Finn hesitate. She'd seen the Aquariian lie before, and the woman wasn't very adept at it. Unless she'd mastered the skill in a few short weeks, it appeared she truly didn't know what was causing Finn's bouts of unbearable pain.

The long-limbed alien got up and sat next to her on the bed, causing Finn to stifle a flinch at her nearness.

"I would never intentionally cause you pain, my child."

Her eyes shone with their candor and some of the left-over tension leaked from Finn's body. She wanted to roll away from the comfort and warmth in the woman's stare . . . wanted to unleash the inferno of anger she'd been stoking for the last few weeks, but a terrible, creeping sense of loneliness snuck up on her and erased her intentions.

"Then . . . what's happening to me, Isis?" she whispered, swallowing past the fear in her throat.

The Aquariian leaned close enough that her warmth soothed Finn, but not close enough to touch.

"I examined you thoroughly. Your body is perfectly healthy."

Even as relief made her sag against the pillows, new anxiety began to fill her.

"Then—"

Isis hushed her with a graceful motion of her slender fingers.

"Your *body* is perfectly healthy, but I have a theory about the rest of you. You haven't been sleeping, have you?"

Finn cocked her head defensively.

"I've been a little busy."

Isis inhaled and released a breath on a sigh.

"You've been unconscious on *Independence* for three days." Finn didn't have time to appropriately react to that outrageous statement before the Aquariian continued. "We've all been understandably concerned. Can you tell me more about this pain?"

Finn blinked. *Three days?* She'd been out for *three days?* That thought led to ones of her crew, and a new wave a panic stole over her.

"Wait," she cried, tearing the covers free from her body and throwing her legs over the side of the bed. "Where are Nova and Enyo? Are they all right?"

Isis hurried to stop her.

"Calm yourself."

Finn stopped her movements with a hard glare.

"I can't calm myself. I need to know what you did with my crew. They need me."

She panted from the exertion as a fresh wave of pain hit her in the abdomen, causing her to double over. In an uncharacteristic show of force, Isis unceremoniously shoved her back into bed.

"You *must*. I believe this pain is a manifestation of your worry."

"My *what?*"

"Listen to me, Finn. Focus on your breathing and think. When does the pain usually strike?"

She watched the Aquariian's chest rise and fall in gentle swells, trying to get her breaths to mimic the action.

"At night," she gasped.

Isis offered an encouraging nod.

"And what are you normally doing?"

Finn sucked in a ragged breath and worried her lower lip between her teeth.

What am I doing? Her mind practically screamed.

What wasn't she doing? There was so much resting on her shoulders. Each night while the worlds slept, Finn plotted. She agonized over every detail of her plans, worrying that one wrong step could cost her and the imprisoned hybrids everything. There was so much at stake. How could Isis even ask the question?

The Aquariian seemed to read as much in her expression as in her shortness of breath.

"It is as I suspected. When I examined you, I could feel the turbulence centered here." A long, slender hand stopped to rest just below the center of Finn's chest. "The task you have undertaken would be difficult for anyone in the most ideal of circumstances, but you have been pushing yourself, forcing yourself into isolation and refusing sleep. With no outlet to release your anxiety, it has manifested itself physically. It is not unusual, though I have never seen a case quite so severe. Perhaps this is yet another unique aspect of your Teslan heritage."

Finn sputtered for a response, coming up empty. She was beginning to think of her hybrid abilities as more of a curse than anything else. Finally, she mumbled, "Great, in addition to not touching people, I can now look forward to bouts of blackout-inducing pain every time I get a little worried."

A gentle smile lifted the Aquariian's lips a fraction of an inch.

"I'd say you were more than a *little* worried. But I expect things will be easier for you now that you're back on *Independence*. You won't be dealing with this alone anymore."

Even as the words fell like a warm blanket of much-needed relief over Finn's weary body, she resisted. That is, until the door opened to her right and a deep voice slightly tinged with token sarcasm cut through the fog of her emotions.

"I couldn't agree more, Isis."

Taking a deep breath to steady herself, Finn turned to meet her newest visitor. The captain of *Independence* looked as polished and handsome as ever, though his blond hair had grown a bit shaggy and his normally clean-shaven face was covered in a smattering of new stubble. He held his tall body in a casual pose, but there were new lines of tension around his green eyes that were impossible to miss.

"Shane." She gave him a smile that ended up more like a grimace. "You've looked better."

Some of the lines eased a bit as he shot a pained grin over at Isis.

"I see our patient is on the mend. Do you mind if I have a moment alone with her?"

Finn's panicked face shot to the Aquariian's, begging her not to go, but the woman merely gave the blankets draping her patient's legs a sympathetic pat and took her leave.

Left alone, Shane cleared his throat a bit awkwardly and shifted on his feet. Seeming to catch himself, he grabbed the steel chair from its spot by the desk and pulled it over to her bedside.

"I . . . *we* are all more than a little impressed at what you have accomplished in such a short amount of time." Finn's eyes widened to the size of dinner plates. Of all the things she expected him to say, a compliment didn't come remotely close to making the list. Shane's gaze left his hands to meet hers. They burned with intensity. "The luxury pod was a clever touch, though I must say I still can't wrap my head around how you managed to take the Sirian hybrid from one of Arcturus's most revered religious emissaries without detection."

Not entirely without detection, Finn thought, as she remembered Enyo's bloody claws sinking into the soldier's flesh with a disgusting gurgle. She ignored both the praise and the obvious curiosity in his tone and sat up straighter.

"Where is Enyo?"

Surprise darkened the olive green of his eyes.

"So, Enyo is her name?" Leaning back in his chair, an affectionate half grin tugged at his lips as he commented, "She was more than a little perturbed at the notion of boarding our ship. A bit like someone else I know. She said she would answer to 'N'Goza' or no one. After she tried to take my eye out with those claws of hers, we had to lock her in one of the smaller cargo holds." Taking Finn in from head to toe with a grin, he chuckled. "It figures you'd find the most foul-tempered blended to rescue first."

Once again, Finn threw the covers off her body and moved to stand.

"Take me to her."

Shane rushed to steady her.

"Hold on. There are some things we need to clear up."

Glaring at him from beneath a fall of auburn curls, she snapped.

"I won't stop rescuing hybrids. I've spent almost every last piece of gold I've earned, and I intend to see my plan through." Quieter this time, she said, "They're suffering out there, Shane."

"I don't want you to stop." The softly spoken admission halted Finn in her tracks. She lifted her stare fully to find him waiting for her, his face gentle with affection. "I want you to help us finish what you started. There's no denying you have a talent for this, Finn, but as the last few days have proven, this was never meant to be a solo job. Let us help you. We can do this together."

Grim's face flashed in her mind:

There is a bigger mission at stake, one you are needed for.

"Is that you talking," she asked Shane on a harsh murmur, "or the *Luminary*?"

At the mention of their leader, the openness in his eyes shuttered before disappearing completely. His tone went flat as he answered.

"The Luminary and *Independence* aren't separate; we're a package deal, Finn."

"What did Grim do to make you so blindly loyal?"

Shane opened his mouth and then closed it. She waited, but an answer never came. Using every ounce of strength she possessed, Finn rose to her feet and stood tall. She hoped that she hid the shaking in her legs as she demanded, "Take me to see Enyo."

She felt certain he would have obeyed her had her legs not chosen that moment to give out. Her body sagged to the floor in a heap, but he managed to catch her around the waist before she could hit.

Shane released a bone-weary exhale, gently pushing her back into bed.

"We'll bring your crew to you."

SEVEN

A ir hissed through the automatic doors, announcing her crew's arrival. Finn had managed to find an acceptable position—propped up and cross-legged in bed. She hoped her strength would return soon. She was certainly going to need it to deal with whatever lay ahead.

Nova came into the room first, her blemished body proudly on display in a pair of short linen shorts and a cropped tank top. Her stringy brown hair hung limply at her shoulders. She smiled brightly at the sight of Finn.

"Hey, boss lady. Feeling better?"

Before she could answer the doxie, an unholy growl shook the walls of her room and Finn caught sight of Enyo being led in by none other than Conrad.

The sight of him was like taking a hit from Grim's *bokken* straight to the chest and it sent her reeling. Thankfully, his glowing, otherworldly blue eyes were focused intently on holding the struggling Sirian hybrid in place as her lithe fur-covered body fought against his control. Conrad's powerful frame dwarfed Enyo. His black dreads were tied away from his face in a messy topknot and his ebony skin shone under the artificial lights.

Shane brought up the rear of the strange group, the doors hissing closed behind him. His blond hair looked more disheveled than it had been mere minutes ago; yes, he was a far cry from the handsome, buttoned-up captain she'd come to know.

"Let me go, you bastard," Enyo spat at the glowing-eyed hybrid. Conrad gritted his teeth in response and his eyes flared brighter.

Before she could stop herself, Finn spoke quietly.

"His parents were married."

Everyone in the room went silent and four heads turned simultaneously in her direction.

Enyo's struggles ceased as her yellow eyes cleared and she regarded Finn for a long, confusion-filled moment.

"You are alive, *N'Goza*. I thought they had killed you."

"I'm okay. How are you?"

"Not pleased with being locked up again," she sneered in Shane and Conrad's direction.

"Sorry about that," Finn apologized, cursing her inability to help her new friend while being missing in action for three days. "It was a misunderstanding. They won't do it again. You can stay with me." She glanced at Shane meaningfully, but before he could respond, a low voice filled the room.

"Like hell she can," Conrad argued. "She almost took your eye out, Shane."

"I'll admit my aim is not what it used to be," Enyo said, offering a toothy grin.

Finn couldn't put it off any longer. She finally turned and looked at the glorious hybrid she'd spent the better part of a month trying to forget. As though he could feel her attention, Conrad's incredulous and angry gaze shot to hers.

No longer focused on Enyo, his blue eyes drank in the sight of her, paralyzing Finn with their intensity. Like Shane, course stubble colored the hard planes of his cheekbones and jaw. He wore a black singlet that hugged the muscles of his chest, leaving the runic markings covering the swarthy skin of his arms and shoulders on full display.

"Let her go," she told him quietly. "She won't hurt me."

Something like pain flashed in his eyes before he shut it down, his face clearing and voiding all emotion.

"Do it, Conrad," Shane ordered. Then, turning to Enyo he said, "There is no violence on my ship. Keep those claws sheathed and we won't have any problems."

The Sirian snarled, no doubt taking offense to the orders.

"It's okay, Enyo. Do as he says," Finn instructed quietly.

A barely perceptible nod was the only acquiescence she gave, but apparently it was enough for Shane. He showed only the barest hint of surprise at her submission, before motioning for Conrad to release her. Though it looked like it physically pained him, the large man complied.

Enyo pulled free from Conrad's hold with a hiss, shooting them both a glare as she moved to Finn's side.

"That was intense," Nova mused from the corner, casually examining her cuticles as though a standoff between hybrids were an everyday occurrence.

Seeming to remember her presence, Shane glanced at the scarred doxie, doing a double take before shaking his head in bemusement.

"Let's give them some time, Conrad. Finn"—he sent a pleading look her way—"think about what I said."

She gave the captain an absent nod, her attention too occupied by Conrad's retreating presence to formulate a genuine response.

Without a backward glance in her direction, he kept pace with Shane's steady strides out the door. If the big half-breed wanted to stay, he did an excellent job of hiding it. Finn tracked his broad back until it disappeared, her heart catching painfully when she lost sight of him.

"What now?"

Finn glanced over to find Nova already seated in the chair Shane had once occupied, legs propped up on the bed and eyeing them expectantly. Enyo's forehead creased in annoyance at the doxie before returning her focus to Finn.

"When will you be ready to leave? The large one's abilities may prove problematic, but I can easily dispatch the captain."

Judging by the sparkle in her eye and the twitch of amusement on her lips, she seemed to be relishing the idea.

"No. We're not *dispatching* anyone. I mean it, Enyo. Most of the crew on this ship are hybrids . . . *innocent* ones." Enyo's body stilled at the revelation. "I'm not suggesting we trust these people," Finn continued, "but they want to help us rescue others like us. They have more manpower, more resources, and they're giving us an opportunity to use both. Not to mention they have the list of hybrids in Reliance captivity."

"If they're so great, what do they need us for?" Nova asked, twirling a strand of lank brown hair. Finn's answer came without hesitation.

"Because a doxie and a Mud Pit thief were able to steal a hybrid prisoner from a high-security estate in the center of the Arcturians' home planet with half the resources and less than three weeks of planning time." Finn locked eyes with Enyo. "You're damn right they need us. Working with them is the best play for us to make right now. If they are planning a double cross, we can keep them close, see it coming, and intervene. Until then, I say we take what they're offering."

They didn't have to like it. Finn sure as hell didn't. The last thing she ever expected was to be stuck on *Independence* again, sharing close quarters with the people who had betrayed her, but Isis had been correct in her assessment.

She'd been pushing herself too hard. Saving the hybrids was an undertaking too large for just one person.

Or three.

The Sirian's mind went to work behind her eyes, her long legs carrying her over to the room's circular window. She remained motionless as she took in the vast obscurity outside.

"An *N'Goza*'s feet belong on the ground, not in the sky." The wistfulness in Enyo's voice surprised Finn. Finally, she turned back to face them. "I do not like this plan, but in this I will trust your judgment. We will work with this captain and his crew, but at the first sign of trouble"—Enyo's hands shot out at her sides, her sheathed black claws elongating in one fluid movement—"we are taking the list and I will tear this ship and everyone on it to shreds."

Finn swallowed at the intensity in her stare.

"Let's just hope for no trouble then, yeah?"

The conversation ended on Nova's fearful squeak of agreement.

EIGHT

Tiri had been noticeably absent since Finn had regained consciousness, a fact the child angrily announced was due to Conrad forbidding her from being in the same room as Enyo. Even telepathically, the girl's temper was unrivaled.

After promising to come see her just as soon as she got her crew settled in their quarters, Tiri finally ended their telepathic connection.

Nova seemed more than pleased to have a space all to herself—especially one as accommodating as *Independence*—and took mere minutes to settle into the room next to Finn's. She'd say this for the doxie, she was turning out to be downright adaptable. Enyo, however, was proving to be a bit more stubborn.

"I will stay here with you, *N'Goza*." Her yellow eyes scanned Finn's quarters as her matter-of-fact statement hung in the air between them. With her colorful hair tied away from her furred face, she looked even younger than Finn had first assessed.

Finn crossed her arms and glanced meaningfully at the bed.

"Right. And who gets the bed?"

Enyo followed her look, quirking a multihued brow.

"You really don't know much about Sirians, do you?" When she didn't answer, the sizable woman continued on a dramatic exhale. "I will be much more comfortable sleeping on the floor."

"Wouldn't you also be more comfortable with a room of your own?"

The Sirian's eyes glinted at the suggestion.

"I hardly think it wise to leave you unprotected in your weakened state."

It would seem that sometime between her rescue on Arcturus, arguing about rules, their arrival on *Independence*, and their three-day separation, Enyo had appointed herself as Finn's personal bodyguard.

She wanted to argue with the obstinate Sirian but given her recent three-day coma and history with *Independence*'s crew—including the attempt on her life during her last stay—Finn was having a difficult time making a case for herself. More to the point, it was kind of nice having someone in her corner this time around (someone other than an eight-year-old mind reader anyway).

Besides, the one thing Finn *did* know about Sirians: they were a pack species. Being on her own without the comfort of a tribe all these years, and at the mercy of Jessup and his torments no less, must have been its own special brand of hell for Enyo.

Finn made a show of throwing her hands in the air and rolling her eyes.

"Okay, fine. You can stay here on one condition." Enyo waited patiently for her to continue, not at all impressed or affected by the theatrics. "Make use of the shower while I get some rest."

She pointed in the direction of the bathroom and watched as a familiar glimmer of excitement flashed in the Sirian's eyes, before she caught herself and shut it down. Finn stopped herself before the laughter bubbling up inside of her could escape.

Casting a long-suffering grimace in her direction, Enyo stretched her neck, dormant muscles popping and cracking as she said, "If I must."

"You *must*," Finn ordered.

She watched the hybrid's retreating form enter the bathroom and shut the door. When the rush of the shower's spray registered, Finn finally tagged the gloves from her bed, turned, and made her way slowly to the door. Her strength was finally coming back to her and the desire to stretch her legs had become overwhelming. Given how long the Sirian had gone without such amenities, Finn felt certain she had plenty of time to go see Tiri and get back before her "bodyguard" was any wiser.

As she made her way to the door, her bare fingers grazed the wall and the ship's layout wrapped around her like a familiar blanket. Being a hybrid certainly had its perks. Finn slipped on her gloves and passed through the doorway. Moving down the hallway, she softened her steps against the metal-grate flooring, stalking as silently as her body would allow toward the third room on the left: Tiri's room.

The ship's lights hummed above her and the familiar vibrations of *Independence*'s inner workings filled Finn with a sense of rightness. She'd spent the last few weeks dutifully ignoring all thoughts related to this vessel and everyone on it, but now she was faced with a truth she couldn't avoid: she'd missed this. No place—not even the Mud Pit back when Grim was still a fairytale and life had been somewhat content—had felt more like a home to her than this one.

As if in direct opposition to her feelings, a slender figure rushed around the corner of the hall, stopping less than a meter in front of Finn. She recognized AJ's pale skin and dark hair immediately.

With her run of bad luck lately, Finn supposed she shouldn't be too surprised to find herself face-to-face with Shane's psychotic kid brother.

"Great," she mumbled. She knew she could handle the half-Anunnaki so long as she avoided eye contact when his black gaze began to swirl with color—she'd learned firsthand the power behind those eyes' hypnotic blues, greens, and purples when the boy had nearly compelled her to float herself in the cold, dark abyss of space—but she was starting to regret taking off without Enyo in tow.

Hearing her, he looked up. Shifting awkwardly on the balls of his feet, he made a point to avoid looking into her eyes. His alabaster hands pushed up the sleeves of a dark gray sweater before balling into fists at his sides.

"There's no docking bay to float me out of on this side of the ship, AJ," Finn pointed out darkly.

His dark eyes darted quickly to hers and then away again. *"You left!"* The words exploded from the teenager in a cloud of manic energy, making them sound like an accusation. When she made no move to answer him, he finally met her stare fully. His black eyes held hers steady. He took a breath, his words slightly calmer as he said, "I didn't get to say thank you."

Finn felt her own eyes widen and her mouth fall open but was helpless to guard her expression; his words shocked her. The angry, arrogant boy she'd grown so used to was gone, an awkward, unsure youth in his place. His stare drifted down to her gaping mouth and then back up as he spoke.

"People are saying you're staying."

Coming unstuck, she offered him a cautious nod.

"For now."

Something like hope flickered across his features as he moved closer, but a low snarl rumbling from behind Finn stopped him in his tracks. Enyo's hard voice cut through the air.

"That's close enough, boy."

That was fast.

Finn spun, taking care to keep herself between AJ and the Sirian. Isis must've been busy making her new guests feel comfortable. Since showering, Enyo had traded in her rags for a clean pair of pants and a long-sleeved shirt.

When her eyes made it up past her friend's new clothing, Finn snorted; she couldn't help herself. While the Sirian's eyes and imposing fangs promised menace, her fur and multihued hair had been hastily dried, causing it to frizz and fluff up in disarray.

At the sound of mirth, Enyo's gaze snapped to her and the fuzzy hybrid's lips curled on a scowl.

Finn grinned.

"AJ and I were just catching up." She turned to find the boy's stance had widened into a defensive position as he eyed the Sirian warily. "AJ, this is Enyo. She's part of my crew."

At her words, he seemed to forget the growling hybrid, his eyes shooting back to Finn.

"You've got a crew?"

She shared an amused smile with Enyo before answering.
"We're working on it."

Sensing Finn's calm, Enyo seemed to relax a little. With no
immediate threat to combat, she crossed her arms at her chest.

"This one seems too pretty to be a hybrid," she mused.

AJ's eyes narrowed at the offhand remark, his body tensing in
the unrestrained anger Finn had learned to associate with him.

"I'm half-Anunnaki and I could make you cut off your own
arm and eat it if I wanted to."

Finn watched in alarm as they squared off on either side of
her, the menace returning to Enyo's shoulders as AJ's eyes began
to whirl in a telltale mixture of purples, greens, and blues.

"You won't be able to do anything if I knock you on your
ass again," Finn interrupted, her eyes focused on his nose. At
the reminder of their first face-off, the color leaked from his
irises, returning to their obscure black. His face reddened and
his chest heaved with frustration as he warred with his temper.

Enyo watched his struggle, her face pensive.

"He does not know how to fight."

The boy's already red face darkened several shades, his
eyes darting between them like trapped prey. Before Finn had
time to predict it, he drew his fist back and punched the wall
of *Independence* with surprising force.

"Shut up, you *dog*!"

Shockingly, Enyo's eyes softened with what looked to be pity.
Seeing it there seemed to be the final straw for AJ and he turned away
from them both, his heavy footfalls stomping down the hallway.

Finn found it hard to believe Shane and Conrad would
neglect to teach their brother something as necessary as
how to defend himself, but given the way their guilt had led
to coddling in the past, she was starting to see how such
instructions may have fallen to the wayside.

"AJ," Finn called out to him. He stopped just before round-
ing the corner, but he refused to turn and face her. Taking it

as a somewhat positive sign, she continued. "Do you want to learn how to fight?"

Back ramrod straight, he lifted his head a fraction of an inch before calling back.

"Shane would never allow it."

"I'm not asking what Shane will allow. I'm asking what *you* want."

Taking a deep breath, he finally turned to face her, his expression set with determination.

"I want to learn how to fight."

Finn nodded once in acquiescence.

"Fine. We start tomorrow."

It was AJ's turn to look shocked. His eyes went wide, hope and disbelief warring with one another.

"You're going to teach me?"

"You better rest up," she warned him, her face stern. "I won't be going easy on you."

Finn tried not to let her fatigue show. She'd have to deal with Shane—and most likely Conrad too—which would be a pain, not to mention the time and commitment involved in training an unstable hybrid with unresolved trauma and anger issues.

But then something strange happened. As she stood there lamenting the huge undertaking she'd just piled on her own shoulders, AJ smiled. She'd never seen him smile before and if she'd thought him painfully beautiful before . . . with that smile he was devastating. It transformed his features and made him look the way a fourteen-year-old boy with his whole life ahead of him should.

"I'll see you tomorrow," he promised before darting around the corner and out of sight.

Sighing, Finn turned to find Enyo's tawny eyes assessing her.

"The boy's temper is going to be a problem."

"I don't know, I've seen worse." Finn offered her a knowing smile. One Enyo returned easily, her fangs gleaming in the artificial light.

NINE

They made it to Tiri's room without further incident. The door barely had a chance to open fully before the little girl was there, green eyes wide with excitement and a sweet smile on her lavender lips.

Finn stifled a laugh as Tiri practically bobbed in place, her tiny body unable to contain the excitement bubbling over. Her bouncing ringlets were pulled away from her face and secured with a pretty purple bow that matched her pale lavender skin. She wore pants and a short-sleeved top, her peculiar vinelike markings in plain sight.

"Finn! Enyo! Come in! I'm so excited you're here."

Enyo cast a confused glance at Finn, who merely shrugged her shoulders and smiled, following the child into the depths of her bedroom. It looked the same as it had weeks ago: a desk littered with paper and colored pencils, an assortment of metal puzzles and stuffed animals scattered throughout, and the blindingly beautiful mural adorning the walls.

Finn heard Enyo suck in a breath at her side and followed her gaze to the plant life Tiri had hand painted all by herself and with expert precision.

"Pretty incredible, isn't it?" Finn asked the Sirian.

The warrior didn't answer. Instead, her bemused expression softened and she turned to stare at Tiri. The child was waiting for her and stepped forward with her hand outstretched.

"My name is Sotiri, but everyone just calls me Tiri. It's nice to finally meet you, Enyo. I can already tell we're going to be good friends."

Enyo eyed Tiri's small hand like it might be some kind of trap and Finn finally released the chuckle building inside of her as she watched the standoff between fierce warrior and determined little girl. Tiri's hand remained steady, her eyes focused, as she waited for the large woman to take it. Eventually, Enyo seemed to come to a decision. Extending a fur-covered hand to grasp Tiri's, she bowed her head to the child.

"Well met, little Tiri."

The girl beamed, a grin taking over her elfin face from ear to ear. Satisfied, she turned to make her way toward the desk against the wall. Watching her go with a puzzled expression, Enyo leaned into Finn and whispered.

"How does she know my name?"

As Tiri fiddled with the papers spread across her desk, she shouted casually over her shoulder.

"I heard it Finn's head."

Enyo's jaw slackened and her brows rose into her multi-hued hairline.

"She *what*?"

"Tiri," Finn called. "I thought we talked about this."

The little girl turned narrowed eyes on Finn and placed her hands on her hips.

"It's not *mind snooping* if I'm trying to save your life. Conrad says so."

Finn's heart seemed to skip a beat and her body went tense, but before she could respond to that interesting tidbit of news, the little girl pulled a piece of paper from the center of the pile and thrust it proudly in Enyo's direction.

"I think you'll like this one," Tiri told the Sirian.

Enyo reached out a tentative hand and grasped the paper. She turned it over to reveal one of Tiri's colored-pencil drawings. In it, the Sirian stood in the dark, her feral stare illuminated by the moons overhead. Her long, intimidating claws were dripping with red and a soldier lay unmoving at her feet.

More hard lines in that deep shade of red colored the immobile man's chest and throat.

Finn's eyes widened in alarm at what the girl had obviously gleaned from her mind and stepped in to confiscate the drawing. Before she could, Enyo folded the paper and stuffed it in her pocket. A genuine smile of amusement lifted her lips.

"You are right, I do like it."

Tiri grinned happily before turning to Finn, her eyes sobering as she did.

"I missed you, Finn. You shouldn't have left without saying goodbye. Everyone's thoughts were so sad when you left."

The solemn little girl's words filled Finn with shame, and she sighed just as the automatic doors opened once again behind them and the energy around the room pulsed with tension.

"I thought I said no visitors, Lil' Bit."

Conrad's low voice washed over the trio. As soon as Tiri saw him, her mouth widened in an unrepentant grin.

"You did."

Finn turned in time to see him shake his head and aim an incredulous stare Tiri's way. Enyo shifted closer to her side, her stance defensive and her black claws elongating almost imperceptibly. Conrad's sharp blue stare took in the Sirian warrior and then finally shifted to Finn.

"We need to talk."

It took some convincing and several promises to return— the guilt caused by Tiri's panicked expression at her departure wreaked havoc on Finn's insides—but the child finally allowed them to leave. Enyo, on the other hand, flat-out refused to give Finn some alone time with the blue-eyed, formidable hybrid.

A small part of her was grateful for the backup, and Finn couldn't muster the energy to fight her on it. Conrad, however, was on the darker side of livid. It was obvious he held no affection in his heart for the Sirian, and given his history with the race, she couldn't entirely fault him.

Regardless, a seething Conrad led Finn and Enyo to the crew rec room. Stopping before allowing them entrance, he cast a dark glower Enyo's way before lowering his gaze to Finn's.

"Is the bodyguard really necessary?"

Finn registered the hurt in his glowing eyes simmering next to the anger. She fumbled for a response as the full force of it washed over her, but came up empty.

Considering the way they'd left things during her last stay on *Independence*, she found his gall at questioning her distrust more than a little strange.

In fact, she found it downright frustrating.

Shaking free from the stupor that had been shrouding her since she'd first laid eyes on him, Finn finally allowed the resentment and betrayal seething within her to surface.

"Can you blame me? Considering the way you played me last time."

Enyo remained uncharacteristically quiet at Finn's back. Hearing her accusation, Conrad's stare widened incredulously.

"*I* played *you*?"

"Please. All you've done since I met you is lie to me. *All of you.* You knew about Grim being the Luminary and you knew he'd sent me here."

Finn pushed her way past Conrad and stormed into the rec room. Her eyes skimmed past the Earthen pool table, holoscreens, and furniture and landed on the neon flashing bar to her left. Charging up to it, she tagged a shot glass and a bottle of bright orange alcohol. Grim would lose it if he saw her drinking, dulling her senses when she should be alert.

The thought made her fill the glass to the rim.

She finished pouring just as Conrad stormed inside. Enyo trailed behind at a safe distance, her yellow eyes watchful.

"None of us knew your relationship when he sent you to us," Conrad launched in, eyeing the shot glass and its contents warily. "I had no idea that *Grim*, as you call him, had practically raised you."

She'd noticed that Conrad had yet to call her by his nickname for her, *Hellion*, and the loss of that intimacy coupled with his anger hurt her more than she cared to admit. Finn tipped the glass back against her lips and swallowed its contents, biting back a wince as it burned a pathway down her throat.

"And why should I believe you now?" Finn hissed. "That day, before we entered Cartan's orbit, you had your chance to tell me everything. *You didn't.*"

The glow of his eyes became painfully intense and Finn backed away instinctively. Before either of them could continue to fan the flames, a loud crunching sounded from behind them, slicing through the tension in the air. Their heads turned at the same time to find one of *Independence*'s pilots lounging on the couch at the far side of the room, mouth full of whatever was making that Gods-awful crunching. Over his tall, lean body he wore his token tan overalls. His spiky hair had been dyed a neon shade of orange and the caramel skin around his mouth was covered in green crumbs.

The young pilot flashed a wry smile and swallowed.

"Jax, get out," Conrad growled.

Jax raised his hands in surrender. Even so, Finn noticed, he made no move to exit. "Hey, don't mind me. I'm a purely impartial third-party witness with no vested interest in how this plays out whatsoever. By the way," he continued, looking at Enyo, "who's the new hottie?" To punctuate his question, Jax wiggled his orange eyebrows and winked at the Sirian.

Enyo looked him up and down, found him clearly wanting, and growled.

Ignoring them both for the moment, Conrad launched back in.

"Can you honestly say you've never stretched the truth for the greater good?" When Finn leveled him with a defiant stare, he ran a hand over his face in vexation. "You're a thief for the love of the Gods, how can you be so sanctimonious?"

"I grew up with a code of honor and decency," she shot back. "One no one else on this ship seems to share."

Jax began to mutter under his breath, his round, amber eyes dubious. "Honor and decency in a galaxy ruled by the Reliance? You must be used to disappointment then."

He dipped his hand into the clear bag of green-dusted spheres and popped a few more in his mouth. The crunching practically reverberated off the walls around them. Though it took effort, Finn dutifully ignored him, focusing all of her fury on Conrad instead.

"I do not lie, not about things like that and not even for the greater good."

"Well"—Conrad scowled, crossing his arms at his chest and sharing a look with Jax—"we fall at your feet in apology then. I had no idea such a sacrosanct member of society was standing in our midst. Do the Gods know they've misplaced you?"

Finn clenched her jaw, feeling the heat rise in her cheeks.

"What the hell are you getting at, Conrad?"

"I think he's calling you a hypocrite, just in a very *round-about* way," Jax answered through a mouthful. Both Finn and Conrad sent death glares in his direction, the fire of their frustration fanning out. In response, the pilot held his hands out in supplication. "Hey, impartial third party, remember?"

Grabbing his bag of snacks, Jax rose from his place on the couch and headed for the door. Just when she thought they were safe to continue their argument in private, the pilot stopped at the threshold and called over his shoulder.

"Would you two hurry up and make a decision on what you're doing? Do you hate each other? Are you a couple? Some of us are still waiting for our *thank-you* lap dance . . . although, I would be willing to accept a substitute if you wanted to tag in the sexy newbie."

Jax grinned lasciviously in Enyo's direction before walking out of the room and leaving them all in stunned silence.

The reprieve didn't last long, however, and Conrad launched right back in.

"Finn, none of us were aware your relationship with the Luminary was anything other than professional. If I'd known"—he paused, the glow in his eyes receding as his stare held hers—"I would have told you and we could have avoided the last three weeks of drama."

"*Drama?*" The whisper was all Finn could manage.

Conrad watched her carefully before expelling an angry huff.

"You ran off without giving any of us a chance to explain. We had no idea where you were or if you were okay; it was impulsive and selfish."

Finn's mouth fell open.

"That's enough." There was an edge to Enyo's voice Finn had yet to hear. The large Sirian took a step toward Conrad, not cowed in the slightest by his size or abilities. "You have said your piece. However, I am free because of *N'Goza* and you will not continue to insult her in my presence, *lafaar.*"

As Finn was not fluent in Sirian, she had no idea what Enyo had just called him, but judging from Conrad's dark look of fury, it certainly hadn't been a compliment.

He stood motionless for long, tension-filled seconds; the blaze of his irises shining brightly. Finally, his stance loosened infinitesimally and his face shut down. The glow dulled and his cold gaze moved past Finn as he marched out of the rec room.

She stared at the spot he'd just occupied, the numbness from the shot she'd taken earlier fading as anger and sadness filled her.

She had expected many things in returning to *Independence*. She knew she'd have to face her sister at some point, and she knew a showdown with Grim was imminent, but Conrad's anger had never occurred to her.

Speaking of my sister . . .

Iliana had been noticeably absent since Finn's return to the ship. Given how their last interaction went—with Iliana using her abilities to see Finn's darkest memories—she supposed her older sister could be steering clear of Finn's wrath. Though, she found it hard to believe the normally tenacious courtesan had suddenly learned the wisdom in giving her little sister space.

"I think it is safe to assume Conrad does not care for me," Enyo mused, interrupting Finn's train of thought.

"I wouldn't take it personally. A Sirian soldier killed his mother; tore her apart while he watched."

Enyo growled, showing her teeth.

"The dogs who serve as guards to the Reliance are not Sirians. They are nothing more than outcasts with no tribe and they bring dishonor to our people."

As interesting as that revelation was, Finn found herself too lost in the tumult of emotions brewing inside of her to comment.

"Conrad was not the same man after you left." Finn's head shot back around to see Isis had appeared in the doorway, her silver eyes assessing the room and her purple robes swaying with her tall body's graceful movements. "We were all worried for you, but Conrad . . . Well, Conrad is not a man accustomed to fear, and when you left us, he wore his like a second skin. Each day I watched him prowl the ship, vibrating like a bomb ready to explode. I watched as he begged Tiri to find you, argued constantly with Shane, and even refused to speak to the Luminary."

As Finn took in that surprising bit of news, it settled in the pit of her stomach. It felt like a bag of coiled serpents had taken residence there, slithering around inside of her and spreading guilt in their wake. Even as she battled with the uncomfortable feelings, the need to defend her actions became too much to ignore.

"I couldn't stay, not after what happened, not . . . after Grim."

Isis's iridescent blue face softened.

"My child, you need not explain yourself to me. It is clear you and Conrad share a bond. I merely wished to offer insight as I would hate to see that bond severed because you are both more hardheaded than you would care to admit. I understand why you did what you did, and were he not so consumed with worry over your well-being, Conrad would too. Let us just say it is in the past and I am relieved to see you back and well." The Aquariian offered Finn a small smile before turning to Enyo. "When you are ready, have Finn bring you to my sanctuary."

With the invitation hanging in the air between them, Isis offered them a solicitous nod before taking her leave. A few beats of silence passed before Enyo broke it.

"I think I like the blue one."

Finn smiled at the understatement, eyeing the empty doorway. Hours ago, he had accused Isis of trying to harm her, but now . . .

"Yeah, me too."

She finally let her gaze drift to Enyo's.

"It seems as though you have much more to tell me about your time on this ship," the Sirian said with a knowing stare.

TEN

Finn spent the next two hours filling Enyo in on the events of the last month. The Sirian guarded her expression, listening intently and nodding every so often to encourage her to keep talking. Finn told her everything, except for her time alone with Iliana after being healed and the secret shame it had revealed.

All these cycles later, she could still feel the recoil of the chancellor's gun in her hand as she fired the shot that ended Sophie's young life. Sophie, her only friend and light in the darkness of her imprisonment at the chancellor's hands. Despite Conrad's past assurances that Sophie's death wasn't her fault, Finn couldn't shake the heavy sense of guilt.

She'd spent the better part of the last three weeks pushing all thoughts of Sophie and the chancellor as far from her mind as her psyche would allow, and she had no intention of bringing them to the foreground now.

Despite some initial discomfort and much to her surprise, Finn found it easy to open up to the Sirian. The only time the large woman showed any reaction to her story at all happened when Finn reached the reason for her hasty departure from *Independence* and thus, Grim's betrayal.

"*Kunyamen*," Enyo spat; her eyes shooting fire.

Finn tensed at the vitriol in her voice.

"I don't know what that means, but it doesn't sound good."

"There is no translation in your tongue, but it is the worst insult my people have for someone like this Luminary . . . for a man who lacks integrity."

Finn nodded her head, unsure how to respond to the vehemence in the Sirian's voice. After eight cycles under his tutelage, it was hard to hear her mentor referred to as a man who lacked integrity—no matter how true it may be. The naïve girl inside of her wanted to jump to Grim's defense, but the bitter woman his betrayal had nurtured held her back.

"I wish to go to the sanctuary the blue one mentioned," Enyo mused, interrupting Finn's thoughts.

Two hours later, Finn had dropped Enyo off at Isis's sanctuary for a visit and spent some time catching up with Tiri in her room. The Sirian only allowed the separation on the promise Finn would go straight to her room and await her new bodyguard's return.

Now, she was finally alone with her thoughts, and she was learning that alone with her thoughts was not a great place to be. Finn flopped on the soft bed and considered the ceiling. Despite her desire to hide away and avoid any inevitable conflict, there was a large part of her that was grateful to be back on *Independence*.

Shane wanted to join forces in saving the hybrids and she was more than happy to share the burden of that particular task. She wasn't sure if she'd ever trust the captain and his crew again, but if Conrad, Isis, and Tiri were to be believed, none of them had known the true extent of Grim's lies.

Conrad was not the same man after you left.

Isis's quiet proclamation rang in Finn's ears, resonating like a sonic pulse. Fueled by righteous anger, she'd felt supremely justified in her actions for the last few weeks. She hadn't once stopped to consider the ones she'd left behind.

She hadn't allowed herself.

You shouldn't have left without saying goodbye. Everyone's thoughts were so sad when you left.

Poor little Tiri; every time Finn moved to leave the room, the child's eyes would light up with a panic she couldn't quite hide.

Conrad, a man unaccustomed to fear, had spent the last three weeks terrified for Finn's well-being. Shane and Isis had worried; even AJ seemed to be affected by her leaving. After cycles on her own, it was both terrifying and oddly touching to realize so many people were in her corner.

If she were really being honest with herself, she would admit that running away and enacting a plan to save the hybrids without help *had* been a bit impulsive and maybe just a *touch* selfish, but Finn wasn't sure she was ready to be that honest.

"I owe Conrad an apology, don't I?" she asked the empty room. As expected, the walls didn't respond, but Finn figured she already knew the answer anyway.

Enyo is going to kill me.

On that dark thought, Finn rose from the bed and headed for the door.

Finn regarded the door to Conrad's quarters, wringing her hands nervously. Should she knock? Should she just walk in, blurt out an apology, and sprint back to her room before Conrad had time to deny her?

It was safe to say that acts of contrition weren't exactly in Finn's wheelhouse. To survive the Farthers, it was necessary to stand by one's decisions and never falter; never show weakness. In those endeavors, she had always been successful. But Finn wasn't in the Farthers anymore, and the father she was starting to remember, her *real* father (Gods rest his soul), had taught her better. So she forced herself to take a deep breath and knock.

Hours seemed to pass in the tense silence that followed. Finally, the door hissed open in front of her and Finn heaved an internal sigh of relief; a relief that died a sure, quick death when she caught sight of Conrad on the other side of the door.

He wore a singlet and cargo pants like before, but he'd recently showered and wet chunks of dark hair fell down to his shoulders, beads of water dripping from their ends and trailing a pathway down dark skin stretched taut with muscle. He registered her presence with mild disinterest, his azure eyes flicking over her with the kind of annoyed apathy one might reserve for a rodent.

"I thought I heard someone lurking out here."

Clearing her throat, she soldiered on. "Can I come in?"

"What do you want, Finn?" he asked flatly, instead of moving.

He wasn't even going to let her in. Well, if the stubborn jerk wanted to have it out in the doorway, she'd just have to adapt. There was no turning back now.

"Through three cycles of hell, I had one person I could depend on," Finn blurted out, "just one." Then, much quieter she said, "And we both know how that turned out." She could feel the tears rising, burning her eyes at the mention of Sophie, but she forced them down. At her words, Conrad's face softened and his eyes flared. He looked like he might interrupt, but she held a hand out to stop him. "After that I was alone . . . until I found Grim. He taught me how to survive; taught me valuable things . . . things I never would have learned without him. I thought . . ." Finn stopped when her breath hitched and shook her head. "It doesn't matter what I thought. When I saw him here on *Independence*, when I found out what he was . . . I realized everything had been a lie. I know I should have given you the chance to explain things, and I'm sorry that I didn't. I shouldn't have run away—"

Before Finn could finish, the big man moved. His hand going behind her head as he pulled her into his solid chest for a tight embrace. Acting on its own volition, her body sagged against his, absorbing the heat. Thankfully, he was careful and their skin didn't touch. Finn wasn't sure she could handle another foray into Conrad's memories; she was light-years away from being able to control her abilities.

Eventually, he gave her body one last squeeze and released her. When her eyes next roved over his face, she found him watching her intently, his jaw no longer tight with tension.

"*Hellion*," he whispered. Finn's head swam as he spoke. "I can't imagine the things that must have been swirling in that head of yours when you found out who the Luminary was. On the heels of everything you had just been through; your memories returning, almost dying . . . I understand why you left. I'm not happy that you did, but I can understand."

The tightness that had settled in Finn's chest over the last three weeks released and she took a full, deep breath for the first time since leaving *Independence*. Conrad's hand moved toward her face, stopping when only centimeters separated his skin and hers.

"Cool. Jax owes me three weeks of kitchen duty."

They both turned in the direction of the awed whisper to find the ship's second pilot, Lex, amber eyes wide with excitement and her signature pink hair styled in twists and braids across her head. When her eyes caught Finn's, a blush rose in her caramel cheeks just above her twin fish marking and she smiled. "Jax and I made a bet about you two. It looks like I won."

"Lex—" Conrad started in with a warning growl, but the pink-haired menace merely shot him a cheeky wink.

"Don't start with me, big guy. You're the one canoodling in the hallway." Before either of them could comment further, she continued, "Dinner is ready and our table seems to be filling up these days. You two better hurry if you want a seat." Returning her dopey grin to Finn, her voice went uncharacteristically soft as she said, "Welcome back, *Finnie*."

Now it was Finn's turn to growl at the Gods-awful nickname Lex seemed determined to give her, but the woman merely turned away and skipped down the hall, whistling a jaunty tune as she went.

ELEVEN

Suffice it to say, Finn was a swirling mess of confusing emotions by the time she made it to the crew dining area. After a rushed, if not slightly awkward, goodbye to Conrad, she'd raced back to her cabin in hopes she might find Enyo there, but the Sirian had been noticeably absent.

The desire to lock herself in her quarters rather than face whatever might be waiting for her at dinner was stifling. Tiri had already let it slip that Grim was no longer on the ship. Apparently he had "important business" to settle in the Farthers.

Whatever that means.

At least she wouldn't have to deal with *his* presence for the foreseeable future.

What about Iliana? She knew she wasn't ready to face her sister; the bitter pain of their last interaction was still too fresh. However, she also knew from experience she couldn't hide forever.

She was so lost to her thoughts of bets, Grim, Iliana, and the future, that by the time she made it inside the elevator, Finn barely registered the claustrophobic ride upstairs. When the doors opened, she nearly took a step back at the sight and sounds that greeted her.

The long dining table with all its mismatching chairs was almost full. Jax and Lex with their neon dyed hair and matching coveralls sat next to each other in their usual seats chatting animatedly with Nova who sat to their right. Nova still wore her shorts and crop top but her brown locks had been pulled up and braided in a style similar to Lex's. By the looks of things, it seemed as though the doxie and the twin pilots were making fast friends.

Every now and then Jax would turn to the large form at his other side and wink. Finn's stomach clenched at the sight.

It was her first time seeing the Khaleerian hybrid since rescuing him from his imprisonment on Senator Califax's estate. It was also her first time seeing him conscious, and he was much larger than she remembered. He nearly took up an entire corner with his massive frame. He looked to be in his twenties, a fall of chestnut brown hair barely concealing two shiny black horns as they curled back and around his head.

While he listened, his tan cheeks flushed pink with embarrassment.

Shane sat at the head of the table with Conrad occupying his usual place at the captain's left. Some of the tension had cleared from Shane's handsome features and he'd taken the time to shave his stubble and comb his blond hair into obedience. Conrad had once again pulled his dark dreads into a messy topknot and his blue eyes shone with amusement. At the other end, Isis and Tiri huddled together, their blue and lavender heads bent as they smiled and whispered next to a subdued AJ. The sight warmed her from head to toes.

Thankfully, Iliana was not present.

On a deep inhale, Finn's eyes searched for an open spot, only to stop short when she caught an eyeful of Enyo seated next to a vacant chair and looking angrier than Finn had ever seen her. She fought a gulp of trepidation, plastered a smile on her face, and headed in the irate hybrid's direction.

As soon as her backside hit vinyl, the Sirian leaned in with a harsh whisper.

"How am I supposed to protect you when you refuse to stay in one place?'

"I'm not an invalid for crying out loud," Finn whispered back. "I did manage to free you from a heavily guarded estate if you remember." At Enyo's hard, unrelenting glare, Finn rolled her eyes and relented. "Oh fine, but just so you know, it was *important*." Finn nodded her head in Conrad's direction as inconspicuously as possible and Enyo's lips twitched knowingly, revealing a row of sharp fangs.

"Do not let it happen again, *N'Goza*, no matter how *important*."

"Yeah, yeah," Finn muttered.

As though feeling her eyes on him, Conrad's stare moved over to the two of them and smiled.

"Finn," Shane called across the table, "you haven't met Axel yet." He motioned toward the horned half-Khaleerian. At his name, the blush on the large hybrid's cheeks deepened and he offered Finn a shy smile.

"Shane says you helped free me back on Cartan. Thank you."

Before Finn could respond to his softly spoken gratitude, Jax leaned closer to the Khaleerian and whispered something in his ear. Axel's face flushed a deep shade of scarlet, even as the corners of his lips tipped up in a smile.

"Oh, get a room, you two," Lex groaned.

"That's the plan, sis," Jax countered with a calculating grin.

His twin sister stuck her tongue out at him and turned to Finn.

"So *that's* a thing," she said nodding in her brother's direction. "I keep telling Axel he can do *way* better, but he refuses to see reason."

This time it was Jax's turn to stick his tongue out, flicking his thumb under his nose in Lex's direction. Axel's dark eyes remained glued to the table and he looked like he might either be fighting back laughter or the urge to vomit from embarrassment. Finn supposed either reaction would be justified given the casual way the twins were discussing his private life.

At the display, Enyo huffed at Finn's side and muttered, "*Recontenses*."

"What does that mean?" Finn whispered. Enyo's disdainful eyes flicked over to her as she bit out,

"*Idiots.*"

Finn expelled a laugh, she couldn't help herself. At the sound, the entire table turned bemused glances her way and the laugh became a soft smile. She'd missed this, all of it: the ridiculous conversations, jabs, and complete lack of privacy. Gods help her, these people were certifiable, but she'd missed them.

The hard grip of anger and resentment around her heart loosened, taking the rest of her tension with it. She'd had five seconds of this blissful peace before Iliana came striding around the corner, gracefully balancing several trays of food in her dainty hands.

Finn's stomach clenched in pain as a rush of feelings overcame her moment of comfort.

Her sister's long, fiery waves were secured with golden pins at the top of her head. She wore an ankle-length blush gown with cap sleeves. The skirt fanned out at the hips and complimented her indigo eyes . . . indigo eyes that matched Finn's own. As usual, nary a hair was out of place and her makeup had been expertly applied.

Finn felt eyes on her and realized several members of the crew had turned their gazes in her direction in a shameless bid to gauge her reaction. She bit the inside of her cheek and focused her stare on the tabletop, taking a page from Axel's book.

One by one, Iliana made her way around the table, dispersing food as she went. As she passed by Finn, she placed a tray in front of her and leaned down to whisper.

"Welcome back, Finn."

Finn's fingertips sank into her thighs in a bid to control her anger. She refused to respond in any way or meet Iliana's expectant look. Instead, she focused all of her attention on the plate of steamed vegetables, rice, and hunk of glazed beef in front of her.

As she prepared to dig in, savoring the scents of a warm, flavorful meal, Enyo once again leaned into her side, her tawny eyes alight with interest.

"*That* is your sister?"

"Not anymore," Finn retorted, glaring daggers of anger at Iliana's back.

After everything they'd been through—together and apart—her sister had thrown it all away at the first opportunity to reach inside Finn's mind and pluck away her darkest sin. She'd begged Iliana to stop, but her wretched sister had refused to listen, too blinded by her own selfish motives.

Now, Finn's past stood between them like an impassable mountain and she would never forgive Iliana for all it had revealed.

Iliana took the seat to Shane's immediate right and a moment of awkward silence fell over the room before it was broken by the lone sound of metal scraping against metal. Finn glanced to her side to find Enyo—either oblivious or impervious to the uneasiness around her—shoving forkfuls into her face.

Finn took a deep breath and joined the Sirian, practically inhaling the delicious contents of her dinner plate. The rest of the room soon followed suit and eventually the low din of conversation filled the space around them.

Finn was content to listen to the familiar and soothing sounds, only chiming in to answer questions directed at her. Most of them had to do with her time away from *Independence* and Enyo's rescue.

By the time dinner was over and the conversation began to lull, Finn was done with answering questions and ready to head back to her room for some much-needed sleep. Lex, Conrad, and Jax were assigned dish duty and stayed behind to clean up. Finn almost laughed at the twins' pouting faces and the stoic glare they provoked in Conrad.

As she moved to leave the room, she shot the blue-eyed hybrid a cheeky wink. He merely shook his head in bemusement, a grin spreading across his face as he followed the twins to the kitchen.

Finn almost made it to the elevator before a blur of pink stepped in front of her and stopped her in her tracks.

"Finn, we need to talk."

Finn's face heated with her anger, and she finally made eye contact with her sister.

"I don't have anything to say to you," she told Iliana flatly.

"Just hear me out, Little One."

At the mention of her childhood nickname, sizzling tendrils of rage began to unfurl and spread throughout her body.

"What's the matter?" Finn seethed. "You didn't get enough of a show last time?"

Iliana's face tightened in pain, but she didn't back down.

"I don't expect your forgiveness for what I did."

"Good," Finn bit out as she shouldered past, "because you're not going to get it."

With remarkable speed, Iliana moved to block her path once again.

"I am the only person who can teach you how to use your abilities. I'm trying to help you, Finn, to give you back some control." The unyielding expression on her face softened as she continued. "I know what it's like to fear these gifts. Let me help you."

The offer ignited a tenuous spark of longing inside of Finn and she found herself hating Iliana even more intensely for putting it there. No matter how much she wanted it and no matter what Iliana's motives might be, she would never trust her sister again.

Moving a step into Iliana's space, Finn narrowed her eyes and bit out a harsh whisper.

"That would be a nice offer if you were someone I could trust. It's too bad you already made sure that will never happen."

With those parting words, Finn moved around her sister and into the elevator. The doors closed on Iliana's dejected expression and Finn felt the weight of it the entire ride down.

TWELVE

Once again, sleep eluded Finn that night. Her thoughts raced and her temper flared at the memory of Iliana's proposal. Not that her sister's readiness to exploit the one thing she knew Finn needed the most really surprised her, but still. The force of her ire swirled in her gut uncomfortably.

As she listened to the sounds of Enyo's deep, even breathing from where she slept on the floor beside her, Finn allowed herself to imagine what it would be like to have control over her abilities. The offer tempted her, to say the least. She'd been living in fear of these *gifts* ever since she'd realized the extent of what they could do.

What if she could touch people without trepidation? Without having to worry about what they might see?

Images began to flood her mind: Finn's hand holding Tiri's, Finn touching Conrad's face . . . Finn kissing Conrad.

It might almost be worth the hardship of working with Iliana if it allowed her to learn control.

Almost.

On that depressing thought, Finn's tired body relaxed into the mattress and she finally fell into a deep sleep.

He is coming. They've removed the chains and given the girls special dresses to wear just for him. It makes Finn feel queasy. Just the thought of him makes her sick with fear, and she knows Sophie feels the same. More and more lately she's been getting this far-off look in her eyes, as if she's going somewhere else, and even Finn can't reach her.

It feels like she is losing her only friend. Finn cannot survive here without her. If only she could find a way to escape. Maybe then there could be hope for them.

The door opens and he walks in, a cruel smile playing on his thin lips. His black eyes find Kyra first. His smile widens, revealing a row of too-white teeth, and her stomach clenches in fear.

She has always been his favorite.

"Are we feeling stronger today, little dove?"

His thinning hair is slicked back. His gray suit is pressed and immaculate, as usual. He removes his black and gold cloak from his shoulders and approaches her with purposeful strides. He is a big man, and the closer he gets, the tinier she feels.

When he is in front of her, he backhands Finn across the face. Hard.

He has not removed his rings, and she feels a line of blood running down her cheek from where one has cut her. Tears sting the backs of her eyes, but she doesn't let them fall. Finn knows this is just the beginning of the pain he has planned for tonight.

"I asked you a question."

Sophie is crying softly in the corner.

"Yes, Chancellor."

He runs his hand across her cheek, smearing the blood there. "Good girl."

Finn's fists clench in a bid to hold down the tiny meal she had eaten earlier. The chancellor begins to remove his suit jacket, rolling up his shirt sleeves. He takes a gun from his belt and lays it down on the table next to her.

Her eyes widen and her chest tightens. He doesn't usually bring guns in with him. Next, he takes out his whip and sets it down. The whip she knows well.

"Are you familiar with the art of gambling, dove?" When she doesn't speak, he lifts his hand as though to strike her again, and she hastens to answer him.

"N—no, sir."

He lays out a few other nasty-looking tools before motioning for Finn to sit on the bed. She obeys quickly, and he smiles.

"Funny, your uncle knows the game well enough. And tonight we are, as a gambler might say, upping the ante."

Despite the terror his attention brings, Finn is grateful that he is leaving Sophie alone for now. She huddles in the corner with a lost look in her eyes. Finn closes hers. She pretends she is back on Gliese, lying in the cornfields, the sun on her face. She can almost feel Iliana holding her hand.

"Open your eyes."

She obeys, afraid of what will happen if she doesn't.

Her heart pounds. She hears him remove something from his belt, but doesn't look down. He runs it down her face, stopping just above her collarbone. It is a blade. Finn struggles not to cry out when he increases the pressure just enough to break the skin. It burns, and she can feel the blood pooling. She tries not to swallow, afraid it will only push the blade in deeper.

At his chuckle, her hands fist in the blankets beneath her. She feels his hot breath in her ear.

"I've been very patient, dove, but I'm afraid I've plumb run out. It's long past time for you to show me what you're capable of, don't you think?"

Finn can no longer hold back a whine of fear. The knife moves lower, stopping at her sternum. He flicks his wrist, and it slices deep. She screams, her voice cracking from the force of it.

"You can stop this, child," he whispers. "All you have to do is show me what you are."

He is still busy cutting when Finn hears a click. She opens her eyes and looks up. Sophie is standing behind the chancellor, pointing his own gun at his back. Tears are streaming down her face and her hands are shaking.

He turns and growls at her.

"What do you think you're doing, you little bitch?"

She sobs and looks at Finn with wild eyes.

Finn sits still, too shocked to move. Sophie doesn't notice that the chancellor is stalking toward her. She is crying too hard and doesn't seem to be able to make the gun fire. The chancellor's spine is rigid, and Finn can see he is beyond angry. Sophie will suffer for this interruption. When he reaches her, she breaks down, dropping the gun and falling to her knees.

His roar fills the room and snaps Finn out of her stupor. He throws Sophie against the wall, his hand gripping her throat tightly.

"You will pay for that."

Sophie can't breathe. Her face is turning purple. At the sight, anger unlike any she's ever known fills Finn, and she gets up from the bed. He doesn't notice her creep over and pick up the gun. He doesn't see her pointing it at him. It's so heavy her arms shake just trying to hold it up.

"Leave her alone."

He turns and bares his teeth at her in a cold smile, bringing Sophie in front of him. She is gasping for air, reaching out for Finn, but he holds her tight.

"That's right, dove. If you want someone to stop, you have to make them. Show me what you are."

He moves toward her slowly, Sophie still in front of him. All she can do is take small steps backward to maintain her distance.

"P—please stop. Don't come any closer."

He doesn't listen, just watches Finn like the predator he is as he stalks closer and closer still. Sophie is crying out her name, and Finn can't stop the tears flowing down her cheeks. She doesn't know what to do. He's getting too close. She takes another big step back, hitting the bed and losing her balance. Her finger slips on the trigger.

There is a deafening crack, and Finn is thrown backward. She lays in stunned silence for a moment. Then she sits up, her eyes searching to find Sophie's. When she does, she can see they are dull and glassy. She is staring into nothingness, a red stain blooming on the front of her pink dress. The *chancellor's brow is raised, but no anger flushes his face. He lets out a surprised chuckle. Finn barely hears him over the pounding in her ears.*

"That's not exactly what I had in mind."

He drops Sophie on the floor. She hits with a thud, unmoving. Finn's throat feels dry, and she is having trouble getting air.

No, she can't be dead. Finn didn't kill her . . . she didn't!

"Sophie! Sophie, wake up!"

There is a high-pitched wailing filling the room. After a moment, when her throat starts to burn, Finn realizes the sound is coming from her.

Sophie doesn't move, doesn't even blink. No breaths enter or leave her gaping mouth.

He kicks her body with the toe of a black boot.

"It's a shame. I paid good money for her. Oh well, there's always more where she came from."

His eyes are gleaming, and he's walking toward her, hands reaching out to touch her. The room spins. Her body is starting to tingle all over, like maybe this is all just a dream. Her legs feel like they're going to give out, but she can't let them. He's still coming.

Finn raises the gun again and aims it at his chest. He stops and raises his hands in supplication. She doesn't think, just pulls the trigger. The force has her stumbling backward again. When she lifts her gaze, he is on his knees, clutching his bleeding chest. For the first time in two cycles, Finn sees fear in his eyes.

Finn takes in the scene before her with a silent scream, allowing one last look at Sophie's lifeless body. Her only friend is dead. She killed her. She is a monster, just like him. She chokes back a sob and drops the gun. Then she runs through the open cell door.

Finn bolted upright in bed. Sweat dripped from her brow and her chest rose and fell with heavy pants.

No matter how far or how fast she fled, she couldn't outrun the memories of that night.

The sound of quiet whimpering pulled Finn from her thoughts and she turned, searching for the source of the sound. It took her a moment before she realized the desperate cries were coming from Enyo.

She recognized the agonized sounds for what they were.

The Sirian was in the throes of a nightmare.

"Enyo," Finn whispered, hoping to wake her as gently as possible.

Enyo's whimpers became sobs of distress, but still she did not wake. Moving quickly, Finn got out of bed, turned the lights to a low dim, and crouched next to the sleeping Sirian's side.

"Enyo, wake up. You're having a nightmare."

When she still didn't wake, Finn looked at her own hands helplessly; she'd removed her gloves before falling asleep.

Not having to worry about my powers would sure come in handy right now, she thought darkly.

Taking care not to touch the Sirian's fur, Finn grasped the nightshirt covering her shoulder and gave it a gentle shake.

"Come on, Enyo. It's time to wake up."

Enyo's answer was a gut-wrenching scream that came from deep within her belly and echoed throughout the room around them. All at once, the Sirian shot up, her claws extending as she grabbed Finn's bare forearms before she could move away.

Finn's last word before everything around her faded to black was a harshly muttered, "*Shit.*"

It is dark.

Finn does her best to tamp down on the panic rising in her chest, but she is unsuccessful.

The walls of Independence *have faded around them, morphing into the jagged, hard crags of a cave. Looking around, Finn can see that it is a whole system of caves, spanning out before her. Mounted torches illuminate wide tunnels extending north, south, east, and west.*

She turns to find Enyo seated upon a straw mat on the hard floor of the cave. A small fire burns brightly beside her. She is young, maybe fourteen, and while her eyes still carry the hard gleam of a warrior, they lack the cold, emotionless glint that has been present since she and Finn first met.

A giant, full-blooded Sirian female stands over her, regarding Enyo with pride.

"You have done well, my daughter. The tribe views you as a mighty and worthy N'Goza, as they should."

At the praise, Enyo's mouth curves in a soft smile she tries to hide.

"Thank you, Mother."

"Do not thank me yet, child. You are a formidable hybrid, and now that the tribe knows your worth, their expectations will be high and their hearts less forgiving of shortfalls."

"I will not let them down, Mother," Enyo promises with a fervent whisper.

The older Sirian nods her head once in acknowledgement before turning and making her way down one of the cave's many tunnels. Enyo's gaze follows her mother's retreating form before she allows herself to settle next to the fire. Her determined whisper reaches Finn a moment later.

"I will not let them down."

Suddenly, the caves around them disappear and Finn is standing on a rocky cliff as three Reliance hover pods circle overhead. The wind whips her hair around her face, the force of its shrill whistle filling her ears like a siren. It takes a moment for her to get her bearings enough to locate Enyo.

The Sirian hybrid has been collared. Several Reliance soldiers hold her by the arms and legs. She kicks, hisses, and fights for freedom, but to no avail.

"Kunyamen!" She yells into the wind, her eyes focused intently on something behind Finn. Finn turns and follows her line of sight to a Sirian soldier watching the struggle unfold, his brown lips twisted in a sneer.

"Not so special now, are you, little mutt," he growls.

Enyo shrieks, an equal mix of rage and terror, but the wind swallows the sound. One of the soldiers makes a closed fist, the movement charging the stunner glove on his right hand. Lights above his knuckles—from index to pinky—begin to glow and with a twitch of his fingers, he sends a blast straight into Enyo's chest.

Her body goes limp, the pods descend, and the soldiers drag her inside the nearest one.

Finn's eyes snapped open and a scream she barely managed to contain clung to the inside of her throat. She looked down to find Enyo had released her, leaving a semicircle of claw marks leaking blood from her forearm. Glancing around the room, she found the female in the corner, her knees tucked up to her chest, multihued hair cascading down her shoulders, and her arms wrapped around her shins.

The sight made Finn's chest ache. How many nights had she spent alone in the exact same position?

Too many to count.

Before she could go to the Sirian, the doors to the room hissed open and Finn looked up to see Conrad's tense body filling the doorway. He had on a tank top and a pair of shorts. His dreads fell down around his shoulders, sticking up in places and looking adorably mussed from sleep.

She went to him immediately, hoping to prevent his presence from upsetting Enyo further. When she reached him, his concerned glowing eyes landed on her injured arm.

"You're hurt," he said, as his angry gaze flashed over to Enyo.

"I'm fine, Conrad," she breathed. She ushered him quickly through the doorway and out into the hall. "Enyo just had a bad dream."

The hard expression on his face softened infinitesimally as understanding replaced the anger in his blue eyes. Their glow dimmed, and he took a deep breath before releasing it.

"I heard screaming," he murmured. "I thought it was you."

Lines of worry etched his brow and tightened the muscles of his jaw. She inched closer into him, her body moving of its own accord.

"It wasn't me." Finn released a humorless laugh. "Not this time anyway."

He frowned and looked over her head back into the bedroom. "Is she okay?"

"She will be." Finn followed his stare. "I just need some time with her."

His eyes found hers again, drinking in the sight of her with an intensity she couldn't quite define. Again, her mind conjured up images of touching him; a gentle caress of her skin against his that wouldn't send her careening down a path of dark memories. Gooseflesh spread over her arms and chest in response and her heart began to race.

After a moment, Conrad's stare fell back down to the blood still dripping freely from her arm and seemed to get stuck there.

"At least let me send Isis to tend to your arm."

"All right," Finn whispered her agreement. "Just give us some time alone first."

Conrad's mouth twitched in a tight smile.

"Convincing you to do things is much easier than it used to be."

At his jest, Finn rolled her eyes and muttered, "Will you get out of here already?"

Conrad's eyes warmed as their glow once again began to wash over her.

"Good night, Hellion."

"Good night, Conrad."

With that, he turned and strode down the hallway. Finn watched him until he was out of sight before heading back inside her room, ignoring the flutter of emotion cascading through her.

With some trepidation, she made her way over to where Enyo still sat on the floor, huddled in a ball. Slowly, Finn took a seat on the ground next to her and leaned back against the wall.

Eventually, Enyo raised her head and met Finn's stare. Finn's stomach clenched at the unmasked pain she saw in the Sirian's eyes.

"Something happened when we touched," Enyo breathed, her voice raw from screaming.

Finn stretched her legs out in front of her, crossed her feet at the ankles, and eyed her hands warily like they might belong to someone else.

"Sorry about that," she told Enyo. "I'm still trying to figure these abilities out."

Belatedly, the Sirian seemed to notice Finn's bloody arm. Her body tensed and the muscles in her face tightened. "I hurt you."

Her tawny eyes began to shine as she gritted her fangs in frustration.

Finn rushed to reassure her.

"I'm fine. Isis will heal me later. No harm done."

At Finn's encouraging nod, Enyo's body relaxed a fraction. Letting go of her knees, she mirrored Finn's posture and stretched her legs out before her.

"It will not happen again, *N'Goza*."

Finn raised her brows and offered Enyo a sardonic half smile.

"Trust me, I've had worse."

A few more beats of silence passed before Enyo broke it.

"They came at night," she muttered, her eyes drilling holes into the floor. "They crept their way through our tunnels like they had been there a million times before and slaughtered my people while they slept."

Finn swallowed hard. Enyo needed her to be strong, but damn if her hands didn't shake from the effort of holding in the storm of emotions the hybrid's story evoked.

"You were betrayed by another Sirian?" Finn asked, remembering the soldier and his menacing smile.

Enyo studied her through the corner of her eye before answering. "You saw that?"

At Finn's nod, she continued, her face pensive. "My people are proud. We do not care for or about the Reliance and their Arcturians. Since the unionization, we have kept to ourselves, building our cities underground within the northern caves of Siri, Tesla, and Gliese where the Reliance could never find us." Enyo brought her knees back up, letting her elbows rest across their peaks. "It is a rare occurrence, but warriors who lack honor or possess weak wills bring shame to the tribe. They are banished, never to return to their people or families."

Finn worried her bottom lip at the revelation. It seemed as though the Sirians placed as much importance on honor as the Khaleerians did. There was so much she didn't know about the Sirians; so much the rest of the worlds had gotten wrong.

Did this ignorance extend to other alien races as well?

"More often than not," Enyo continued, "the exiles seek out the Reliance. Joining their army is the closest thing to a tribe many of them will ever find, but none before have ever betrayed our locations or way of life to the Reliance . . . until that *kunyamen*, Argo."

"What happened?" The question fell from Finn's lips before she could stop herself.

"Argo was my mother's child and my half brother. She bore him to our chieftain years before I was born. He was ordinary; neither too strong nor too weak to really stand out. For the son of a chieftain, such mediocrity is considered disgraceful. It made him mean and jealous of those stronger than him. There were times when his cruelty nearly got him banished, but it wasn't until he expressed his desire to venture out into the worlds away from our people that the moment finally came. Sirians believe we gain our strength from the earth. It is why we do not like flying. The closer we are to the ground, the greater our power. When the chieftain learned of his desire and could not dissuade him from it, he was cast out, free to follow his whims in exchange for exile from his tribe." Enyo swallowed hard, her face darkening in anger. "It was only a matter of months before he betrayed our people to the Reliance and sold me into slavery."

She'd been handed over by her own brother. Finn knew firsthand the kind of mark such a betrayal left behind in its wake. She hoped wherever the traitorous Sirian was now, he was suffering.

"I'm so sorry, Enyo."

"It is over now," Enyo huffed, refusing to meet Finn's gaze. "You touched me and saw my memories. That is a powerful gift, *N'Goza*."

Finn noted the abrupt subject change, but she didn't force the issue. Instead, she exhaled a breath and muttered, "I don't know if I'd call it a *gift*."

Enyo finally allowed herself to look at Finn. Her eyes were shining and the hope Finn glimpsed there hit her hard like a punch to the stomach.

"Still, is there a way you could use it to erase my memories of that night?"

Finn's breath caught in her lungs and refused to release.

"I'm sorry, Enyo. I don't know how to do that."

"Then, it is not impossible?" the Sirian persisted.

"I don't know," Finn answered quietly.

The conversation died with her admission.

Ten minutes later, when Isis had arrived to tend to her wounds, Finn was still thinking about Enyo's question. Even if she couldn't erase the warrior's memories, what if there was a way to use her gifts to help the Sirian? What if Finn could learn to control her abilities and use them for good?

She loathed the idea of working with Iliana, but perhaps time with her sister was a necessary evil if it meant she could have the power to help Enyo and others like her. As Conrad had already pointed out, Finn's stubborn nature was no longer a luxury she could afford.

She groaned as the weight of her decision settled deep within the confines of her chest.

THIRTEEN

"Focus, AJ."

Finn reached out a gloved hand to pull the boy up from the crumpled heap she'd just left him in.

That morning, she'd awoken feeling stronger and more level-headed than she had in recent memory. Now that she had a plan, control over her abilities was becoming more of an eventuality than an abstract idea. Calm had settled over her, chasing away the remaining dregs of anxiety.

As promised, that morning AJ had been eagerly waiting for her outside her door.

She'd already shown him the proper way to punch. Now, they were working on AJ's stance and refining his technique in an old cargo hold that had been converted into a weight and weapons training room.

Finn knew Conrad and Shane's physiques couldn't have been maintained by genetics alone, and she was pleased to find the room fully equipped, with targets, mats covering the floors, weight machines bolted to the steel deck in the corner, weight suits for strength and endurance training, and an impressive selection of weapons—from throwing knives to pulse guns.

Enyo watched them quietly from a corner as AJ rose to his feet and gritted his teeth in frustration. Finn could tell the Sirian was visibly uncomfortable with everything that had been revealed the night before, but it seemed as though she was still determined to continue her duties as bodyguard.

"I can't focus if you keep talking at me," AJ snapped petulantly, as he blew a fall of black hair out of his face. Sweat glistened on his alabaster skin and his dark eyes narrowed angrily, making his beautiful features harsh in the artificial lights.

Finn grinned at him, tightening the ponytail of auburn waves at the nape of her neck and giving him time to find his stance once again.

"Do you expect your opponent to politely face you in silence and let you gather your concentration?"

Enyo snorted from her corner of the room, and AJ's black eyes hardened with angry resolve. He bent his knees to balance on the balls of his feet like she'd shown him and brought his hands up in front of his face. She could see the wheels spinning in his head and easily slapped away the telegraphed punches he launched in her direction.

Breathing heavily, he went wide with a jab and Finn blocked it, closing the space between them. Grabbing his shoulders, she kicked his legs out from underneath him at the knee and took him to the ground, shifting her hips to straddle his torso.

She aimed a hard punch at his face, stopping just before she made contact.

"What did you do wrong?" she asked him.

AJ's face flushed a deep shade of red as his chest heaved.

"I thought it was your job to tell me what I'm doing wrong."

Finn hopped to her feet and stared down at the boy.

"I could, but then you'd never learn." She watched him stand, eyeing her warily as he did. "You're letting your anger get the best of you. Aggression is good in moderation, but if you let yourself get bogged down by it, your fighting will always be erratic when it needs to be calculated."

He seemed to hang on her every word, his mind going to work as he turned over what she'd said. "Go get some water and take a breather," she ordered. "I want you back in fifteen minutes and the next time you flail a telegraphed punch at me, I'll knock you on your ass for real."

AJ rolled his eyes and offered her a shy grin. Seeing it on his usually angst-ridden features nearly stole the air from her lungs.

"You're on." He chuckled as he made his way over to the water.

Finn caught herself before she shook her head in stupefaction. She'd never heard the kid laugh before. She caught Enyo's eyes across the room and found the Sirian's were warm with admiration.

Who could have predicted Finn would have such an affinity for training the youth? The question turned her thoughts to Grim and her time under his tutelage. She supposed with how adamant he'd been in her training, it made sense she would be the same way with AJ.

Finn let memories of the past wash over as her pupil took his break.

Grim carefully sets down a stack of old tomes on the desk in front of Finn. She inhales the scent of aged leather and paper.

"Go on, Dhala. *Touch them," he instructs.*

Finn obeys, focusing her mind and running her fingers over the cracked covers and ancient lettering. With a delicate touch, she opens a page and just as it is when she touches maps, Finn's mind is filled with images and sensations. They have been doing this more and more, incorporating the odd activity into their daily routine.

Finn's affinity for touching objects and gleaning information from them has only been getting stronger the more they practice. As her palms drift over the title page, an image of a man with dark hair and eyes fills her mind. He is wearing a strange uniform of white pants and what looks like a short, white belted robe. She can feel his calm, calculated aggression as he squares off with his opponent. They each bow before circling one another.

Finn pulls her hand away as she reads the title page, struggling slightly to pronounce the odd word.

"Kyokushin? *What's that?*" Her confused eyes flick over to Grim to find him watching her carefully from his seat in the corner.

"*It is an old Earthen fighting style. Each of these books details a different one I have learned and adopted over the years. You will read them, and once you are finished, we will begin your training.*"

A small smile breaks out across her face at the prospect.

"*You're going to teach me to fight? But why old Earthen styles? I thought you said Khaleerians were berserker fighters.*"

"*It is true that my people find strength in their rage. Consequently, they lack patience and foresight. I have learned how important both are in defeating the enemy. Aggression is good in moderation, but too much of it makes your fighting inconsistent.*" Finn nods her head, her smile growing. His gaze falls to it and then hardens as it meets hers once more. "*Start reading,* Dhala.*"

Finn was so lost to her memories, fifteen minutes passed in a matter of seconds. She came back into awareness as AJ's fist flew toward her nose.

The boy stopped just before contact, mimicking Finn's earlier actions. He let his hand fall, a grin eating up his beautiful face.

"What the hell was that?" she growled. "We hadn't even started."

AJ squared up, his eyes dancing with humor.

"Did you expect your opponent to announce himself so you can gather your concentration?"

Finn almost smiled . . . *almost.* He was learning and he was doing so with a willingness and appetite she never expected to see in him.

Instead, she grabbed AJ by the wrist, put her leg behind his, and used the momentum of their bodies to take him to the ground. By the time she met his eyes again, his smile had become unrepentant.

"I wouldn't be so cocky," she told him. "Your form is crap."

AJ remained unfazed and Finn rolled her eyes, a reluctant smile tugging at her lips. She stood and reached out a hand to help him up but was stopped short by the pounding of footsteps and an angry yell.

"What the *hell* do you think you're doing!"

Finn turned to find Shane's angry gaze aimed at AJ on the floor. When it shifted in her direction, his green eyes practically burned with the force of his ire.

"AJ, Shane and I are going to need a minute," she told the boy. "Why don't you and Enyo practice defensive techniques?"

AJ glanced at Shane cautiously before rising to his feet and following Enyo to the far side of the room. Finn motioned for Shane to join her outside the cargo hold. There, she found Conrad leaning casually against the wall, his blue eyes watchful.

Before she could get a word in, Shane had already moved to her side. He ran a frustrated hand through his blond hair and launched in.

"What were you thinking, Finn? Did you even stop to consider running this by me?"

"AJ wants to learn how to fight," she said, pointing out the obvious.

"What AJ wants and what AJ needs are two very different things. He doesn't need more violence in his life. His abilities make him dangerous enough as it is and after everything he's been through . . . That kind of trauma would make anyone aggressive. Why stoke that fire?"

"What, you're afraid he'll become even *more* homicidal than usual?"

Shane didn't appreciate Finn's flippant comment if his dark glare and the tightening of his hard jaw were any indication. She crossed her arms at her chest.

"That's exactly why he needs to know he can rely on more than just his abilities, Shane. You're writing the kid off before you've even given him a chance." Shane looked like he was about to argue so she cut him off before he could get started again. "Have you thought about how helpless he must feel?" she asked him. "He spent the first part of his life as a prisoner, only to gain his freedom and grow up never learning how to defend himself. He's aggressive because you aren't allowing him to have any control when it's pretty obvious he could benefit from more of it."

"She's right, Shane." Conrad's quiet but gruff agreement washed over the two of them. Shane ignored it.

"*I* know what's best for him," Shane bit out. "Someone like you couldn't possibly know what it's like to try and give him a normal life after what he's been through."

Finn stiffened and her eyes narrowed.

"Watch it, Shane," Conrad said, taking a step forward to stand by her side.

"What exactly is that supposed to mean?" she asked the captain quietly, ignoring the way her heart sped up and her stomach clenched.

Shane blinked, most of his anger deflating from his body as he seemed to realize what he'd just said.

"I'm sorry, Finn, I didn't—"

Sometime during their argument, AJ had joined them in the hallway. He stood behind the captain with his hands balled into fists and his dark eyes blazing.

"You can't tell me what to do, Shane. It's *my* decision."

Shane held out a conciliatory hand and approached him.

"AJ—"

"No!" AJ cut him off with a shout. "Everyone on this ship is afraid of me except for Finn. She makes me feel normal. She's the only one who doesn't look at me like I'm some broken *thing*."

Shane's eyes softened with pain as he reached out to his half brother. "AJ, that's not true."

"It *is* true," the boy yelled, "even on a ship full of blended, I'm still a *freak*!"

Finn's heart stuttered.

"You're not a freak, AJ," Conrad told him gently. "Shane just wants you to have a normal life."

The boy turned on Conrad. Glancing between him and Shane, he expelled an angry bark of laughter.

"What's normal about a ship full of blended fugitives?"

Both of his brothers seemed to be at a loss to answer his question and Finn pitied them a little, especially Shane. He was trying to raise a traumatized teenager the best way he knew how and was only just now realizing he'd fallen short of the job. For a man like Shane, who'd grown up the way he did (with the father he did), it had to hurt.

"Kid," Finn called out. AJ's enraged stare found her, his chest rising and falling with frustrated breaths. "Go clean up. Shane and I will work things out and I expect you back here tomorrow morning. Your form is still crap."

The tension leaked out of AJ's body, replaced by relief at her command and his lips quirked in a half smile.

"Still almost got you though, didn't I?"

Finn tried and failed to glare at the boy.

"*Almost* is the key word there, kid."

AJ's smile widened and he shook his head, making his way down the hallway to the elevator without a single parting word for Shane or Conrad.

Shane watched him go like he'd never seen the boy before. The bemused expression remained stuck on his face as he turned to Finn.

"He smiled," Shane told her. "I've never seen him smile."

"Does that mean you're going to back off?" Finn asked him.

He took in her defensive posture and tense jaw and his face fell.

"Finn, I'm sorry. I shouldn't have yelled at you like that. I just . . . Things have been so hard for him. I guess I'm a little overprotective."

Finn's mouth fell open.

"A little?"

Shane finally smiled, causing his eyes to crinkle a fraction at the edges.

"Thank you for helping him."

He looked like he might want to say more, but seemed to think better of it. Finally, he gave Finn and Conrad a parting nod before following AJ's steps down the hallway.

Finn looked up at the man standing next to her and threw her arms up.

"Don't tell me I'm being stubborn or I'll be forced to slap your pretty face."

Conrad stepped into her space, his warm breath fanning her cheek as he grinned down at her.

"You think I'm pretty?"

Finn rolled her eyes. It was all the response she could muster as she struggled to keep her racing pulse in check as he moved closer.

Slowly, Conrad brought a hand up. It was only then that Finn noticed the black tactical gloves he wore. Seeming to read the question in her expression, he smiled and cupped her cheek with a large, gloved palm.

"You like them? I picked them up at a trading post on Gliese a couple of weeks ago."

At the contact, Finn's breath became uneven and she leaned into the touch without even realizing it. He'd bought them after she'd left *Independence*. Had he always known she would come back, or had he planned on coming after her?

Finn brought one of her own gloved hands up and rested it against his where it still cupped her cheek. His gaze warmed as his eyes began to glow brightly.

"I figured it would be a good first step, at least until you start your training with Iliana," he whispered.

"How did you know I decided to train with Iliana?" Finn asked, frowning.

Conrad's smile widened as he brought his free hand up, holding her face in his gentle grasp.

"I didn't, but I hoped. I'm glad to see it paid off."

Finn let her eyes flutter closed, losing herself in the feel of his hands holding her. The quiet moment lasted precious seconds before the door to the training room opened behind them.

Enyo exited, dragging a weight suit behind her. Completely ignoring their intimate embrace, she unceremoniously hefted the suit over her shoulder with a surprising show of strength— even for the Sirian.

"I'm taking this," she told Conrad as she passed.

Conrad dropped his hands as his bewildered eyes followed Enyo and her pilfered equipment down the hallway. Finn bit her lip in a bid to control the laughter bubbling up and shaking her chest.

They were really going to have to start remembering that on *this* ship, they were never alone. Sensing her mirth, Conrad's eyes returned to Finn and narrowed, but there was no real anger behind them. At the sight, she stopped fighting the giggles and erupted with laughter.

FOURTEEN

A few days after her confrontation with Shane, Finn found herself pacing anxiously in front of the door to Iliana's pod. With each step, her sore muscles screamed in protest.

Training with AJ was going well and as soon as Lex and Jax caught wind of their sessions, they'd begged to join in until Finn finally grew tired of listening to their whines. Even Axel had asked to participate.

Though he was painfully shy, the half-Sirian was also incredibly strong—if not a little clumsy—leaving Finn in charge of training all four inexperienced hybrids. At least she had Envo's help—and Conrad when he could get away from his other duties on the ship. Though the two seemed to have set aside their differences, the tension between them was still merely tolerable.

In fact, life in general had been going alarmingly well as Finn and her crew settled into a routine of sorts. The day after their arrival on the ship, Finn had given Nova an ultimatum: stay on *Independence* as a contributing member of its crew or take the gold she'd earned and a pod to her destination of choice, parting ways for the foreseeable future. If she chose to stay, she would be doing so of her own volition and would no longer be paid by Finn.

The doxie had genuinely surprised her by choosing to stay on the ship. She'd already made fast friends with Jax and Lex, and Finn often found the three of them laughing and cavorting at the ship's helm.

The only dark spot in the last week had come during one of Finn's training sessions with her students.

Jax and AJ were sparring on the mats while Lex and Axel trained with Enyo on the weight machines. As usual, Jax had been goofing off, earning laughs with his off-color jokes when he should've been paying attention to his opponent.

Rather than reprimand him, Finn waited, watching to see what AJ would do. Just as she'd taught him, the boy took advantage of the pilot's inattention and sent a quick, controlled jab straight to the center of Jax's solar plexus. The pilot lost his breath and doubled over with an "oomph" of pain before falling to the ground.

Finn's chest had warmed with pride at AJ's triumphant smile and she'd just been preparing to lecture Jax on the importance of focus, when she was interrupted by the deafening sound of weights crashing to the floor so hard it vibrated.

They'd all turned to see Axel in the corner, his chest throbbing with angry breaths and low snarls of aggression. Finn watched in dumbfounded silence as his skin began to darken to an inhuman shade of red and his muscles began to swell, bulging and tearing against the constraints of his clothing.

If Finn hadn't been watching with her own eyes, she might not have believed it.

In a matter of seconds, Axel had transformed from a timid, heavily muscled hybrid to what looked to be a full-blooded Sirian whose sheer size and muscle mass rivaled that of Grim's.

His rage-filled eyes honed in on AJ as he stomped around the weight machine and made his way over to the boy. Enyo and Finn locked eyes, knowing they'd need to take the Sirian down before he truly hurt someone.

Fortunately for them all, Jax had chosen that moment to find his feet, striding over to Axel with slow, steady steps and a grin eating up his face.

"Is all that for me, big guy?"

At the question and the sight of Jax's devil-may-care smile and glittering amber eyes, something seemed to shake loose in Axel's brain, his skin returning to its normal tan hue and his body deflating until he'd returned to his normal size.

He'd seemed genuinely embarrassed by his reaction, but it was blatantly obvious to Finn that his abilities were volatile and unpredictable. She'd made the decision on the spot to train Axel separately from the group. He and AJ could learn a few things from each other, including how to get a handle on their trigger-happy emotions.

She'd already asked them to meet her tomorrow for their first session together.

The incident only furthered Finn's determination to train with Iliana and learn to control her own abilities. After all, how could she teach others what she didn't know herself? The idea of spending any amount of time alone with her sister practically set her teeth on edge, but she'd made her decision and intended to see it through.

Hence the pacing.

After long minutes of hesitation, Finn finally raised her hand and knocked on the door. She listened for sounds of movement on the other side but heard nothing. The longer Finn waited, the stronger the urge to run became.

Her palms began to sweat beneath the material of her gloves and her heart pounded. Finally, the door opened and Iliana stood before her.

She'd gone for a more casual outfit today—for Iliana anyway—and Finn took in the pair of maroon harem pants, jeweled halter top, and black shawl draping her shoulders. Her long, red curls hung loosely around her shoulders.

"Please come in, Finn." Her smile was somewhat strained, but it was the only clue to how she was feeling. Finn followed her into the pod she used as both a bedroom and an office.

It looked the same as she remembered: a four-poster bed with silk sheets, orange and red silk draping down from the ceiling, elegant furniture, and a crystal chandelier. Candles burned on top of the bureau and vanity, illuminating the room in their warm glow.

Two chairs and a small table had been set up in the center of the space, draped with one of the yards of silk. On it sat a small bowl of steaming liquid, billows of cloying vapors wafting up from its surface.

Iliana motioned for Finn to take a seat at the table. She obeyed, giving the boiling bowl a wary glance. Noticing Finn's caginess, Iliana motioned toward the pungent liquid.

"I have found that the best way to avoid losing myself while using my abilities is to focus on something that anchors me to the present."

"So you picked *that*?" Finn asked with distaste.

"The sights and sounds can be overwhelming when we are experiencing someone else's memories. However, our sense of smell remains unaffected. I usually carry mine with me here."

Iliana tugged on a golden chain around her neck. It hung low, tucking into the space between her breasts and below her top.

Hanging from the end was a tiny silver vial.

Thinking on it, Finn realized that while she saw and heard everything when lost to a memory, her sense of smell had never been triggered. It stung to admit, but she'd been with her sister for less than five minutes and already she'd learned something new.

Perhaps this quality time would be worth it after all.

"So how long did it take you to learn to control it? I'd like to manage my expectations for how long I'm going to be stuck doing this with you."

Iliana ignored Finn's snarky tone, meeting her eyes with sincerity.

"It took me many cycles. I worked at it every day with the tutor the Luminary hired for me, and even then, it was at least two cycles before I had any semblance of control."

At the mention of Grim's alternate identity, Finn gritted her teeth.

"Well, I'm a fast learner."

"Indeed," Iliana muttered. As she took a seat across the table, her gaze fell to Finn's hands. "I'd like to avoid starting you out with skin-to-skin contact. From what I've seen, you have the ability to connect with the residue left behind on inanimate objects. It's a gift I do not possess and, as far as I can tell, it is one unique to you. I'd like to start there."

Finn tensed as she thought about her upbringing with Grim and all the times he'd asked her to touch a book here or a map there. At the time she'd been grateful for his interest in honing her skills for survival.

Knowing everything she did now, she was beginning to see her education in a different light.

Had he been grooming her from the beginning? Had he been trying to hone her abilities without her even realizing?

Sensing her disquiet, Iliana went motionless.

"Finn?"

Without any other target for the storm brewing inside of her, she unleashed it on the only person available.

"Grim knew the whole time, didn't he? He knew what I was . . . *who* I was to you?"

"He wouldn't do that to me . . . to us," Iliana defended sharply. "He knows what I went through thinking you were dead. He wouldn't keep us apart intentionally."

Finn scoffed. It seemed as though hardheadedness was turning out to be a family trait. She eyed her sister carefully, pushing to break through the stubborn woman's careful veneer of calm.

"How many half-Teslans are running around out there?" When Iliana remained silent, her expression unreadable, Finn pushed harder. "Touching objects for information was part of my daily studies with Grim. Which means he knew I was Teslan, and if he knew I was Teslan, he knew the chances were good—no, better than good—that I was your sister."

Iliana's careful mask of composure finally slipped as her indigo eyes hardened with anger. Her voice was a harsh whisper as she said, "If he kept you from me then he will pay."

Interesting.

It looked like Grim's little squadron of loyal hybrids was beginning to crumble at the edges. Iliana continued to regard Finn with intensity and she had to look away, else risk getting seared by its heat.

There was only one other time she'd seen her sister look that way: the night of Axel's rescue on Cartan when she'd saved Finn from certain death. With Finn seconds from passing out with a giant meteorhead strangling the life out of her, Iliana had touched the beast's skin and left him in a sputtering, useless heap.

You will pay for touching my sister.

Even though she wanted to change the subject—given the way Iliana's body had gone tense and the hard glint in her eyes had intensified—Finn asked her about it anyway.

"You mean he'll pay like that meteorhead back on Cartan did? What did you do to him anyway?"

"I may not be able to glean information from objects like you can, but I still have a few tricks of my own."

Iliana seemed to regain some of her self-control. The tension slowly leaked from her shoulders until her face returned to its usual detached expression. Finn was starting to think of it as her "default courtesan setting."

At the continued silence, she narrowed her eyes and waited for Iliana to continue. Her sister released a barely imperceptible sigh.

"All of the blended are unique in that our genetics seem to manifest differently depending on the individual." She nodded in Finn's direction. "Like you and the way you can read objects as well as people. You see, everyone leaves behind an emotional residue, whether on the skin or a beloved doll. It's like a fingerprint; one our people can read.

They call themselves *siphons*, but really we are more like sponges, absorbing any emotional residue we come into contact with. It's a passive ability that allows us to gather information discreetly."

"Then how did you flatten that bodyguard?" For the moment, Finn's curiosity outweighed her anger and distrust for Iliana.

"I have learned to take what I've absorbed and project it. The beast I 'flattened,' as you so eloquently put it, had killed many people. Most of them with his bare hands. Each one left behind the memories and terror of their last moments. I took those memories and forced him to relive them."

Knowing firsthand what it was like to be forced to watch memories she didn't want to see, Finn almost felt sorry for the meteorhead.

Almost.

"Can you teach me how to do it?" she asked Iliana.

"One step at a time, Little One."

Iliana's smile was small but genuine and Finn found herself too excited by the prospect of all the things she could learn to get her hackles up at the nickname.

She felt a familiar wave of determination wash over as she stared into Iliana's eyes.

"Then what are we waiting for?"

FIFTEEN

"Focus on the lilydung root," Iliana ordered, referring to the syrupy vapors wafting around them.

They'd been practicing for the last three afternoons, working on Finn's siphoning ability with inanimate objects, a talent that seemed to be unique to her.

"It smells worse than the Mud Pit," Finn complained, fighting the rising wave of lightheadedness and nausea the sickly sweet scent caused. After three days, she still hadn't gotten used to it.

"Well, it's all we have to work with until you find your own anchor scent. I don't understand why you're hesitating. The sooner you select one, the stronger your control will be. Now, focus, Little One."

Finn groaned and rolled her eyes. She didn't know what she was waiting for either. Iliana had said that her anchor scent had to be something meaningful, something powerful enough to keep her anchored in the present. The problem with that was Finn had no idea what the hell to choose.

She inhaled deeply as her bare hand made contact with the gold-handled hairbrush Iliana had presented her with. Instead of her vision going black, a strange buzzing filled her ears and her eyesight went fuzzy; distorted images began to fill her mind.

With the sweet lilydung to keep her rooted in the present, the memories didn't overtake her like they usually did. Instead, it felt more like watching scenes play out on a holojector than living them.

"Now, tell me what you see," Iliana ordered.

Finn's eyes moved rapidly behind her lids as she studied the images flashing there, forcing them into focus.

A woman sits gracefully before the mirrored vanity in Iliana's pod.

Finn inhaled the scent of lilydung again, focusing harder on her vision. She'd learned that the more concentration she applied, the clearer the images became.

The reflection in the mirror comes more clearly this time. It is Iliana. She uses the brush on thick strands of her red hair, humming quietly to herself.

"I see you brushing your hair," Finn told her flatly as she opened her eyes. "It's absolutely *riveting*."

Iliana huffed in exasperation. During their training sessions, she would often abandon her courtesan decorum and act more like the sister Finn had grown up with.

"Now I want you to try to siphon deeper. What can you tell me about the person who owned the brush before me?"

Finn closed her eyes once again and concentrated. Fuzzy images began to circle in her head. As Iliana had taught her, she fixated on one, beckoning it toward her.

Iliana sits at the foot of a bed, her back to Finn. While she easily recognizes her sister's cascade of fiery locks, everything else about Iliana is different. She is smaller and much younger, perhaps only four or five cycles. Her little shoulders are hunched as she fiddles with a stuffed animal and her short legs swing off the edge of the bed.

The room is small and modest with a medium-sized dresser and walk-in closet to the left. The sun's warm glow cascades over them through a large bay window.

A woman with dark auburn waves flowing down past her shoulders stands behind Iliana, brushing the young girl's hair gently as she hums a melody. Something about it is familiar and Finn allows herself to slide deeper into the vision until she too is standing in the room.

Taking another deep breath and inhaling the lilydung, she sidesteps around the bed, trying to see the woman's face. She makes it to her side and takes in a pair of sparkling indigo eyes and pale skin. The noticeable bump of her abdomen tells Finn she is heavy with child. Dark purple veins run a pathway up her arms and over her neck and chest. Her full lips are also a deep shade of purple and the same hue contours the blush of her cheeks.

Finn opened her eyes and stared at Iliana, her breaths coming almost as quickly as the pounding beats of her heart.

"Who is she?" she whispered.

Iliana held her stare carefully, a sad expression shadowing her face.

"That's our mother, Finn."

Finn dropped the brush and scooted back in her chair, watching it like a pulse gun she knew was about to misfire. Her hands shook so hard they trembled, as the threat of tears stung her eyes. She'd been so young when her mother was killed that she'd had no memories of the woman to hold on to.

Did Iliana understand the gift she'd just given her?

Her sister cleared her throat and met Finn's gaze, lines of worry creasing her brow.

"I'm sorry. I just wanted you to know her in some small way."

Apparently, Iliana knew exactly what she was doing and the kindness nearly undid Finn, taking the mess of emotions she already felt for her sister, tossing them in a bag, and shaking them violently.

As their training sessions progressed, her respect for Iliana had continued to grow and it was becoming harder and harder to keep her at a distance. She seemed to be trying to make amends for her betrayal, and rather than make things clearer, it only confused Finn's feelings further.

Finn shoved gloves over her hands. Jumping up from her chair, her eyes darted around the room before meeting her sister's.

"I have to go."

Iliana's arm extended toward Finn before dropping back to her side. Her brow puckered in concern and she whispered, "I'm sorry."

Glancing down at the table one more time, Finn's hand shot out and snatched the hairbrush. She didn't bother looking back for her sister's reaction as she sprinted for the door and out into the hall.

Finn spent long hours locked away in her room clutching her mother's hairbrush and letting the memories of the woman she'd never known shroud her. She'd already sorted through images of her mother and father laughing together, her mother by herself, and even images of her mother carrying around a fussy baby that she knew had to be her.

Enyo had allowed Finn privacy when she'd seen the manic look in her eyes as she paced the confines of her room and told the Sirian everything that had transpired during her session with Iliana. The longer they trained and spent time together, the more willing Enyo seemed to be to relax her bodyguard duties and allow Finn some blessed moments of solitude.

She finally released the brush from her grip and tucked it tenderly underneath her pillow, realizing belatedly that she had no idea how much time had passed while she'd been deeply rooted in memories of the past.

Her mother was a unique beauty with more grace in her pinky finger than Finn possessed in her entire being. Yet there were moments: an annoyed glare when one of the pigs ran screeching through the house covered in mud or a soft laugh when one of her girls did something she found amusing. Finn realized she may have inherited more from her mother than a knack for siphoning.

Sliding on a pair of gloves, she made her way out into the hall. As though operating on autopilot, her feet carried her starboard in the direction of Conrad's room.

Iliana had given her a gift today and Finn still reeled from the weight of it. She could see her mother any time she desired. It would only take a mere touch of her fingers.

Her mind was full with all she'd learned and seen. Like a swarm of tambiflies caught in a net, each thought beat its wings furiously as it collided with the one next to it. Though it scared her to admit, she found she *needed* to see Conrad, needed his comforting presence as she processed all that the day had revealed.

Finn reached his door and didn't bother knocking. He would be expecting her. Each day they grew closer, their bond stronger, and every day they made a point to spend time with one another.

She had no idea what the future held for them or what their time together even meant. She just knew she needed him more than she was comfortable admitting.

The door opened before her and she stepped inside, her eyes searching out Conrad's form. He sat at the desk on the far side of the room, his back to Finn as he stared out the window and into the vast nothingness of space outside.

"You're late," he pointed out as he turned around. His blue eyes sought out Finn's as he turned and stood, meeting her in the middle of the cabin. Whatever he saw in hers made him ask, "Are you all right?"

She released a deep breath.

"I saw my mother today," Finn told him.

His brows drew together in confusion. "I don't understand."

"Iliana gave me a hairbrush that used to belong to my mother. When I touch it, I can see her memories."

Understanding began to light his eyes and his lips lifted in a gentle smile.

"This is a good thing, right?"

"Yes, it's a good thing. I'm just trying to reconcile the fact that my sister is responsible for something good happening to me," Finn remarked drily.

Conrad's smile widened. He lifted a gloved hand to her face, stroking her cheek gently.

"I know you don't want to hear this, but she loves you, Finn."

Her eyes fluttered closed at the contact and she found herself unable to dismiss the statement as she usually did. Instead, a confusing mix of anger and sadness filled her.

"She made me relive what I did . . ." Finn trailed off. She still couldn't bring herself to say Sophie's name aloud. "If that's how she shows her love, I don't want it."

Hearing the pain in her voice, he brought his other hand to her shoulder and squeezed gently. Her heart fluttered at the touch.

"I understand, but hopefully someday you will learn to see what happened to your friend the way I do." Finn tensed as the familiar shadow of doubt crept over her. Conrad sensed it and he forced her to meet his eyes. "It was an accident, nothing more."

When she continued to face him in stubborn silence, his hand dropped from her face and he led her to the bed. As they sat down side by side, he shot her a warm smile.

"You sat here not that long ago, doing your best to convince me that AJ's fate wasn't my fault. Even though it was hard to hear, you were right."

Finn sighed in frustration.

"I *killed* someone, Conrad. My only friend. You did everything in your power to save AJ. It's not the same thing at all."

Conrad hung his head as he whispered, "I hid in a vent and watched Shane's father murder my parents. It might not be the same, but I know what it is to live with guilt."

Finn's heart squeezed with pain and she leaned into him.

"Conrad," she murmured, "that wasn't your fault. You were just a child."

He turned to face her and raised his brows.

"That sounds familiar," he told her, offering a small smile.

Finn bit her lip. The man wasn't playing fair. She decided to turn the subject back to him.

"Tell me more about your parents. How did they meet?"

Conrad's eyes shone with amusement, letting her know he was keen to exactly what she was doing.

"They met on my father's home planet. His people were from Merlidia before the unionization. The Reliance recruited him at an early age. He was a handsome boy and his abilities made him a useful asset to the army."

"Your father was a soldier for the Reliance?" Finn failed to keep the shock out of her voice.

Conrad's smile waned slightly.

"He wasn't given much of a choice. They took him from his parents before his eleventh cycle. But yes, my father was loyal to the Reliance for most of his life. Eventually, he ended up stationed on Merlidia. My mother was there, working as a seamstress for the wealthiest women in the Inner Rings. They fell in love almost immediately. My mother used to say 'almost' because she had no intention of ever giving her heart to a 'Reliance lackey.'" Conrad chuckled to himself before continuing and Finn smiled. "Obviously her conviction didn't last long. When she became pregnant with me, my father knew what the Reliance would do to them both. He went AWOL and took my mother to the Outer Rings. We were happy there for a time, until Shane's father tracked us down."

"I'm so sorry, Conrad."

He shook his head as though to clear it and changed the subject. "How is training going with Iliana?"

Finn shrugged as a frown tugged at the corners of her mouth.

"I'm sure it would go a lot better if I could find an anchor scent. We're still in the 'touching objects' phase. I don't know how much longer I can sniff lilydung and siphon from tea-cups and hairbrushes when all I really want to do is touch someone without showing them my worst memories."

Conrad put an arm around her, his side warm against hers. She glanced up to find a broad grin stretching his face.

"Anyone in particular you were hoping to touch?"

Some of the tension left Finn's body as she shoved into him with her shoulder.

"Yeah, I'm just dying to hold Shane's hand." She chuckled.

Conrad's laughter filled the room and they both savored the moment. Being close to him like this, his unique scent hung in the air between them, erasing her stress and filling her with a sense of well-being.

She closed her eyes, letting the mixture of mint and oil wash over her as the tension of the day sagged from her shoulders.

Wait a minute . . .

Finn leaned in closer and sniffed at him, ignoring his confused glance as she found the source of his scent: his hair.

"Are you going to clue me in here, Hellion?"

A blush rose to her cheeks.

"The scent in your hair, what is it?"

If he was at all surprised by her question, he didn't let it show.

"It's wax for my dreads."

"Do you have more of it?"

He studied her carefully, as if trying to ascertain whether she'd lost her mind, but Finn was too focused on her goal to be properly embarrassed. Eventually, he seemed to decide she was sane and moved to the far wall. He opened the top drawer of his dresser and motioned for her to come over and look at the contents.

Inside, there were at least a dozen small black jars arranged side by side.

"I like to stock up since I can only find the good stuff in the Inner Rings," he told her.

Finn carefully lifted one into the palm of her hand and screwed off the top. As Conrad watched her in befuddlement, she inhaled deeply, letting his scent wash over her.

Smiling, she put the top back on and met Conrad's gaze.

"I'm taking this."

SIXTEEN

"We come to you now with breaking news from Senator Califax's estate. It has been weeks since the Unionization Ball, but the Reliance is no closer to finding the fugitives who robbed the senator of six priceless Arcturian artifacts."

Images of the Toad and his meteorheads, looking as stoic and violent as ever, flashed on the rec room's holojectors.

"Carserus, one of the fugitives and a Yellow Faze addict, was caught fleeing from the senator's estate the night of the ball."

The Toad and meteorhead Number One disappeared from view as an image of meteorhead Number Two filled the space before them. A gaping hole marked where his right eye should have been. His left eye had a dazed expression clouding it and his slackened jaw hung open as spittle dripped down his yellow chin.

She recognized that look. Apparently, the Reliance authorities were doing their best to keep the giant subdued. Given his unnatural strength, Purple Faze and the trancelike state it induced would be the best way to do it.

Finn returned her focus to the pool table and steadied the wooden stick in her hand. She took aim at the bright yellow ball with a glossy number one painted on it. She needed this break from her training with Iliana and no amount of Reliance propaganda would ruin it for her.

"Six Arcturian artifacts my ass," Lex spat from across the table. Her bright pink braids fell to her naval and moved hypnotically with her head. "I can't believe the Toad and his

Yellow Faze freaks are getting all the credit for the job we pulled off."

Finn hit the white ball with such force it missed the yellow ball completely and shot off the table. Jax ducked just in time before it went careening into his face. He feigned terror at the close call and ran his hands over his spiky orange hair to make sure it hadn't been messed up.

"I don't think I like this game," Finn muttered to no one in particular. Conrad and Axel held back amused grins from their seats on the couch, their large bodies taking up the space to the point they nearly touched. Conrad's blue eyes sparkled as they held Finn's. Lex ceased her angry tirade long enough to shoot Finn an amused smirk. She returned the female pilot's look with a stern glare. "You should be grateful the Toad is taking the fall. Do you actually want the Reliance on our tails?"

"No"—Lex frowned—"but it would be nice to get some credit. No one even knows about Axel or Enyo . . . or any of the blended we're going to save."

"Which is a good thing, sis. This way, they'll never see us coming," Jax reminded her as he threw a lean arm around his sister's shoulder.

"I wouldn't count on it," Finn prompted. "Good luck doesn't last forever."

"Good luck and a tech genius could," Jax reminded her with a rakish wink and a wiggle of his fingers. To punctuate his not-so-subtle reference to his hybrid abilities, the fish marking on his cheek began to glow and the holojector behind him flashed in time with his movements before shutting off completely.

"Hey, I was watching that," Lex pouted. With a snap of her fingers, the female pilot's marking also began to glow and the holojector flashed back on. The volume was even louder this time around.

"I don't understand." Enyo finally broke her silent assessment of the pool table to interrupt the twins' spat. Her tawny eyes narrowed as she bared her fangs in a confused grimace. "What is the point of this game?" the Sirian asked.

Lex sighed and moved away from her brother to stand next to Enyo.

"The point is to knock the balls into the holes."

"But why?" Enyo growled in frustration.

"Because it's fun."

Lex shoved into Enyo playfully with her hip before taking her place next to Nova at the other end of the table. The doxie—dressed in a pair of pants with the legs cut up to the knees and a thin scrap of material just barely managing to cover her breasts—shot the female pilot a conspiratorial wink. As Lex aimed, she stuck her tongue between her lips in concentration.

The stick went wild in her hands as she took her shot and the white ball rolled a measly few inches before stopping at the center of the table.

"That's it," Lex shouted as she threw her hands up in frustration. "We're done playing this stupid game."

"I thought it was supposed to be fun," Enyo murmured to herself.

Finn grinned at the Sirian and suppressed a chuckle. She felt warmth at her back and turned to find Conrad had risen from his spot on the couch to join her. His posture was relaxed and the ghost of a smile played at the corners of his mouth.

Lex grabbed Nova by the hand and raced her over to the bar where a holopad rested, unused. Mark still glowing, she twisted her fingers a few inches above the pad in graceful movements and closed her eyes in concentration.

Soon, bright neon lights in pinks, oranges, and purples began to flash on the walls around them and the sounds of frenetic music filled the room, thumping so loudly Finn could feel the beat in her throat.

Jax grabbed a blushing Axel by the collar of his shirt and led him to the center of the room where Lex and Nova had already begun to jump around holding hands and bobbing their heads to the rhythm. Jerky hops and furious head bobs matched the beat.

Though their spasmodic movements made them look ridiculous, their giant grins and uninhibited dancing said they couldn't have cared less.

"Come on, boss lady!" Nova yelled over the noise.

"I don't dance," she shouted back to the doxie. "Just ask Conrad."

In direct defiance of her statement, Conrad pushed Finn between the shoulders and followed her stumbling steps into the madness. She turned to glare at the big hybrid but found him already grinning unrepentantly and moving his body in time with the song.

Finn rolled her eyes and crossed her arms tightly over her chest.

Conrad took no pity. Pulling her gloved hands away from her body, he spun her in a fast circle, forcing her to comply or else fall to the ground. Finn's dark auburn hair flew around her face from the force of the spin. Lex shrieked with amused glee at the sight and mirrored Conrad's trick with Nova.

The doxie spun, albeit less gracefully than Finn, before landing on her backside with a thud. Her cackle of laughter filled the room and the rest of the group soon joined in.

Enyo watched them darkly from the safety of the corner, her furred arms crossed at the chest. Finn couldn't hear the Sirian over the music, but she could read her lips as she muttered on an eye roll, "*Recontenses.*"

Finn laughed at the sight and closed her eyes, letting the music take over. She flailed her arms and shook her head, looking like the idiot Enyo thought she was and not caring the least bit.

SEVENTEEN

Finn plopped the oddly shaped teacup in her hands down on the table with a little too much force. Fortunately, it survived unscathed.

"I'm sick of this! When are you going to teach me how to stop showing people my memories every time I touch them?"

She and Iliana had been at it for nearly two weeks and she still hadn't graduated from siphoning memories from whatever mundane objects her sister could get her hands on.

Now that Finn had found an anchor scent all her own in Conrad's dread wax, her abilities were becoming sharper.

Patience had never really been one of Finn's strong suits and now more than ever she felt the urgency to learn whatever Iliana could teach her.

Her sister's eyes glinted knowingly. She wore another one of her fine silk dresses—this one a deep shade of scarlet—and her red hair was pulled away from her face in a chignon. They'd reached a truce of sorts ever since she'd handed Finn their mother's hairbrush, and though their relationship was still more than prickly, they were beginning to settle into a somewhat comfortable routine in one another's presence.

"In order to teach you, we will have to touch. I wasn't sure if you'd be receptive." Finn tried to ignore the vulnerability lurking in the depths of Iliana's eyes as she spoke and forced her face to remain relaxed and devoid of emotion.

"That's why I'm here, isn't it? I'll do whatever it takes."

Iliana nodded once, bringing her hands up to the table from her lap. Finn eyed them warily.

"When you touch someone, it is important that you build a wall around yourself. Keep all your feelings inside, especially the bad ones. When you are angry or frightened, you are more likely to project your memories onto others. You must learn to control what you are feeling. Each emotion goes into a box that you keep carefully closed."

Maybe this wouldn't be so hard after all. If there was one thing Finn knew how to do, it was compartmentalize her feelings. However, the anger and fear part would take some work.

"Put emotions in a box . . . got it." Finn gave her sister a sarcastic two-finger salute.

"Are you sure you're ready for this?" Iliana asked hesitantly.

"I don't remember you being this trigger-shy a month ago," Finn grumbled.

At the mention of the debacle resulting from the last time they'd touched, Iliana's gaze narrowed and her full lips pursed.

"For this to work, you're going to have to let go of the past and your resentment."

Finn sighed as she met Iliana's intent stare. Her sister wasn't backing down on this and though Finn wanted to argue, she was learning the importance of relaxing her stubborn nature for the greater good. Letting go didn't necessarily mean forgiving and she certainly would never forget, but if she wanted to hone her abilities, she was going to have to meet Iliana halfway.

Finn threw her hands up and tossed Iliana a half-hearted glare.

"Fine, I'm letting go as we speak."

Iliana's answering smile was small and somewhat tentative but the tension that had been weighing her down the last two weeks seemed to evaporate.

"When I take your hand, focus on the memory I show you. Relax your mind and your body and let go of emotions."

Iliana's hands inched nearer across the table and Finn's stomach clenched in anxiety. As though sensing it, Iliana reassured her.

"I will disengage if any of your memories slip through. Now, do you have your anchor scent ready?"

Finn pulled the small jar from her pocket and set it on the table. Twisting off the lid, she took a small dab of wax and rubbed it between her fingers. Conrad's scent immediately filled the air around her. She gave Iliana a tight nod and stretched her shaking hands across the table.

"Remember all that you've learned so far, Little One."

With that last piece of advice, Iliana's hands closed the space between them and grasped Finn's. As a low buzzing sounded in her ears and images began to flood Finn's mind, she inhaled deeply, letting Conrad's scent keep her grounded in the present.

She imagined every feeling and thought tucked tightly away in a large metal box, imagined the lock snapping into place, and then sat on the thing for good measure.

On another inhale, she beckoned the images closer, squeezing Iliana's hands as she did. It was something she used to do as a child when she was nervous but didn't want to admit it. She'd squeeze her sister's hand and her sister would squeeze back to let her know everything would be all right.

She felt Iliana's return squeeze an instant before the images came into focus.

A young Iliana holds a crying auburn-haired toddler in her arms. She rubs the child's back in soothing circles. Eventually, the small girl hiccups and pulls from the embrace.

"Want Mama," she tells Iliana in toddler speak, a frown marring her brows.

"I know, Kyra. I know." Iliana wipes the tears from the child's face with gentle fingers and begins to stroke her hair. The toddler's lower lip begins to quiver when she realizes her big sister cannot magically make their mother appear. As the tears begin to pool in her eyes once again, Iliana pulls her into her lap and begins to sing a lullaby.

Finn was so young in the memory she couldn't have been more than two or three cycles. She didn't remember much about that time, but she *did* remember the way their father had changed when their mother died.

He became a shell of the affectionate, effervescent man he'd been.

He rarely played with his girls or tucked them in at night. He'd been too busy protecting them from a galaxy that would see them dead.

As a child she'd thought her father paranoid. As an adult, she understood the depth and scope of his fear.

However, with or without her father's attention, Finn's childhood had been filled with love and affection thanks to Iliana. Her eyes began to sting uncomfortably as she took in the scene from her sister's memories. She'd been taking care of Finn and putting her comfort first since Finn was a baby.

She took another deep breath, filling her nostrils with Conrad's scent as the memory began to shift and change. As it did, Finn realized she was in control this time. Iliana had opened herself up, allowing her to siphon whatever memories she chose. Finn let one memory come into focus for a moment before moving on to the next, sorting through them like one would leaf through the pages of a book.

When she reached one that seemed different from the rest, she paused. Unlike the others, this memory pulsed before her, gray and ominous. She stopped, beckoning it to the forefront, the edges of her vision blurring as she tried to concentrate.

Darkness began to overtake her as the memory overwhelmed Finn's careful control. Her heart beat a furious, panicked rhythm in her chest. With Conrad's scent long forgotten, Iliana's memory pulled her from the present and sent her careening into black.

It is cold and someone is screaming. Finn can barely make out the shapes in front of her as her eyes adjust to the dimness. The feminine screams become whimpers and Finn wraps her arms around herself in a bid to ward off the chill in the air.

Suddenly, there is light. A door is being pushed ajar from the inside by a large man with a potbelly and a dirt-streaked face. The fluorescents from the other room illuminate him and what appears to be a small hold on a ship. When he looks back at the sobbing form huddled in a ball on the ground, Finn's heart clenches. Bile begins to rise in her throat as she takes in the torn, raggedy dress and the bright fall of red hair shadowing the woman's face from view.

"Li-Li?" Despite knowing her voice won't be heard, Finn can't help but whisper her sister's name into the shadows.

Holding the door with his foot, the man buttons his pants and watches Iliana for long seconds. Eventually, his voice cuts through both the room and Iliana's cries.

"You belong to me and the crew now." Reaching into a back pocket, the man pulls out Finn's singed dolly and throws it to the ground by Iliana. "Your sister is dead. You have no family, no one to miss you. You might as well embrace your new role on the ship."

With that, he turns and exits through the doorway. As the shadows swallow up the remaining slivers of light from outside, Finn sees Iliana's shaking hand reach out and snatch up the doll. She pulls it to her chest just as darkness falls over them.

Finn's eyes snapped open, dropping Iliana's hands as though they were ablaze. When her shocked face panned up to Iliana's, she found her sister's eyes and cheeks wet with tears.

"I'm—I'm sorry," Finn stammered, choking back her own rising tears. "I didn't mean to . . ."

With one carefully drawn breath, Iliana regained her composure and the pooling wetness in her eyes receded.

"It's all right, Little One. I could have prevented you from seeing it."

But she didn't.

Though it was only one memory amidst a sea of thousands, it was enough for Finn to glean what her sister's life had been like before Grim came into the picture and helped her become a courtesan.

Sharp pain lanced Finn's heart as she thought about what she'd seen.

"How long?" she whispered, deceptively calm despite the storm raging inside her.

Her sister's forehead creased with confusion.

"I don't understand."

"How long were you on that ship before Grim found you?"

Finn winced at the sharpness rising in her tone, but amidst the pain in her heart was a growing rage on behalf of Iliana and all she had endured.

The wrinkles in her sister's forehead smoothed in understanding.

"Too long."

The small flames of rage became an inferno in Finn's chest.

"Iliana—"

She wasn't sure what she wanted to say but it didn't matter. Iliana cut her off before she could finish.

"It is in the past Finn; let us leave it there." Iliana's eyes grew solemn as she held Finn's. "Please understand when I siphoned your memories without your permission, I just needed to know that you'd had a better life than I did. I know it's foolish, but I hoped if I looked into your past and saw happy memories while we were apart, then everything I endured would be worth it. To learn you had suffered just as greatly . . ." Her voice broke and the tears Iliana had been holding back finally began to fall without restraint.

She understood Iliana's intentions better than she ever would have dreamed. Right now, in the confines of her pod with no witnesses to put on a façade for, she was showing Finn exactly who she was. Finn had been ignoring the glaring evidence as best she could for the last few weeks but there was no denying it now.

Iliana was a woman who loved her little sister more than anything in the world.

Knowing what she'd been through and knowing her desire to spare Finn from the same fate, the remaining dregs of Finn's resentment faded into oblivion.

"I love you, Iliana," she whispered. The words shot out of her mouth before she even knew she was saying them. Iliana sucked in a breath, her eyes widening in shock before sliding shut, fresh tears cascading down her cheeks. When she next opened them, they shone brightly, and a soft smile spread across her face.

"I love you too, Finn."

EIGHTEEN

"Good," Finn called. "Remember to keep your guard up and don't be afraid to use your legs."

She watched as Lex squared off with Enyo, bouncing in place with her fists at her chin. At Finn's compliment, she smiled wide and straightened her legs. Enyo, taking advantage of her inattention, tackled the dainty girl around her waist and took her to the ground.

The air left Lex's lungs on a loud grunt. It took a moment for her to catch her breath, but when she did, her amber eyes sparkled and she shot the Sirian a grin.

Finn shook her head as Enyo reached down and helped Lex to her feet.

"You should've seen that coming, Lex," Finn scolded.

The girl tightened the pink ponytails at the top of her head.

"You distracted me," she said, pouting.

Finn sighed and rolled her eyes, moving on to the next sparring duo. Jax and AJ feinted and rolled around the training room mats, doing their best to avoid hard kicks to the lower body and jabs to the face. The boy and the young pilot had tossed their shirts to the side, sparring with their chests bared in a blur of alabaster and caramel.

Axel worked with the weights, watching quietly from the corner. Though he trained separately with Finn and AJ, he was desperate to prove he could be present for the group's sessions without having another episode.

AJ launched an uppercut at Jax's chin, but the pilot saw the punch coming and ducked out of the way with impressive speed.

"Nice, Jax. Make him work for it," she called.

Not one to be outshone, AJ switched tactics, mimicking a move he'd learned from Enyo. He dipped his head and tackled Jax's midsection. As they struggled, AJ curved his leg around Jax's ankle and took him to the ground.

Joy swelled in Finn's chest at the sight and she grinned with pride. She made her way over to Axel as she watched the boys struggle for leverage on the ground.

"You doing okay, Axel?"

The half-Khaleerian took a deep breath and released the weights he'd been holding at his shoulders with ease. The kid's strength seemed to know no limits. He ran a hand over his horns and tore his eyes away from the sparring duo.

"I'm good. Now that I know what to expect, I can control my temper. Besides, Jax is doing great out there."

His face lit up with a shy smile and Finn returned it.

"Fortunately for me, you've all proven to be fast learners."

The hulking hybrid turned toward her, his smile fading and replaced by an earnest expression.

"It's not us. It's you. You're a great teacher. Where did you learn all this stuff anyway?"

Grim's face appeared in her mind's eye. It was strange to hate someone and be completely indebted to them at the same time. None of this would be possible without her mentor, yet his betrayal and lies were like a poison in her bloodstream she had yet to purge.

"I used to read a lot," Finn told Axel dryly.

"Focus on what you saw when you read the books, Dhala. *Concentrate on re-creating the movements."*

Grim's hulking form stands before her unarmed. His dark eyes search hers carefully as he circles her where she stands. His dark red skin and glossy horns shine in the candlelight.

Finn closes her eyes, conjuring up images from the long study sessions he'd been putting her through lately. Every time she laid her hands on the tomes, images of controlled aggression and graceful fighting styles filled her mind.

It isn't just a parade of images though, and it isn't like watching the scene from a safe distance on a holojector. When she touches the books, she becomes a part of the people inside them. In the recesses of her mind, there is no such thing as a safe distance; she lives inside the moment with them.

She can almost feel the emotions of the strange-looking warriors she glimpses, and it frightens her.

After a moment, she releases a frustrated sigh and opens one eye to glare at Grim.

"This is stupid. I can't just learn how to fight by reading a bunch of your old books."

Grim clucks his tongue at her outburst.

"You're doing much more than reading. Besides, that is why we are sparring, Dhala. You already have the knowledge you need, now we must put it to use."

Finn fights back a smart remark and closes her eyes once again. Grim is giving her the opportunity to learn how to defend herself, something she desperately needs, and she doesn't want to seem ungrateful.

She focuses her mind, shutting everything out but the knowledge she has gained reading Grim's books. She inhales deeply, forcing her limbs to relax. Her eyes shoot open when she hears movement to her right.

Grim moves with incredible speed, his massive frame launching itself at Finn. On instinct, she ducks low and dives out of striking distance. Rolling to her feet, she eyes the Khaleerian warily.

"I thought we were starting slow."

"Slow gives you time to think, it clouds your mind," he says as his eyes narrow. Finn gulps in trepidation, watching her mentor circle her with a predatory gaze. The fear is nearly overwhelming and her hands shake at her sides.

He throws a punch and she barely manages to dive out of the way. He swings for her again and again; she dives out of the way with milliseconds to spare.

"Stop running and fight, Finn."

Her heart pounds in her chest, and her vision goes fuzzy with the onslaught of panic.

In a blur of motion, Grim spins and launches a kick at her face. Finn's hands come up to block his leg. With a grace she didn't know she possessed, she releases him and spins into his body. Her foot darts behind his ankle as her right fist hits his chest with surprising strength.

Grim loses his balance and falls to the ground with a thud. Finn freezes.

"Grim?"

Slowly, the big man lifts his eyes to hers, low laughter shaking his chest.

"Very good, Dhala.*"*

NINETEEN

"Axel, keep a lid on that rage," Finn ordered as she followed his retreating steps.

It was early morning during their regular training session. The large half-Khaleerian had just taken a jab to the jaw, and she hadn't been holding back. His skin was already darkening and the black of his pupils had begun to bleed into his irises.

AJ's eyes flitted over to them from his sparring match with Enyo and Finn tossed him a stern glare.

"Focus on your own fight, AJ."

Suddenly caught unawares, the boy's eyes shot wide and he turned quickly back to Enyo.

He wasn't quick enough.

The Sirian tackled him around the midsection with a move that was becoming her signature and took him to the ground, pouncing on his chest as he landed and holding one long claw to his pale throat.

Finn shook her head and turned back to Axel. She found him watching her intently as he struggled to control the heaving breaths filling his barrel chest. He clenched his jaw tight in a bid to control the raging emotions.

Eventually, his skin returned to its normal pallor and his eyes cleared.

"I don't get it," he said on a frustrated exhale. "Why is it so important I learn how to fight without using my abilities? When I get angry, I feel strong . . . I feel *powerful*."

His eyes darted away at the admission as though embarrassed. Across the room, Enyo had helped AJ to his feet to square off again. Learning from his mistakes, this time the boy gave the Sirian his full and undivided attention.

Finn took a step toward Axel and gentled her voice.

"Your anger makes you strong, Axel, but a Khaleerian's true strength lies in their ability to control that anger. With that control, you are like a rifle, powerful but accurate. Without it, you're a grenade and you will blow up anything and anyone in your path."

"How do you know so much about Khaleerians?"

"I was trained by one." Finn clenched her jaw as she added begrudgingly, "He learned to master his anger and his strength became a finely honed weapon. He was one of the best fighters I've ever known."

"Was?"

Before she could muster up a reply, movement at the door caught her attention. Conrad and Shane entered. Shane had given their training sessions a relatively wide berth in an attempt to respect AJ's wishes, but it appeared as though his patience had run out.

She was honestly surprised he'd lasted as long as he had.

AJ dutifully ignored his brothers' interruption and ducked out of the way just as Enyo's fist came flying at his face. He spun to the left and countered, just barely missing the Sirian's jaw with a well-timed right hook.

Shane watched closely, making his way over to Finn without ever taking his eyes away from the sparring duo. He came to a stop at her left and Conrad joined them a moment later.

"Don't tell me you need me to train you too, Shane," she said evenly without taking her gaze from the fight.

The captain let out a breath that was half sigh and half chuckle.

"Conrad has assured me you are a very capable teacher but—"

"You had to see for yourself," she finished for him, finally letting her eyes drift over in his direction.

"Yes." He smiled.

"I tried to keep him away as long as I could, Hellion," Conrad remarked through an amused smirk. Finn rolled her eyes before stopping to size the captain up. His lean frame sported a pair of tan pants and a long-sleeved shirt. A pair of dark brown boots completed the look.

"You know," she told him, "there's really only one way to know for sure if I'm cut out to teach AJ."

Shane's blond brows arched in confusion as he regarded her. "What's that?"

"You're going to want to take those off." She inclined her head and stared meaningfully at his boots. Shane's green eyes followed hers, his expression perplexed.

"You want me to take my shoes off?"

"Yeah," she said over her shoulder as she made her way to the center of the mats. "We don't allow shoes on the mats."

Across the room, AJ feinted half-heartedly and Enyo countered with a lazy uppercut that didn't even come close to landing. Both of them had diverted their attention to watching the conversation in front of them unfold and both were doing a terrible job at pretending otherwise.

AJ looked dumbfounded.

Enyo's eyes gleamed with amusement.

"I don't understand," Shane called to Finn.

She stretched her left arm followed by her right and shifted on the balls of her feet.

"What's to understand? You're going to fight me."

The captain's mouth fell open comically wide. He looked to Conrad for help, but the big hybrid merely folded his arms and smiled.

"I can't fight you, Finn. I'm a trained soldier. And I'm twice your size."

Finn smirked.

Shane would never relax and trust her to instruct AJ if he doubted her skill. There was only one way to show him he had nothing to worry about.

Maybe then the poor man could finally relax a little.

"Do it, Shane," Conrad ordered quietly.

The captain eyed them both warily. Eventually, his shoulders sagged slightly and he relented. She watched as he kicked the boots from his feet and rolled up the sleeves of his shirt.

Enyo and AJ gave up the charade and watched Finn and Shane with rapt gazes. The captain made his way to her on the mats and stopped a few feet away. His eyes assessed her warily.

"Finn, it's fine; I trust you to train AJ. We don't need to do this."

"No, you don't," she said as she circled him, "and yes, we do."

His head turned to track her movements and his body tensed as he readied himself for an attack.

He wasn't going to make the first move. His stance was purely defensive.

If this was going to work, she needed his full participation.

Finn feinted low and stepped into his space, throwing an elbow into the center of his hard abdomen. He grunted and caught her other fist as it came speeding toward his nose.

Finn purposefully left her guard open, waiting to see what he would do. Shane merely released her fist and stepped away.

This time, Finn sent a well-placed kick to Shane's midsection. As he huddled over groaning, she grabbed him by the hair and kneed him hard in the face. His head fell back as she released him, blood dripping from his nose.

"Stop holding back," she growled.

Anger flashed in his green eyes and Finn grinned. He stood to his full height, squaring his broad shoulders. He cracked his neck and wiped the blood from his face with the pad of a thumb.

His eyes tracked her movements, gauging her next step.

As she swung high, he ducked low and pivoted out of her way, kicking her hard behind the knees. She stumbled before righting herself.

He moved again and she managed to duck under the hard punch he launched at her temple. Before she could recover, he came running at her. She found the way he moved with such deadly elegance both intimidating and impressive in equal measure.

Shane had finally stopped pulling his punches and he was proving himself to be a worthy adversary.

The captain dipped his shoulder and attempted to wrestle Finn around the midsection. She anticipated the move. Using Shane's momentum against him, she bowed her upper body and sent him flying over her. He landed on the mat with a hard thud.

In a testament to speed, he was up and on his feet in record time. Each time they made contact, he seemed to be studying her movements, calculating them, and recalibrating before their next exchange.

It was thrilling to have such a skilled opponent.

She kicked out at his legs, aiming for his kneecap. Shane predicted the move and caught her around the ankle, twisting as he sent her flying to the floor.

Finn rolled to her back and hopped to her feet just in time to see him barreling at her once again. She dove into a somersault and evaded him, jumping back up and throwing herself at his upper body.

Her hands grabbed onto his shoulders and she used her momentum and body weight to curl her lower half just below his hips, shooting her legs down and around his knees.

Shane fell backward . . . hard. She landed atop his midsection and aimed a fist at the space between his eyes. She held it poised in midair and waited for his reaction.

They both panted for air, their chests surging from exertion.

Suddenly, the aggression cleared from his expression and his lips began to widen with a growing smile.

"That was fun."

TWENTY

Finn took her time tidying up the training room, relishing the alone time, something she'd gotten precious little of since returning to *Independence*. Her students had been released and Enyo, Conrad, and Shane had gone off with them in search of breakfast.

She pushed the mats up against the wall and sat down on one of the weight machines, turning abruptly when a throat cleared behind her.

AJ stood at the room's entrance, his dark eyes darting around and his posture uncertain.

"I thought you were long gone, kid. Training is over for the day," Finn told him.

The boy looked at the ground and scuffed his shoe on the floor.

"I know. Shane wants everyone on the bridge in five. I offered to let you know."

A meeting on the bridge?

Finn's heart sped up.

"Thanks. I'll be up in a minute."

Several seconds passed in silence and AJ's eyes darted around the room nervously.

"Was there something else?" she asked him.

AJ bit his lip hesitantly.

"Spit it out, kid."

His words left him in a rush.

"It's just that, I heard Shane and Iliana talking. The things the Reliance did to you when you were a kid . . . is all that true?"

Finn swallowed hard past the dry lump that had formed in her throat and did her best to sound casual.

"Depends on what you heard."

"They tortured you?" he asked softly.

Tension filled the air and Finn struggled to respond. Finally, she simply nodded in affirmation.

"Me too. Did they . . ." He hesitated slightly before the question spilled out of him. "Did they make you kill someone?"

AJ's hands had balled into fists and his spine straightened as he awaited an answer.

"Is that what they made you do, AJ?" she asked him gently.

It took him long moments, but eventually he nodded his head, tears welling in his eyes.

"They made me use my abilities on people . . . Made me convince them to do horrible things. I didn't want to," he added in a rush. "They made me do it."

Finn's heart ached for the boy as she remembered the Reliance brand she'd seen burned into his chest.

"It wasn't your fault, AJ; you never had a choice back then, but now you do."

"Yeah, thanks to you," he murmured as his eyes brightened. "Training with you is . . . Well, it's the happiest I've ever been. I finally feel like I'm a part of something, you know?"

"You've always been a part of something," she told him. "Shane and Conrad have given you a chance to help other people like you. Not many of us get a chance like that."

AJ's eyes narrowed angrily.

"They don't understand what it's like."

"Maybe not, but they love you. That's got to be worth something. Besides, they've both suffered in their own ways. It may not be the same as what you or I went through, but it's suffering all the same."

He seemed to think over what she said, his mind going to work behind those dark eyes. A tiny sparkle appeared there and he grinned with reverence.

"I've never seen anyone take Shane down like that. It was incredible."

"Your brother is a skilled fighter."

Some of the light left his eyes and his smile faltered.

"I never knew," he admitted quietly. "I guess there's a lot I don't know about Shane."

"You should take it easy on him. He's trying his best." His face relaxed slightly as he gave her a sharp nod. "Good. Now go get something to eat," she told him softly.

She watched the boy's exit as anger filled her. She'd done her best to keep it together during their conversation, but now that he'd departed, the rage at all he'd revealed was hitting her hard.

The things the Reliance had put him through, and at such a young age no less, were abhorrent. But the worst part, the part that kept her up at night . . . There were so many others out there suffering the same fate.

Finn just hoped they could reach them all in time.

TWENTY-ONE

Finn made her way to the bridge with steady strides. When she arrived, she found the rest of *Independence*'s crew waiting for her. Shane stood with the twins at the ship's helm while Iliana, Isis, Tiri, Enyo, Conrad, Nova, Axel, and AJ sat in the crew's seats facing them.

The captain had cleaned the blood from his face, but a purple bruise had already begun to form at the corner of his square jaw.

She shot a wry smile at him and hurried to take a seat in between Conrad and Enyo. Iliana noticed the exchange and shook her head, causing her loose red curls to sway with the movement.

Finn's smile merely widened to a grin.

Since their most recent training session, things had shifted significantly in their relationship. She now understood Iliana in a way she'd never dreamed she would and, slowly, they were learning to trust one another.

Shane watched them for a moment before addressing the room.

"The ship needs fuel. We'll be docking on Kreet shortly to refuel and restock the ship."

Lex let out a whoop of excitement.

"Freedom!" she cried dramatically.

Jax offered his sister a high-five and Shane shot them both an exasperated glare.

Finn had no idea why the twins would be so excited to visit an Outer Rings planet, especially one as desolate as Kreet, but she supposed the energetic duo had been cooped up for so long they had to be chomping at the bit for any change of scenery.

And Kreet would certainly be a change of scenery. The planet was nothing more than desert and rocks. The only reason it received as many visitors as it did was the giant market the upper castes had set up on the planet's craggy surface.

Hundreds of them gathered daily to sell their wares, which ranged from synthetic food, fuel, and secondhand clothes, to the more rare finds like stolen upper-caste jewelry and tech. The place put the Mud Pit's black market to shame with the sheer quantity of merchandise.

She'd been there a few times over the last cycles, but she always kept her visits short in a bid to get back to the Mud Pit.

Shane eyed the neon-haired twins as he announced, "Not everyone will be leaving the ship." Lex crossed her arms at her chest and began to pout. "Tiri, Enyo, Isis, AJ, Axel, and Jax, I need you to stay behind this time."

Lex let out another excited cheer and eyed her brother.

"Sorry, bro. I'll bring you back something nice."

"I'm sure we'll find a way to entertain ourselves."

Jax ignored his sister to shoot a heated stare Axel's way. The giant half-Khaleerian's cheeks flushed a deep scarlet and he bit his lip nervously.

Finn rolled her eyes and looked over the rest of the crew.

Tiri sagged in her seat, her round eyes downcast. She fiddled with one of the ribbons around her pigtails and bit her lavender lip.

"Don't you worry, my child, we'll have plenty of our own fun while they're away," Isis soothed, wrapping a long blue arm around the girl's shoulder.

On some level, Finn understood the prudence of Shane's decision. They needed crew to stay behind and, in Tiri's case, the child was far too conspicuous with her lavender skin and odd markings. Still, she reacted to the sadness in the little girl's eyes.

Don't worry, kid. I'll steal you something pretty, she thought loudly.

Tiri's eyes shot up to meet Finn's and she frowned.

It's not nice to steal things, Finn, she reprimanded.

The child looked so indignant, Finn couldn't help but laugh out loud, earning several stares from the surrounding crew.

Enyo hadn't moved at Finn's side and she gently nudged the Sirian.

"He's right. It makes sense for you to stay behind," she told the hybrid.

Enyo's glittering eyes flitted past Finn to Conrad.

"You will keep *N'Goza* safe," she told the big man in a harsh tone that left little room for argument.

Conrad nodded slightly, his blue eyes assessing the Sirian. "I will."

Finn bit back a sigh and muttered, "*N'Goza* can take care of herself."

Belatedly, she noticed AJ had tensed in his seat. Anger seeped off him in waves, and he held his hands in tight fists on his lap.

Somehow, he managed to make his tone sound even as he locked eyes with Shane.

"I'd like to go to Kreet," he told his brother through clenched teeth.

Shane observed the boy warily.

"I don't know if that's such a good idea, AJ."

Rather than explode as she and most likely everyone else expected, AJ forced himself to take a deep breath.

"I've been working hard, Shane. I can handle this."

The captain's brows shot up in surprise as he took his younger brother in. She could see the wheels spinning in his head as he weighed his options. Finally, his gaze moved to Conrad first, then Finn. She gave him a subtle nod of encouragement.

Releasing a deep breath, Shane's features softened and he relented. "Okay, AJ, you can come to Kreet." Shooting a stern look at the rest of the crew, he commanded, "We dock in an hour. Be ready to leave."

TWENTY-TWO

Finn stood in the cargo hold between Iliana and Conrad as the ship's doors opened to reveal the planet of Kreet. They had all changed in preparation for the arid climate. Iliana had slipped into a magenta hooded sari draping her shoulders and waist. She wore a pair of rose gold wraparounds over her eyes. The captain, Conrad, and AJ sported sleek black wraparounds, and Shane looked rugged in a pair of tan cargo pants and matching shirt.

All three men wore scarves over their noses and mouths.

The women wore saris or capes and varying styles of wraparounds.

Finn smoothed a wrinkle in the silk blouse she'd borrowed from Iliana and secured the hood of her cape over her head and around her mouth as she took in the rocky cliffs and sandy hills as far as the eye could see.

Endless rows of tents the same shade of tan as the sand had been set up, and hundreds of passersby shuffled between merchants and peddlers, their high-volume haggling filling the space with a delightful din.

The scent of countless spices and various meats smoking over a fire filled Finn's nostrils and her mouth watered.

Adjusting her gloves, Finn watched Lex practically vibrate in place with her excitement.

"I bet they have that special sugar bread you can't find any-where else," Lex told no one in particular.

"Everybody meets back at the ship in an hour, got it?" Shane pointed to his watch as he looked the group over. "We stay in pairs so nobody goes wandering off too far. Conrad's with me, Iliana and Finn are together, and AJ, Nova, and Lex . . . stay together . . . and stay out of trouble."

Shane eyed Lex sternly as he finished his command. The pilot tossed him a distracted wave and an innocent smile, locking arms with AJ and Nova as she dragged them out of the ship.

Shane ran a hand through his hair in vexation.

"Let's get this over with," he muttered.

Finn bit her lip in an attempt to hide her smile at the poor man's obvious anxiety. Conrad leaned down low to whisper in her ear.

"Be good. I'll find you out there as soon as I get a chance to get away."

Finn lost the fight and grinned up at him.

"When am I ever *not* good?"

The corners of Conrad's lips turned up in a smile. He lifted his gloved hand slightly to squeeze hers and then followed Shane out of the ship.

Iliana sidled closer to her sister, her eyes shining with humor.

"That seems to be going well," she teased sardonically.

Finn shoved her shoulder lightly and headed for the doors.

"Wait," Iliana called. "Leave the gloves behind. I have something I want to try with you."

Finn turned and eyed her warily.

"There are tons of people out there. I'm not so sure that's a good idea."

"Do you trust me?" Iliana asked with uncharacteristic vulnerability.

They'd certainly come a long way together in the short time she'd been back on *Independence*, but Finn never went anywhere without her gloves. Even when she removed them for their training sessions, she felt exposed in a way that had her breaking into a cold sweat.

"Finn," Iliana repeated quietly, "do you trust me?"

Finn sighed and tore the gloves free from her hands dramatically.

"Fine, have it your way." She shoved them in her pocket and glared at her sister. "Now can we go?"

Iliana's answering smile was resplendent as she whispered, "Yes."

Iliana steered them into a corner between two tents selling brightly patterned rugs and dishware respectively.

"Okay," Iliana whispered as she eyed the crowd. Between the yells of merchants, their customers' chatter, and the pods and ships passing overhead, Finn had to strain to hear her over the hubbub. "I want you to start by picking an object. It can be anything. Practice staying present as you siphon from it."

"Okay," Finn breathed. "That sounds easy enough."

She unscrewed the top of Conrad's hair wax inside her pocket and dabbed a little on her finger. She rubbed the wax above her upper lip, just below her nostrils, and inhaled.

Her eyes scanned the tents past rows of spices, racks of red-and-gold clothing, and countless other odd commodities. Finally, her gaze landed on a tent selling wooden jewelry; carved within the beads were runic markings similar to the ones on Conrad's shoulders and back.

Keeping her hands close to her sides, Finn worked her way through the crowd until she made it to her desired destination.

Her eyes locked on a black, wooden bead bracelet with a small runic totem attached. She reached out and grasped the thing between her fingers, inhaling Conrad's scent as she did. Images flashed in her mind, but she was able to sort through them easily, keeping focus on the crowds bustling around her.

A small, older woman bends over a rectangular table covered in wooden beads. She holds a small laser the size of a pen in her hand and uses it to burn carvings into the beads. Her eyes narrow and her tongue dips out between her lips as she carefully strings them together one by one. Finn leans closer to study the woman's movements. As she does, she can see the bright blue runic markings covering her face and hands.

Finn held the bracelet tightly in her hands as she searched the interior of the tent. Sure enough, she found the old woman watching her.

"You're Merlidian?" Finn asked her. The old woman nodded, but said nothing. "How much?" she asked, motioning toward the bracelet.

The woman held up two fingers and Finn dug around in her pocket for the remaining stash of gold she'd stuffed there, tossing two pieces to the old woman.

Finn shoved the bracelet into her pocket and ignored the trace of memory remnants left behind from the Merlidian woman's touch.

She got distracted on her way back to Iliana as she passed a tent with a small wooden structure in front of it. Its rectangular shape had been painted a deep shade of red and four yellow wheels had been mounted to the bottom.

Small curtains had been pulled aside from the structure's center revealing a small window-like space where several marionette puppets danced and twirled haphazardly.

Two of the puppets sported bald heads, red button eyes, and shimmering gold bodies. They were flanked by brutish-looking soldier puppets as they toppled wooden props and sent the other marionettes running in the opposite direction.

Finn finally tore her attention from the odd spectacle and returned to Iliana's side.

"That was good," Iliana praised her as she sidled up next to her sister.

"What's next?" Finn asked.

"Now you choose someone."

"Choose *someone*?"

"Yes, you're going to practice siphoning from a person who isn't me," Iliana murmured.

Finn's stomach dropped and her palms began to sweat.

In the distance, she spotted Lex's pink braids—the girl still dragging a dazed AJ around—as she stopped at a tent billowing smoke from the fresh bread baking there in a stone oven.

Where the hell was Nova?

Lex said something to the vendor and squealed with delight at whatever the man said. AJ recoiled at the sound, but Lex was oblivious to the boy as she handed the seller a piece of gold in exchange for a loaf of bread covered in glittering sugar crystals piled so high they looked like mountains.

Finn's eyes darted through the crowd once again, but Nova was nowhere to be found. Seeming to sense her disquiet, Iliana leaned close to whisper, "What is it? Is something wrong?"

She did her best to shrug off her concern. Nova probably snuck off to find some customers of her own. Kreet was as good a place as any for the doxie to earn her gold.

"Nothing," she told Iliana, "I'm just looking for my next victim."

Across the way, she spotted a male vendor with a wrinkled face and white hair. He stood proudly next to several hanging racks of bright-yellow, synthetic coats. Finn made her way over to him, pretending to be distracted by the jackets as she bumped into the old man and grabbed his hand to steady herself.

She is in a barn. Inside, rows of pens house handfuls of multicolored, horned mammals called ramans. Their hooved feet stomp the ground and harsh bleating fills the air. Finn struggles not to let the sound overwhelm her. In the back, the old man sits next to a large bucket filled with liquid.

He takes his time dipping piles of jackets one by one into the bucket, using a large wooden paddle to stir and keep them submerged. A magenta raman covered in blue and black spots chews on hay at his side and the old man looks the creature in the eyes as he laughs maniacally.

"They love my coats," he says with a toothless grin. "I wonder if they'd still love them if they knew where they got their color."

He lets loose with another round of inane cackling and Finn eyes the bucket of yellow liquid with growing disgust.

Raman piss? Seriously?

Finn released her hold on the man and struggled to mask the disgust on her face.

"Excuse me, missy," the old man stepped back out of her way. "See anything you like? It's three gold pieces for the coats."

"Not bad," a deep voice murmured behind her. Finn spun to see Conrad admiring the man's wares. "Not really my color though."

He reached out a swarthy hand to stroke the yellow material and Finn hustled to his side. She slapped his hand away and began to steer his big body in the opposite direction.

"No!" At Conrad's arched brows of surprise, she forced herself to take a breath. "I wouldn't," she whispered.

She could tell Conrad's lips twitched with bemusement beneath the cover of his scarf as he allowed her to lead him from the crazy old man and his urine coats. She slipped the gloves from her pocket and back over hands.

Iliana hurried over to them.

"Where is Shane?" the courtesan asked Conrad.

"He had to take a meeting," he told her, "but he asked me to give you these."

Conrad pulled from his pocket a pair of delicate hair pins in the shape of tambiflies. They'd been carefully hand painted in an alluring shade of orange, and tiny glittering crystals covered their wings.

Iliana reached out hesitantly to touch the pins, her mouth slightly ajar and her indigo eyes wide with surprise.

Belatedly, she seemed to remember her audience. Taking the pins from Conrad, she carefully masked her features and addressed them both in a breathy voice.

"I think I'll head back to the ship. You did great Finn, but I think you deserve a little fun time."

With that, she turned on her heels and sped away. Finn watched her retreating form with narrowed eyes before turning to Conrad.

"What the hell was that about?"

Conrad looked from Iliana to Finn and shrugged his big shoulders.

"Nothing I plan on touching with a ten-foot pole. If I tell you I got you something, are you going to run away too?"

Finn's eyes widened and her skin prickled with an unfamiliar sense of anticipation.

"You got me something?" she whispered.

Conrad grinned and pulled something from the back of his pants. As Finn watched, he presented her with a small, curved knife. The blade glinted in the sunlight and her chest swelled as she noticed the hilt was covered in a smattering of blue gems forming the shape of peacock.

"It reminded me of the way you looked at the Unionization Ball on Cartan," he murmured, taking the knife and dipping down to tuck it into her boot. "I figured you'd get more use out of that than a pair of hair pins."

Finn grinned at the beautiful man in front of her, her chest swelling with emotion. Suddenly, she remembered the bracelet in her pocket.

"I got you something too," she told him, fumbling around until she grasped the wooden beads and held them up for him to see. "They're Merlidian. I thought you might like them."

Conrad carefully took them from her, his face soft but unreadable. After long moments of silence, Finn felt sure she'd made a mistake. She was just preparing herself for a hasty exit, when he slipped the bracelet over his wrist and smiled down her.

"My father used to have one just like it," he said softly.

She couldn't see his eyes, but she could tell from the soft curve of his lips that she'd pleased him. Seeing the emotion on his face made her pulse pound.

"So, tell me about Shane's meeting."

The awkward subject change seemed to amuse him, and he smiled widely.

"I'd rather show you around instead."

With that, he grabbed her gloved hand and pulled her into the fray.

"Wait, we have to stop," Finn yelled to Conrad. Thirty minutes later, she still hadn't managed to finagle any information out of him about Shane's meeting, but she found she was having too much fun to care. Conrad had taken the time to show her the entire market. They'd made their way through countless tents, pausing to admire the sheer volume and diversity of goods—from clothing and jewelry to strange tools Finn had never seen before and even handcrafted weaponry.

At one point, Conrad had stopped to purchase them steaming chunks of delicious spiced meat and vegetables speared on a wooden stick.

Now, they were on their way back to the ship with full bellies and bags of goodies when Finn spotted a tent lined with shelves and shelves of hand-painted porcelain dolls. She led Conrad over as her eyes landed on one with white-blonde ringlets and green eyes almost the exact same shade as Tiri's.

The doll's delicate features had been painted with near-perfect precision and she wore a fluffy, emerald-green satin gown and white fur stole around her dainty shoulders.

Conrad arched his brows as he followed her.

"I didn't have you pegged for a doll collector, Hellion."

She rolled her eyes and pointed the satin-gowned doll out to the merchant.

"It's not for me. Don't you think Tiri will love it?"

Conrad's face softened as he looked the doll over.

"It's perfect."

Finn couldn't agree more. Remembering Tiri's indignation at thievery, Finn smiled as she handed the merchant the last of her gold and tucked her purchase safely under arm.

"Hey guys!" Lex shouted over to them as she sprinted to their side with AJ and Nova in tow. All three of them had their hands full of purchases and AJ still looked slightly stupefied.

"Where were you?" Finn asked Nova quietly.

"Around," the doxie answered cryptically.

Finn's eyes narrowed but she didn't comment further as they made their trek away from the market and back to *Independence*.

TWENTY-THREE

"**E**nyo, you're being ridiculous."

Lex chastised the glaring Sirian and pushed an armful of clothing in her direction.

Jax and Axel cuddled together closely on the rec room's couch while sharing bites of sugar bread, fresh candied fruit, and more of those crunchy green spheres Jax seemed to be so fond of.

"Leave her alone, sis," he called around a mouthful.

Lex ceased her tirade long enough to shoot her brother a deadly glower.

"She has no clothes and we picked these out especially for her." The pilot pouted, motioning toward AJ with her free hand as she said *we*.

The boy's alarmed expression shot to Enyo as he rushed to say, "I didn't pick out anything, I swear. It was all Lex."

The pink-haired female rolled her eyes and stuck out her tongue while Nova watched the drama unfold from a distant corner. The scarred doxie examined her fingers as though bored with the whole exchange.

"An *N'Goza* does *not* wear a dress, *choya*."

Enyo sounded like she might be choking on her nickname for the fiery pilot. Finn had asked what it meant. It turned out *choya* roughly translated to *little pest*. Naturally, Lex had no idea what the word meant and thought it was a splendid endearment.

The Sirian scowled in distaste at the fluffy pink satin in Lex's arms. Finn thought she could make out a few feathers in the pile as well and bit her cheek to keep from laughing.

"But we bought them for you," Lex countered through gritted teeth.

Enyo folded her arms over her chest and stared the pilot down.

After several long minutes of tense silence, Jax exhaled loudly and unfurled his lean frame from his spot on the couch, wiping green dust from his hands.

"Did you buy her anything without cap sleeves and a skirt?" he asked his twin sarcastically.

She eyed him for a moment in shared understanding as her eyes began to sparkle.

"Maybe," she told him suppressing a smile.

Jax snatched the pink frilly dress from his twin's arms and shot Enyo an exasperated look.

"You try one on, and so will I." He motioned toward the glittering, feather-covered pink dress in his hand.

"I'm not wearing that," she bit out harshly.

"No, you're not," he shot back. "I am. You'll have to find something less exceptional."

The room went quiet as the two regarded each other. Enyo's gaze darted between Jax and the dress as her mind went to work. Finn looked to Conrad to gauge his reaction.

He sat at the bar holding a drink in one hand, the bracelet she bought him on Kreet hanging from the wrist of the other. He merely smiled and raised the glass, taking a long swig as his blue eyes danced with humor.

Eventually, Enyo seemed to come to a decision.

"Fine," she said on a huff.

Lex squealed with delight and led them both out of the room.

By the time they returned, Finn and the others had already moved on to a new round of pool. Axel and Conrad seemed to have a knack for the game, though Finn was almost certain Conrad was using his abilities to cheat. Lex entered the room first, sweeping her arms up dramatically as she announced,

"Ladies and gentlemen, I need your full attention." She motioned toward the empty doorway and bowed low. After a moment of nothing but the sound of Lex's excited breathing, she cocked her head and blinked. "Any minute now, guys."

Another moment of silence passed and the doorway remained empty. Lex held up a finger to the room and ran out into the hallway.

"Will you two hurry up?" they heard her grumble in the hall. "You're making me look bad."

Jax made his appearance first, strutting into the rec room with confident strides. His lithe body was draped from shoulders to ankles in pink satin. The shoulder straps of the dress were covered in bright pink feathers and the rhinestones covering the garment's long skirt sparkled and glistened in the artificial lights.

Axel let loose a loud bark of laughter before catching himself and going silent.

"Well," Jax said on an overexuberant twirl. "What do you think?"

"Quit looking for flattery, Jax, we know you're pretty," Conrad smirked. "Let's see Enyo."

Jax winked and executed a perfect curtsy before joining Axel at the pool table.

There was a scuffle outside followed by a loud thud. After a beat, Lex and Enyo came tumbling through the doorway. The caramel flesh of Lex's face was completely flushed and her breathing had become ragged from exertion but her amber eyes glistened with excitement.

Finn wanted to roll her own eyes in vexation, but she found herself too busy staring slack-jawed at the Sirian. She had on a pair of black, formfitting pants tucked into a pair of shiny, gray boots. A white silk shirt with flowing sleeves draped her body, covered by a tight black vest with several pockets below the chest. Her long multihued hair had been pulled away from her face by two silver barrettes and the flowing mane gleamed and shone under the lights from a recent bout with a hairbrush.

She looked beautiful . . . and formidable.

Well done, Lex, she thought, smiling.

"You like it, don't you?" the female pilot asked knowingly.

A myriad of emotions seemed to be warring within Enyo's eyes: gratitude, dismay, hesitant joy.

Finn took pity on the Sirian. She walked over to the duo and, in one fluid motion, she tossed a pool stick at Lex, giving her no choice but to divert her attention and catch it.

"Take the win, Lex."

Blessedly, the pilot cooperated, grinning as she nodded enthusiastically and skipped over to the table.

Finn shot Enyo a conspiratorial wink that the Sirian returned, along with a grateful smile as she took her place next to Conrad at the bar.

As Finn made her way over to return to her game, Nova—uncharacteristically quiet throughout the recent parade of insanity—left her corner to approach.

She finally noticed the parcel in the doxie's hands.

"Here, boss lady. I got you something." Devoid of her usual exuberance, the doxie's voice was abnormally soft.

Finn swallowed her shock and took the parcel from Nova with wide eyes. As she opened it, she caught sight of deep-blue fabric. She pulled it away from the paper, recognizing the material immediately.

She ran her hands over the shiny, thick raman-hide coat much nicer than the other synthetic ones she'd seen on Kreet and fortunately *not* dyed in raman piss. Finn held it up in front of her to examine the intricate detailing. The seams and the sleeves had tiny royal blue embellishments and the waist tapered in elegantly before fanning out below the thighs.

"I owed you a coat," Nova shared quietly. "Or two," she added on a shy smile.

The supple hide was soft in Finn's hands. She'd never owned anything like it before.

"Thank you, Nova," she whispered, emotion choking her. She tried to force it down with levity. "You didn't steal it, did you?" she asked the doxie lightly. When Nova didn't answer, Finn's eyes narrowed, staggering emotions forgotten. "Wait, did you?"

Nova shot her an unrepentant wink and hopped off to the couches where Jax, Lex, and Axel chatted animatedly, leaving Finn to stand alone with her "liberated" jacket draped over her arm.

TWENTY-FOUR

Finn gently held the padded bag with the fragile porcelain doll inside in her hands as she made her way to Tiri's room. The girl had spent the day with Isis in her sanctuary and had returned to her room to shower away the dirt and grass stains. Lex's antics had already made Finn late for her promised visit and she had no doubt the little girl was ready and raring to give her hell for the tardiness.

Still, on her brisk walk there, Finn couldn't help but feel staggered by the events of the last week. Everything in her life was changing with a swiftness that frightened and excited her in equal measure: her relationship with Iliana, the ease with which she was beginning to accept *Independence* as home, her abilities.

After her test run on Kreet, Finn's confidence in her newfound aptitude at controlling her Teslan powers was growing steadily. She'd even left her gloves behind in her room, a monumental step considering she'd never gone a day without them.

As she began to make her way around the corner to Tiri's room, the sound of muffled voices slowed her pace. Down the hall, Shane and Isis huddled together, speaking in hushed voices.

Finn ducked into the nearest doorway as quietly as possible. Daring a peek around the corner, her eyes locked on the duo. They were so deep in their conversation they were completely unaware of their audience. Isis's tall, robed frame was fraught with tension; her silver eyes narrowed into scary slits as she hissed at Shane.

"Three quarters of the galaxy depends on Reliance tech for the very air they breathe and the synthetic food they eat. They saw to that decades ago with the systematic removal of plant life from the Inner and Outer Rings. They left just enough to keep their fat bellies fat and ensure they never had to eat synthetic like the rest of us. They cannot know of Tiri's existence, Shane, let alone what she is capable of. Not while she's still so young and vulnerable. My people promised the Luminary we would aid his cause, but not at the cost of our most precious creation's safety. She's just a child, Shane."

Creation? What exactly was Tiri capable of?

Isis was more agitated than Finn had ever seen her, her eyes glinting with anger. She could only see Shane's back where he faced off with the tall Aquariian, but the captain's spine was ramrod straight and his hands were balled into fists.

"She is much more than a child, Isis. You know it, I know it, and the Luminary knows it," Shane said, leaning in closer. "But hear this: she is part of this family and I would never let anything happen to her, Isis. *Never.*"

On his fervent vow, Shane turned from Isis and made his way down the hall. Finn ducked back into the doorway and held her breath, listening to the sound of receding footsteps. When she felt safe peering around the doorway again, she found the hall empty.

Independence was a ship bursting with secrets and it seemed Finn had just inadvertently stumbled upon another one.

Did this have something to do with Shane's secret meeting on Kreet?

What else were he and Isis hiding and what did it all have to do with Tiri? The parts of the conversation she'd overheard made little sense to her.

Moving from her hiding spot, Finn continued to Tiri's room. Maybe the child could provide some answers.

As the door slid open in front of her, Finn found Tiri standing off to the side and wringing her small hands with anxiety.

"I take it you were listening?" Finn asked her as she moved into the room.

The little girl bit her lip, her eyes wide with fear and worry. "Were you listening too?" she whispered.

Finn nodded in affirmation, her eyes assessing the child's fragile state.

"I can't say it made a whole lot of sense though. You want to tell me what's going on?"

Tears began to pool in Tiri's eyes as she bit her lip. After a moment of hesitation, she extended a dainty, green hand.

"I'd rather show you."

Finn tensed on reflex but forced her body to relax. She could handle this. After all, this is exactly what she'd been training for all those long hours with Iliana. Finn inhaled deeply, the scent of Conrad's wax still fresh in her nostrils.

"I guess you're finally getting that handshake you always wanted, kid," she told Tiri with a half smile and a wink. She set the bag and the doll on Tiri's bed and held her hand out to the girl, palm up. The child remained uncharacteristically serious, a strange sadness filling her expression as Finn clasped it.

The instant their skin touched, a loud pop filled the air and a bright blue light flashed behind Finn's eyelids, drowning out the rest of the room.

She felt her body go limp and then she felt nothing.

Finn came into consciousness slowly, her limbs and eyelids heavy with sleep.

No, not sleep.

As the memory of how she came to be unconscious returned to her, she sat up quickly and almost head-butted Isis where she peered down at Finn's prone body.

The bright lights within the Aquariian's sanctuary nearly blinded her as she took in the lush greenery cushioning her body and the various scents of newly bloomed buds and blossoms.

"We've got to stop meeting like this," she told the woman in a wry tone as she struggled to sit. "How did I get here?"

"Take it slow, child." Isis frowned with concern as she helped her into a seated position.

Finn leaned against the fuzzy bark of a tree and regarded the Aquariian with a watchful gaze as she waited for the blue woman to break the silence and tell her what the hell was going on. Sensing her disquiet and growing impatience, Isis took a seat across from her, taking the extra time to cross her long legs elegantly.

"My sweet Tiri is not one of the blended like you and the others," she told Finn after a beat.

She had been prepared for many things, but the Aquariian's softly spoken admission came nowhere near to making the list.

"What . . . what do you mean? She's *not* a hybrid?"

"My people are peaceful. Many years ago, we chose not to take part in a war we had no stake in. But then the Reliance came for our planet; for the life we spent eons cultivating. And just like that"—she snapped her long fingers—"they destroyed it. Without a second thought." Her silver eyes met Finn's with an intensity that left her squirming. "Aquariians are a peaceful people until we are pushed too far."

Never underestimate the depths of an Aquariian's rage.

Grim's warning echoed in her ears as Isis continued.

"When the Luminary approached us with a plan for revenge—a plan to take back our planet—Aquarii's highest-ranking priestesses brokered a deal."

Finn's mouth went dry as she whispered, "What deal?"

"Aquariian's have always maintained the balance of living things. One flower blossoms while another dies, returning to the earth to start anew. We have always cultivated this cycle, but it was never in our power to *create*. Something like that requires a great sacrifice."

Isis reached out a slender hand, her fingers grasping Finn around the wrist.

Instantly, images began to take shape in Finn's mind. She focused on the strength of Isis's grip and the soft grass beneath her body as she beckoned the images to the forefront of her mind.

The stone pillars of an Aquariian temple extend to a vaulted ceiling painted with beautiful murals of multicolored plant life. Everywhere she looks, vines and blossoms wind their way around the stone building, stealing her breath with their beauty. Voices catch her attention and she steps forward to see a small group of people standing near a large stone altar. Grim stands before four Aquariian priestesses known as doonas, *their silver robes heavy with the multifaceted chains marking their rank.*

"I understand this comes at a great cost to each of you," Grim states gruffly. "Know that your sacrifice will not be in vain."

One of the doonas *with deep-set wrinkles around her eyes and mouth locks eyes with Grim. Her voice is no more than a low rasp as she says, "You must vow to protect her, Khaleerian."*

"I vow it," he answers readily.

They all nod in unison, seemingly satisfied.

"Come forward, child." The doona *at the center of the quartet beckons to someone hidden in the shadows and a young Aquariian moves forward with unsure steps, stopping next to Grim. Finn immediately recognizes Isis. "Isis will join you, once the ceremony is complete, as the child's protector," the* doona *explains. "While I trust that you intend to honor your vow, Isis will be there to ensure you do."*

Grim nods in acquiescence as the four Aquariian doonas *form a circle around the stone altar. One by one they join hands. Finn watches on, transfixed as they bow their heads in unison and begin to mumble indecipherably. This continues for several moments before a bright blue light begins to emanate from their center, washing over the altar and consuming everything in its path.*

Finn jumps when a loud popping sound fills the temple. The blue light becomes unbearably bright, forcing her to shield her eyes with her hands. She keeps them there for long seconds until the glow recedes. As her eyes adjust, she realizes that the doonas are gone and four small piles of ash stain the ground where their feet had once been. Her eyes shoot to Grim and Isis, but they don't seem to notice the strange anomaly. Their eyes are studiously fixed on something small squirming at the center of the stone altar.

A loud cry echoes off the stone walls around them and Finn nearly chokes on her rising heartbeat. She takes tentative steps closer at the same time Isis hurries with uncharacteristic clumsiness toward the altar. A small baby with pale lavender skin covered in green, vinelike markings and a shock of white-blonde curls squirms in place. Her bungling fists try to find their way to her mouth and her face scrunches with the onset of tears when she can't seem to get her body to cooperate.

Isis reaches the baby and places her finger in the infant's grip, cooing and smiling down at her. As the baby soothes and coos up at Isis, the stone floor beneath the altar begins to crack. Finn watches on in stunned silence as thick vines, grass, and multihued blossoms begin to grow, sprouting through the floor and clamoring toward the ceiling.

Finn felt Isis release her and her eyes shot open, searching out the Aquariian's.

"What *was* that?"

"*That* was the sacrifice my people made to aid the Luminary in his cause."

"I don't understand."

"Our oldest and wisest *doonas* gave their lives to bring Tiri into this world. She carries their knowledge and wisdom inside of her and with them, the ability to do the impossible."

Finn struggled to take it all in, her wide eyes fixated on Isis.

"Everything you see here," the Aquariian continued, "was *created* by Tiri. This room was once sterile and barren, until I brought her to it. With no more energy than you would exert to go for a brisk walk, the child created life from nothing."

Finn thought about the mural on the walls of Tiri's bedroom and how closely it resembled the murals within the Aquariian temple.

I saw it in a dream. Finn had listened to the child's whispered admission all those weeks ago having no idea they were anything more than the musings of an imaginative child.

If what Isis was saying could be believed, Tiri was the most valuable being in all the galaxies.

"She can bring it all back," Finn breathed, thinking of the synthetic grass and plant life covering the Inner Rings.

"The galaxy remains reliant on the Arcturians and their government and technology for food, air . . . everything. In a matter of cycles, Tiri could change all of that. She could tip the balance away from the Reliance's favor. She could give us independence."

A galaxy free of Reliance control? Was such a thing even possible? Finn thought about the synthetic plants, intense vacuum ultraviolet light, and laser turbines replacing the existing plant life on every planet in the Inner and Outer Rings. They truly did depend on the Arcturians and their tech for the very air they breathed.

"The Arcturians would never let it happen," Finn countered.

"That is why they *must not know.*" Isis leaned in closer, spearing Finn with her stare. "We have to protect Tiri until the time is right, regardless of the Luminary's plans."

Finn nodded absently, the weight of this most recent revelation sinking in. Grim's endgame was all that mattered to him. She had no idea what his plans were, but she would not let him endanger Tiri in his selfish bid for revenge.

Before she could comment further, the door to the sanctuary opened and Shane, Conrad, and Iliana filled its frame.

The captain gave Isis and Finn a quick once-over, crossing his arms at his chest as his eyes finally met Finn's.

"We need to talk."

TWENTY-FIVE

F inn followed the somber trio to the dining room. As she crossed the threshold, she found herself face to face with the rest of the crew.

Two meetings in one day?

All of them were seated around the table in their usual places (save for Isis and Tiri). Even Nova perched quietly in a chair between Jax and Lex. Finn's eyes flitted through them until she met Enyo's alert gaze.

The Sirian gave her a nod, her expression serious. Finn offered her a weak smile and took a seat next to Conrad. The big man's body was stiff with tension, adding to Finn's growing feeling of unease.

Shane cleared his throat and let his eyes rove over the group before finally breaking the tense silence.

"I received some information on Kreet. We've been given the go ahead from the Luminary to begin our next rescue."

Finn straightened in her chair.

"And will the *Luminary* be taking part in this rescue?" she asked in a sharp voice.

Shane barely spared her a cursory glance.

"As you all know, I took a meeting on Kreet. While there, I received confirmation of something called the Dome located on Aquarii. Several of the blended from the senator's list have been moved there."

Aquarii?

She hadn't been to Aquarii since . . . Finn shuddered as she struggled to keep the unpleasant memories of Sophie and their imprisonment with the chancellor at bay.

A heavy silence filled the room and Finn let the subject of the Luminary drop for a moment, refocusing her attention on Shane, who looked as tightly strung as she had ever seen him.

"What's a dome?" Lex asked with furrowed brows.

"*The* Dome is a prison," Shane responded in a flat tone. "The Reliance ships the blended there and forces them to exhibit their abilities in violent challenges and fights to the death. It's modeled on the old Colosseum in ancient Rome. Our intel reports at least eight blended being held prisoner there as we speak. There were more, but the most recent games killed three and several others were sold off."

A low growl turned Finn's attention. Everyone looked shocked and horrified by what Shane was saying, everyone except Enyo. Enyo had breezed past shock and horror and careened straight for rage.

"Apparently," Shane continued, "successful fighters are bought and sold by high-ranking officials to keep and use their abilities as their new owner sees fit. Those who are killed in the Dome are labeled as weak stock and considered better off dead."

"What are we waiting for?" the Sirian hissed. "We are wasting time talking when we should be tearing that Dome to shreds."

Shane eyed her carefully before continuing.

"The Dome is more heavily guarded than any other Reliance building we've infiltrated. We need to send a team down to Aquarii for reconnaissance before we can plan an effective rescue." His eyes flitted over to Finn's once again. "Finn, do you mind if I speak with you privately?"

The table went silent. Finn nodded absently before standing and following Shane out of the dining room. As she passed, Conrad shot her a look she couldn't quite decipher and the heavy tug of anxiety pulled at her.

She trailed behind Shane as they made their way through the corridors of *Independence* and up to the bridge. Once there, he motioned for her to take a seat and leaned back against some free space near the ship's consoles.

He didn't waste time with small talk.

"I'd like you to choose a small team and take your luxury pod on-planet. With your abilities, you can gather enough intelligence to map out the Dome and lead this rescue when you return."

Lead the rescue? Finn's heart pounded precariously in her chest.

"You want *me* to lead the rescue?"

Shane nodded.

"You've already demonstrated a knack for this, and with what Iliana has shared with me about your abilities, you're our best shot at success."

"Is this *your* decision or the Luminary's?" she asked suspiciously.

"It was mine," a familiar deep grumble sounded from behind her and she turned to find Grim's towering frame filling the bridge's doorway.

His shiny horns and red skin glinted in the light and his dark eyes showed no hint of emotion as they held hers. It was the first time she'd seen him since his betrayal so many weeks ago and she tried unsuccessfully to tamp down on the rage burning a hole through the lining of her stomach.

"*Dhala*," he said gently, "it is good to see you."

Finn released a sardonic laugh. She couldn't help herself.

"I wish I could say the same," she told him through a clenched jaw.

"Still," he cleared his throat. "Shane tells me your training with Iliana has been progressing."

At the casual mention of her sister, Finn's anger boiled over and she finally snapped.

"I'm not doing this with you. I'm not going to stand here and pretend like I don't hate you." She took an angry step in his direction. "You kept me from my sister all these years.

You knew what I was, and instead of helping me get back to my family, you turned me into a puppet in whatever game it is you're playing with the Reliance."

Grim's face remained devoid of any decipherable emotion.

"You needed time to heal," he told her evenly.

"Is that what you were doing all those hours you forced me to siphon from your books? Helping me *heal*?"

Grim sighed and sucked air through his teeth as though Finn were an errant child throwing a tantrum.

"I know better than anyone the horrors of this galaxy. I gave you what was necessary to survive them."

"What's the point of all this, Grim? What do you want with all these hybrids? How does a Farthers middleman get the kind of resources needed to infiltrate planets like Cartan and Aquarii?"

She found the questions pouring out of her before she could stop them. There were so many unanswered, so many things she'd wanted to ask these last few weeks.

Rather than respond, his stoic face shut down even further. His hand went to his pocket to touch something there before he seemed to realize what he was doing. Finn caught a glimpse of metal as he removed his hand and let it drop to his side.

"Now is not the time. Choose your team; you leave for Aquarii tomorrow."

At his casual dismissal of her—the girl he'd raised from feral child to capable woman—Finn lost her last shred of control.

She stomped past him through the doorway, her shoulder roughly bumping his midsection as she did.

Ignoring his grunt of surprise, she stopped her retreat and turned to level Shane with a hard stare. If she was going to do this, she might as well get something out of it and there had been one thought plaguing her mind since Enyo woke up screaming in their room all those nights ago.

"I'll do it on one condition."

The captain's eyes drifted over to Grim briefly before returning to her.

"Name it."

"There's a Sirian named Argo employed by the Reliance Army. I want you to use your contacts to find him for me."

If Shane found her request odd, he didn't let on.

"Consider it done."

TWENTY-SIX

Finn clutched the chain she'd lifted from Grim's pocket. It was the necklace. The one he'd sent her on a wild goose chase to find all those weeks ago when he'd prodded her to chase down Iliana to recover it. The necklace that had kicked off this entire mess and stripped her of everything she'd known to be true.

She eyed it for several minutes, almost as though if she stared long enough, it would tell her everything she wanted to know.

Well, it would . . . but she'd have to touch it first.

Finn removed the glove from her hand and crossed her legs on the bed. She inhaled the scent of Conrad's wax and closed her eyes. Her bare hand reached out and clasped the chain of the necklace. Almost immediately a loud buzzing filled her ears and images began to flood her mind so quickly she had a hard time focusing.

She caught hazy glimpses of a pretty woman with hair the color of wheat and blue eyes so pure, they rivaled the sky on Gliese. Her smile lit up her entire face as she held a squirming bundle of blankets in her arms.

And just like that the image was gone.

Finn sighed in vexation. As soon as she would catch sight of something she wanted to examine further, the memory would evaporate. Every time she tried to grab on to them, they would slip out of her grasp.

Finally, a memory clearer than the others came to her and she latched onto it in a death grip. She pulled it closer, allowing it to envelope her.

* * *

Grim sits in his office. A book rests poised in his hand as he reads aloud in a low murmur. Finn can't help but be soothed by the deep timbre of his voice.

He pulls something from his desk and puts it around his neck. The chain and Khaleerian gemstone rest just below his throat. It seems small on him, as though the necklace were made for someone much slighter of build.

Finn can tell from the dim glow of candles that it is nighttime. Still, she can make out his dark eyes as they stare into the shadowy corner. She takes a step forward, her eyes straining in the low light.

What she sees has her stopping short. Curled up in the corner and resting atop a pile of blankets is a small child with a fall of dark red hair. She is sleeping soundly and snoring gently.

That's me.

From the looks of it, this memory is taking place a few months after her arrival on the Mud Pit.

"I assumed you would have sent her away to her sister by now." Adult Finn turns to find Doc—the resident bartender at the tavern Grim owned on the Mud Pit and an old friend of Finn's—watching the Khaleerian from the office's entrance. His bespectacled gaze is thoughtful. "You've never kept any of the others this long," he remarks.

Grim finally tears his stare from the sleeping child and gives Doc his full attention.

"Is there a question in there somewhere, Doc?"

The reptilian alien smiles imperceptibly and adjusts the glasses where they perch on his nose.

"Just wondering what makes this one different."

"She reminds me of someone," Grim says in a low, pained whisper.

"Will you be keeping her, then?"

"She's not a pet, Doc," Grim growls in annoyance. Doc merely continues to stare deep into the Khaleerian's eyes knowingly. Grim expels a frustrated breath. "Would it be so crazy if I did?"

"Yes," Doc answers immediately.

TWENTY-SEVEN

Tiri murmured quietly to the doll pressed tenderly against her chest. She seemed to be in better spirits now, though Finn's gift had surely helped.

The little girl's eyes had beamed with joy when Finn finally gave it to her, paying special attention to the doll's hand-painted face.

"I love her! I'm going to name her Allora."

Isis paused her pruning of a fat purple flower to share a soft smile with Finn.

It had been tempting to lock herself in her room and obsess over the memory she'd siphoned from Grim's necklace, but Finn was doing her best to block out all thoughts related to the giant Khaleerian.

Instead, she spent the better part of her afternoon working out a plan for wandering through the streets of Aquarii undetected. All the plotting, combined with the upper-caste clothing and discreetly placed comm devices and weaponry provided to her by Shane and Iliana, had her feeling somewhat confident about their chances.

Now, she found herself seeking refuge with Tiri and Isis in their dreamlike garden.

The lights were set to dim, showing night had fallen in the sanctuary. Somehow it was even more beautiful, even more magical in the duskiness.

"I don't understand," Finn commented as she examined a bundle of intertwined purple stems stretching skyward. "What's so special about this one?"

Apparently, one of Isis's rare flowers was set to bloom tonight and since the plant only blossomed once every six cycles, Isis and Tiri were camped out on the soft grass until the special moment arrived.

The plant looked ordinary enough to Finn, though she supposed the deep purple of the stem and sepals was quite extraordinary.

"The flower's pistil can be harvested and used for its healing capabilities. I've made extracts from it that can knit a wound together within hours," Isis noted without looking up from her ministrations.

"And the flower's insides glow and fly through the air." Tiri made the excited announcement as she spun Allora in dizzying circles.

"The flower's *stamen*," Isis corrected, smiling indulgently.

Tiri merely spun faster. Her circles became clumsy until she eventually fell to the ground and landed on her backside, erupting in a fit of giggles.

Finn shook her head and chuckled.

It was hard to believe the carefree little girl in front of her possessed the wisdom and knowledge of the Aquariian *doonas*.

It was even harder to believe that same little girl had created the paradise surrounding them.

"I'm going with you, Hellion!"

They turned in unison at the bellowed exclamation to find Conrad—Enyo close on his heels—storming through the tall grass near the sanctuary's entrance.

"As am I," the Sirian growled.

The interruption shattered their quiet reprieve. Finn barely had time to appreciate that the two had finally put aside their differences, united as they were in their anger at being left behind.

Conrad stomped to her side where she sat against a tall tree.

"You're not going to Aquarii without me."

"I take it you heard," Finn grumbled.

Finn had chosen a small group for the mission; selecting Nova to pilot the pod to Aquarii and AJ to join her in casing the Dome. The boy's Anunnaki abilities would surely come in handy, given how tight security was supposed to be on-planet.

Shane took her decision in stride; better than she'd expected. However, so far, it appeared as though AJ and Nova were the only ones truly happy with her choice.

Finn sighed and met their angry gazes.

"No, you're both staying here." Before either of them could argue, she raised a hand to silence them and moved to stand. "You two are the best warriors on the ship. You're needed here to keep the crew safe."

To keep Tiri safe, she thought to herself as her eyes involuntarily shifted to the child. She held Allora close and watched the trio with wide eyes.

"Come, child." Isis rushed to Tiri's side and began to usher her away. "The pistils will be here tomorrow and I've got a dress in my room I can't wait to alter for Allora."

Completely unfazed by the abrupt change in plans, Tiri yelped with glee and held the doll over her head.

"Allora says she can't wait!" Tiri held the toy's mouth up to her ear. "And she hopes it's purple." The child's smile faltered for a moment as she seemed to remember Finn and her predicament. "Will you be okay, Finn?" she asked hesitantly.

She gave the girl a wide smile and nodded. "Go get Allora her dress," she said warmly.

She watched as Isis and Tiri skipped hand in hand from the sanctuary and out into the hall. Finn met Conrad's glowing eyes pointedly.

"I need to know you're both here protecting the ship and everyone on it."

"And who will be protecting you?" he asked angrily.

"Enyo, can you give us a minute?" Finn asked quietly, not daring to break Conrad's stare. She could sense the Sirian was less than happy to be dismissed, but she obeyed, turning on her heel and leaving in a huff. When she was out of earshot, Finn continued. "I know about Tiri, Conrad. Isis showed me." He reared back in surprise, but she didn't give him time to process. "Right now, Tiri is more important than any of us . . . than you or me. I need to know you're here keeping her safe. Please," she pleaded.

He watched her for long moments, his eyes stormy as he warred with his conflicting feelings. After a few beats he relented, his big shoulders sagging as he took a deep breath.

"Just promise me you'll be safe," he whispered.

Finn forced a smile that didn't quite reach her eyes.

"I'll be safe," she assured.

He saw her struggle and his eyes softened, their glow dimming. He reached out a gloved hand to caress her cheek and she leaned into the touch.

Finn could have stayed that way all night, but a low hissing turned their attention and interrupted the quiet moment.

They turned toward the source of the sound to see the petals of the purple plant expanding and separating. On a sigh, the flower bloomed and grew to reveal iridescent plum-purple petals. Tiny blue and pink tubes extended into the air and little clusters of yellow at their peaks began to glow.

Their radiance filled the space around Finn and Conrad, lighting their faces in luminous purple and yellow.

With a short pop, the shining clusters separated from the plant and began to float skyward in a slow, deliberate ascension.

"It's beautiful," Conrad muttered.

"Have you ever seen anything like it?" she asked, unable to tear her eyes from the splendor.

"Never."

Their eyes met as the plant's soft glimmer washed over them and all around them from above.

Conrad's eyes once again began to glow, enhancing the incandescence.

He was still being so careful not to touch her skin to skin whenever they were together.

He hadn't slipped once.

Now, surrounded by his scent, the beauty of the sanctuary, and with her departure for Aquarii imminent, Finn was feeling brave.

She moved closer into his embrace, her bare hand reaching out to touch his cheek and then trailing the runic markings down his shoulder. His brows shot up in confusion as his eyes began to glow even brighter.

Slowly, Finn inhaled all that was Conrad. Ignoring the din of memories poking at the back of her brain, Finn pulled him closer.

Conrad wrapped his arms around her and pulled her tighter. His head tilted down at the same time hers lifted upward and their lips met. Finn was bombarded with a rush of emotion and sensation she'd never felt before.

She clung to him, her body pressed against him as she lost herself in the contact.

They stayed that way for a long while, kissing and reveling in the joy they felt to be in each other's arms.

Eventually they had to come up for air, their chests heaving. Conrad's eyes burned brightly as they held hers.

"Come back to me," he breathed.

"That's the plan," she told him, grinning.

TWENTY-EIGHT

Enyo proved a little more difficult to placate than Conrad, but by the time Finn, Nova, and AJ were ready to leave the next morning, most of her ire toward Finn seemed to have dissipated. She couldn't risk telling the Sirian about Tiri, not yet anyway.

Instead, she focused on convincing Enyo that her considerable talents as a warrior would be put to better use protecting the crew remaining on the ship.

The rest of *Independence*'s crew—save for Grim—came to bid them farewell at the pod's entrance. Thankfully, the Khaleerian was smart enough to keep his distance and remain in his quarters on the ship out of respect . . . at least that's what Shane claimed.

As the captain finished loading the pod with supplies he'd picked up on Kreet, he reached over and clapped AJ on the back. Shane muttered a gruff "Good luck" to the boy. Nova and the twins shared jokes and hugs. Iliana stood back, wringing her delicate hands nervously as she watched Finn.

Finally, she seemed to come unstuck and made her way to Finn's side. She stood there awkwardly for a moment before throwing her arms around her younger sister in a tight hug. Finn squeezed her back, inhaling the flowery sent of Iliana's curls.

"I'll be back before you know it," she told Iliana as she pulled away and tried to ignore the tears pooling in her big sister's eyes. "Besides, aren't you sick of me yet?" She shot her a grin, and Iliana choked on a surprised sob before her body relaxed and she finally smiled.

"Never, Little One."

Once they were ready to depart, Conrad gave Finn one last wink and the trio took their seats at the ship's helm.

Surprising everyone—including Finn—Nova maneuvered the pod out of the docking bay with near perfect precision.

The doxie winked cheekily and said, "The twins have been giving me pointers."

Once the pod had officially detached from *Independence*, Finn extricated herself from her seat and headed to the back room to prepare. She had just reached the door's threshold when AJ's voice stopped her.

"Finn?" She turned to face the boy and waited for him to continue. After a moment, he said, "Thank you for choosing me. I won't let you down."

"I know you won't, kid," she told him.

AJ's dark brows furrowed, wrinkling the porcelain skin on his forehead.

"When are you going to stop calling me 'kid'? I'm not Tiri."

"I call kids 'kid.' It's not that complicated," Finn pointed out, smiling softly at the boy's indignant expression.

"Yeah, well you'll change your mind after this mission. I'm going to show you I'm not a kid."

Finn sighed and gave the boy a hard stare.

"Don't do anything stupid, AJ."

Finn spent the next few hours mentally preparing for the monumental task ahead of them, forcing thoughts of Tiri, Conrad, and Enyo as far away as she could as she poured over the maps Shane had given them.

She filled in AJ and Nova as the flight progressed, stressing the importance of traveling through Aquarii unnoticed. This was an information-gathering mission only, and she looked AJ dead in the eyes as she warned against rash actions or heroics.

Nova had already changed into what she lovingly referred to as her "upper-caste costume."

Finally, after they had all changed into fancier garb, Finn slipped her brand-new knife into a boot and paced with anticipation.

Fortunately, Nova chose that moment to announce they were nearing Aquarii. Finn and AJ took their seats at the ship's helm and waited in tense silence for Nova to land the pod.

While Nova remained with the ship, Finn and AJ made their way through the streets of Aquarii. Despite it being such a large planet, Finn was surprised to find very few people inhabiting it. It would seem the Dome was the planet's main draw and, aside from a cadre of Reliance soldiers, only the highest-ranking, most-important members of the Reliance seemed to be visiting the planet at any given time.

Naturally, it made blending in a bit of a challenge.

Fortunately, those same high-ranking officials rarely traveled without a large number of servants and slaves to see to their every need, giving Finn and AJ the perfect cover. They'd been doing all right so far, and as they silently drew closer to the Dome, most of Finn's tension had begun to ease.

The planet was a far cry from its once lush and fertile land. The ancient Aquariian stone temples had been torn down, replaced by glass skyscrapers, marble monoliths, gaudy fountain displays, and holojectors. Ostentatious chariots much like the one she'd seen on Arcturus—pulled by mechanical horses—passed by occasionally

The sparse plant life that remained was synthetic.

On every street corner they passed, holojectors projected three-dimensional images of lower-caste alien races. Their reverent voices told the story of where each of them had been when the unionization began.

Aquariians, Goslans, Khaleerians, and so many others spouted off their histories in stilted tones, all the while praising the Arcturians and their arrival.

She wondered how many of them had been reading a script at gunpoint during their recordings. She'd never heard a member of the lower castes speak about the Arcturians without bitterness and vitriol dripping from their tongues.

Finn made a point to run her hands over the marble pillars and walls as she passed, memorizing as many details as she could. She battled with the swarm of images that flooded her with each touch, taking care to breathe deeply. She dabbed a small amount of Conrad's wax above her upper lip and inhaled, sorting through indecipherable flashes of violence and screaming intermixed with raucous laughter and applause.

As her hand brushed the glass pane of a window, a vision began to fill her, overtaking all the others.

She is standing amidst a crowd within a vast arena. Looking around, Finn finally understands why Aquarii seems so empty. The entirety of its population is gathered around her inside, in a display that transports the planet into a high-tech version of one of the pages from Grim's tomes about ancient Rome. A dome overhead, made from advanced hard-light projections, shields the space from the elements and separates the spectators from the dozens of hybrids currently engaged in battle at the Dome's center. The specially tuned hologram refracted light through a prism that gave the Dome true mass, allowing it to be felt as well as being seen.

Pods hover overhead with cameras affixed to them. Their small lenses capture incredibly clear images of the chaos taking place inside. A multitude of holojectors mounted within the Dome display the closeup video feed of bleeding hybrids engrossed in the brutal battle royal below.

Between each screen is a massive laser gun, all of them pointed at the melee below. Around her on all sides, rows of seats house thousands of raucous spectators dressed in a tide of red and gold so massive Finn can hardly distinguish one person from the next. She follows their hungry gazes back to the center of the arena where the commotion has intensified.

A female with long silver hair and spindly limbs holds the decapitated head of her opponent up for all the spectators to see. Spittle forms on her lips as she lets loose a victory cry.

Finn released her hold on the window with a gasp.

AJ noticed the change in her demeanor and stepped closer, a look of concern on his face.

"What did you see?"

Her somber eyes landed on the boy.

"It's bad," she whispered back.

His eyes narrowed in understanding, sparking with anger. The sight sent waves of unease throughout Finn.

"AJ, are you going to be okay to do this?" She hadn't considered the boy's past and how his torture and imprisonment might affect his emotions during their mission.

At her question, the anger cleared from his expression and he nodded firmly.

"I'm fine. Keep touching stuff. We need to know what security looks like in the Dome."

Finn watched him for a moment longer before nodding and turning back to the building behind her. She placed her hands on a nearby doorknob and focused on the images filling her field of vision. Like pulling on a single string in a sea of yarn, she navigated her way through the memories attached to the door until she found one she wanted.

She is in a control room filled with small-scale holojector screens. Each of them displays different images of hybrids locked within glass cages. Some are bound or blindfolded while others lie unconscious. Ten armed soldiers surround her on all sides talking distractedly as they scan through the images.

"Shift change is in ten, boys," one of them tells the others. "We're on perimeter duty tonight."

Another soldier, younger than the rest, groans and rolls his eyes.

"When are we on Dome duty? I want a shot at the big one during the games."

He points at one of the screens, but Finn is too far away to make out the image.

"Like you could take him," another soldier scoffs. The others join in his laughter, ribbing the younger man until his face is as red as his uniform.

Finn pulled away and turned to AJ.

"There are at least ten soldiers in a control room monitoring video feeds of the arena at all times. There are another ten walking the perimeter, and dozens more in the Dome during the games."

The boy's eyes widened as he let loose a low whistle.

"I hope Shane knows what he's doing," he mused.

I'll second that, Finn thought darkly.

"What are you two doing out here by yourselves?"

Finn spun in place to face a dark-haired Reliance soldier. His handsome features were pinched in anger as he stormed over to where they stood and raised a hand covered in a stunner glove. As he neared, his other hand pulled a heavy reinforced staff from his belt.

From the corner of her eye Finn saw AJ's stance widen and he reached for one of the weapons strapped to his belly.

"No weapons, AJ," she ordered through her teeth as she forced a smile. She had faith in the boy's ability to throw down and defend himself, but this was not the ideal scenario for a showdown. "You'll draw dozens more if we're not careful."

She released a deep breath when his body relaxed slightly and his hand fell to his side.

How the hell were they going to talk their way out of this? She'd said no weapons, but they might not have a choice in the matter.

Finn watched the soldier draw closer, closing the distance between them in record time, but before she could come up with a decent excuse, his body stopped abruptly. It was almost as though he'd walked into an invisible wall. The anger slowly erased itself from his expression, replaced by a look of pure awe.

Finn followed his rapt gaze to AJ. The boy stood with his shoulders squared; his black eyes now swirled in a mix of greens, blues, and purples. On instinct her own eyes flew away from his and back to the soldier's.

"Shit," she muttered. "AJ, what are you doing?"

"Getting us out of here," he answered shortly, keeping his focus on the soldier. "Keep a lookout."

Finn didn't bother getting worked up over the boy's bossiness. Instead, her head shot around in all directions, looking for more soldiers to come out of the woodwork.

"We're clear," she told him. "Make it quick."

AJ didn't hesitate. His voice deepened as he commanded, "You never saw us here. You're going to go to your barracks and have a nice nap."

"Yes, I think I'll have a nap," the soldier droned flatly.

Finn remembered what it felt like to be stuck in the boy's hold and felt a slight twinge of pity for the man. Slowly, he turned on his heel and walked away with stilted, robotic movements. He set off in the opposite direction and never looked back.

AJ's eyes were back to their usual black when he turned to her and smiled.

"That was close."

Despite her misgivings with his abilities, Finn couldn't help but be impressed with the boy.

"Quick thinking, kid." His smile widened at her praise even as he rolled his eyes at being called "kid" yet again. "Now let's get the hell out of here before we run into any more puppets for you to play with."

"What about the mission? Do we have enough intel for Shane?"

Finn's stomach tumbled uncomfortably; she grimaced.

"We've got all we're going to get."

She didn't say what she was really thinking: *Going into that Dome is a suicide mission.*

It was a good thing she specialized in suicide missions.

As Finn and AJ made their way back to the pod, they kept wary eyes on their surroundings the entire way. When they reached the clearing where Nova had landed, they found the doxie waiting for them, leaning casually against the pod's exterior. Oddly, she'd changed out of her borrowed clothes and back into her shorts and half-shirt, proudly displaying her scarred body for all to see. She greeted them with a cheeky wave and a smile.

She was going to get them caught.

Finn shook her head angrily and picked up her pace, closing the distance between them and escape. When only a few feet separated them, Finn tracked movement from behind the pod.

As she watched, a large group of Reliance soldiers began to make their way around the back of the ship, lining up on either side of Nova. Rather than looking afraid as any fugitive doxie in her right mind would, Nova greeted the soldiers with an even wider smile before her calm gaze returned to Finn's.

"Nova, what are you doing," Finn hissed.

The girl ignored her, walking straight up to the highest-ranking Reliance soldier as he approached, extending a scarred hand.

"Do you have my gold?" she asked him impatiently. "These are the half-breeds I promised back on Kreet, and I've already given you the coordinates to a ship full of them. That's got to be worth my weight in coin."

She blinked coyly at the man and as her words sank in, Finn's heart dropped in her chest. Everything around them seemed to move in slow motion as the pounding of it filled her ears.

The coordinates of the ship? Oh Gods.

"I guess now I know what you were really doing on Kreet," Finn hissed at the doxie.

"You traitor!" AJ yelled suddenly, attempting to shove past Finn.

She stayed him with a hand on his shoulder as panic began to blur her vision. In his anger, AJ's eyes started to swirl with color once again, and the surrounding soldiers began to yell over each other.

"Don't look into its eyes!"

Nova had been thorough in her betrayal.

One of the soldiers on the far side of the group sent a blast at AJ from the fist of his stunner glove and the boy hit the ground in a lifeless heap. Finn struggled to remain motionless, her mind swimming as her panic-stricken brain searched for an escape, or at the very least, a way to warn the crew of *Independence.*

Carefully flicking the comm device on her wrist, Finn prayed to the Gods someone was listening. Nova looked in their direction, her pockmarked face devoid of any emotion save for the obvious relish at earning her weight in Reliance gold. How could Finn have been so stupid? So careless? Enyo had been right. She should have known not to trust the doxie's loyalty.

Now, not only was Finn about to pay for her own carelessness, but the entire crew of *Independence* would pay as well.

Since Nova was looking away, she missed the soldier behind her as he unholstered his plasma gun. Before Finn could exhale, he pointed it at the back of the doxie's head and pulled the trigger. The front of Nova's head exploded in a macabre fountain of blood, smoking tissue, and bone. Her unseeing eyes went skyward as her body fell to the ground in a heap.

"The Reliance thanks you for your service," the soldier told Nova's lifeless form.

Finn used their moment of distraction to bring the comm to her lips, yelling, "They're coming for *Independence*! Get out now!"

The soldier's eyes flicked over to Finn. "Take them," he commanded.

The remaining soldiers aimed their stunner gloves at where Finn stood frozen. Before she could move to flee, their fingers closed into fists and a barrage of blasts hit her from all sides.

The world went dark and Finn collapsed next to AJ.

TWENTY-NINE

Finn came to with a horrific headache. Her mouth was uncomfortably parched, and a loud buzzing sounded in her ears. Remembering the soldiers and their stunner gloves, she sat up quickly and immediately grabbed her head in agony.

Something hard and metallic slammed into her temples; a cry of pain escaped her dry lips. Finn pulled her hands back and examined them. They'd been covered with steel boxes that were locked at her wrists.

Her clothes had been changed, and her possessions—including her knife and Conrad's hair wax—had all been removed. She fought down nausea as she examined her new garb. An itchy pair of dark burgundy pants and a matching long-sleeved shirt covered her body and her feet were wrapped in dirty cotton socks . . . no shoes.

Tiri? Finn called out to the girl in her mind. *Tiri, can you hear me?*

She waited long minutes for a response but none came. Finn tried to tell herself the child was merely out of range, but dread sat heavy in the pit of her stomach.

Her eyes struggled to take in her dark surroundings. She was underground, alone in what appeared to be a small glass cell with a tiled floor. One of the panes had a small, closed slot she assumed was used for food. More cells lined the floor as far as her eyes could see through the dimness. She could make out the blinking lights of cameras—all aimed at the glass cells—spread throughout the space.

"AJ?" she called, trying to ignore the rising dread in her voice. "AJ?"

"Finn?" She followed the boy's voice to a cell several feet away. She could just barely make out his still form huddled in the corner and a large strip of silicone that had been wrapped and fastened around his head, covering his eyes. "Finn, I can't see," he yelled in panic.

"Will you two shut up? I'm trying to sleep." Finn flinched as an unfamiliar, mildly annoyed voice called out into the darkness.

"Where are we?" Finn asked the voice, too frightened to be cautious.

This time, a different voice answered her. It was deep with a slight rasp.

"You're in the Dome. Well, under it to be exact."

Finn's head shot from left to right, searching for the source of the sound. It appeared to come from one of the cells to her immediate right, but the figure inside was shrouded in darkness.

Finn's heart fell, and she muttered a low expletive under her breath. She shifted awkwardly on the ground, struggling to move properly with her hands covered in the clunky boxes. Frustrated, she slammed her back against the cell wall and exhaled a puff of air.

She fought to force her panic and all thoughts of Nova's treachery and the fate of *Independence* to the back of her mind. It would do them no good. When her breathing had somewhat evened, she turned to call through the glass.

"Everything is going to be okay, AJ. Just try to stay calm."

AJ's voice echoed around her, breaking as he struggled to speak.

"The soldiers know where the ship is. They're going to kill them all, Finn."

Tears pricked the backs of her eyes and a lump formed in her throat. She fought it down and tried to answer as calmly as possible.

"It's going to be okay, AJ." She strained to sound confident as she said, "It's going take more than a few Reliance soldiers to get the best of your brothers."

"Somebody shut her up!" A gruff voice yelled out into the night and Finn flinched.

"Get some sleep," she whispered to AJ.

Given what she'd already seen of the Dome, they would need all the rest they could get. She leaned back against the wall, the sounds of soft snoring and bodies shifting in the dirt filling her ears.

Her mind raced in the darkness. Without her hands, she was at a significant disadvantage. There would be no escape tonight, but hopefully tomorrow they'd be leaving their cages, allowing for more possibility. She wasn't sure how many hybrids surrounded her on all sides, but if she could convince enough of them to work together, they just might stand a chance.

Finn closed her eyes and let her mind work on a plan. She relaxed her body as much as her constraints would allow and took a deep breath.

Tomorrow.

Tomorrow she would get them all out of here.

How hard could it be to convince a handful of hybrids to work together?

Finn stirred in the early morning as the sounds of movement, coughing, and the low buzz of artificial lights above her filled her ears. Now that the night had passed, she could finally make out her surroundings.

The underground space was lined with twenty ten-by-fifteen-square-feet glass cages; ten on either side. Each cell had a toilet and small sink in the corner and a small, rectangular drawer that opened out from the other side.

Her eyes sought out AJ and she found him a few cells away curled on his side on the floor. His deep, even breaths told her he had at least found sleep at some point during the night.

Inside the cell next to his, a bald man sat awake in the corner with his elbows resting on his knees. His giant body was strung tight with hard muscle, but his casual pose gave him a deceptively calm appearance. He wore a jumpsuit in the same burgundy color as Finn's shirt and pants.

The parts of his skin it exposed were such a dark shade of black he almost looked blue. He watched her intently, the irises of his eyes shining a deep yellow ringed with red. Something about his stare unsettled her, and an involuntary shiver stole up her spine.

"That's the Solidarian," a voice to Finn's left declared. She turned and found a pale young woman resting casually against the wall of the cell next to hers. Unlike Finn, she appeared to be unrestrained; a deep-burgundy jumpsuit identical to the Solidarian's covered her body. Her dark hair was matted and pulled into a snarly ponytail.

She turned oval eyes to Finn and smiled.

"You won't get much conversation out of him. He's been here fifteen cycles and word is he never says a peep. I wouldn't either to be honest. I heard he took down a whole company of Reliance soldiers . . . burned their barracks to the ground. He's been here ever since. Too dangerous to be sold, but too violent and entertaining to kill." The young woman leaned up against the glass and whispered, "My advice? Steer clear of him in the Dome."

Fifteen cycles in a cage?

The man must be certifiable at this point. Finn knew she would be. Could this Solidarian be the same one she'd heard whispered stories about on the Mud Pit? The one who was supposedly executed with steel boxes around his hands? The thought didn't bear thinking about.

"Who are you?" Finn asked the young woman.

She shrugged her bony shoulders and stated, "In here, I'm Supersonic."

Supersonic?

At Finn's questioning gaze, the hybrid blew a fallen strand of dark hair from her face.

"You're wondering about the nickname," she stated matter-of-factly. "No one lasts long in the Dome. It's easier to remember nicknames. Plus, it helps me remember what everyone can do out there. So . . ." She eyed Finn. "What can *you* do?"

"He doesn't get one?" Finn ignored the question and motioned with her head in the direction of the Solidarian's cage. Supersonic shuddered dramatically.

"I'm not touching that with a ten-foot pole."

Finn scooted closer to their adjoining glass wall.

"Have you tried to escape?"

Supersonic tipped her head back and let out a ringing laugh that set Finn's teeth on edge. She glared as the hybrid took a few moments to compose herself before shooting Finn an amused grin.

"Outside of this place, I could run laps around the Dome and be back on my ass in this cell before you could blink. I'm half-Xandar, which means"—she leaned in close, her breath fogging the glass between them—"I'm *fast* . . . hence *Supersonic*."

Finn knew a little about the alien species from the planet Xandar. They had once lived on a high-gravity atmosphere within the Outer Rings. When the Reliance unionized the Inner and Outer Rings, the Xandar people found that the lower levels of gravity on their new homes gave them increased speed and endurance.

"So, have you tried to escape then?"

She looked at Finn like she might be missing half her brain and motioned toward a grouping of lasers mounted and spaced out around the ceiling of her cell.

"Those things are motion sensitive. The Reliance rigged them to go off if they detect any movement faster than average walking speed. So, to answer your question, no. I haven't tried to escape." She took in Finn's shocked if not defeated expression and continued matter-of-factly. "We all have them. The more dangerous the half-breed, the more intense the measures." She nodded in the direction of the intimidating Solidarian. "His cell is heat sensitive. It's rigged to rain freezing foam over the poor bastard if he even sweats too much."

She supposed that explained why the space was free of Reliance guards. She hadn't clocked any cameras in the underground space either. If the cells were so cleverly triggered, they wouldn't need to worry about constant oversight.

"And the others?" Finn asked quietly, her eyes scanning to the rest of the cells.

Supersonic's unblinking stare assessed her carefully.

"Fine, I'll give you a rundown, but don't expect any more favors from me. It's nothing personal, but once these cells open and they send us out to the Dome, it's every half-breed for themselves."

Finn nodded in understanding, hoping that she could convince the cheeky hybrid otherwise before that happened. If the Gods favored them, it would be days before they had to face each other in the Dome. At her acquiescence, Supersonic pointed to the cell on the other side of Finn's.

"She's new. Got here a few hours before you."

Finn followed until her eyes landed on a small girl, probably no older than eleven or twelve. She was huddled in her cell like a frightened animal, a cascade of yellow waves falling around her painfully young face. Like AJ, a band of silicone covered her eyes, and her hands were secured tightly behind her back.

As Finn took in the terrified child's form, she had to stifle a gasp. Running up the length of the girl's neck and past the confines of her jumpsuit were runic markings identical to those of Conrad; their blue glow made even starker against the pale white of her skin.

Forcing her tone to sound casual, she spoke to the child.

"Hi. What's your name?"

Her little head turned left and right as if to find the source of Finn's voice.

"Carrow," she finally whispered softly. "Micro," Supersonic corrected. "I'm calling you Micro." At Finn's harsh glare, the dark-haired hybrid shrugged her shoulders innocently. "What? She's tiny."

Finn shook her head and focused on the little girl in her cell.

"Hi, Carrow. My name is Finn. I'm new here too. How old are you?"

"Eleven," she breathed.

Finn's stomach clenched hard.

Gods, she is so young.

"I know someone with markings just like yours," she told the child gently.

Carrow's mouth opened in surprise. "You do?"

"His name is Conrad. He's really good at moving things with his mind. What about you?"

The child bit her lip.

"I can move things sometimes, but I have to concentrate really hard."

Before Finn could offer any additional words of comfort to the girl, Supersonic interrupted.

"So, you can *sometimes* move things with your mind?" She teased with a harsh laugh. "I'm sticking with Micro." Rather than wait for the meek child to answer, Supersonic drew their attention to the cells across the way. "The unconscious one over there is Bedlam, at least that's what I call him. The Reliance keeps him knocked out with a steady stream of narcotics until it's time to enter the Dome. I've never seen anything like him before. As soon as he wakes up, his skin turns dark red and he bulks up until he's gigantic. Apparently, he's half-Khaleerian. All I know is he's stronger than forty of me combined and angrier than a drunk Goslan."

Finn could just barely make out the hulking form of the man in question on the floor of his cell. Two long horns wrapped his head and glistened in the artificial lights. His chest rose and fell with deep, heavy breaths.

Another half-Khaleerian?

Finn's heart ached at the onslaught of information, but— true to her nickname—Supersonic never slowed down to offer her time to adjust.

"The one in the cell next to him is Viper," she continued. "You can barely see her through all that latex covering her, but her skin is poisonous. I saw her touch a guy in the Dome once . . . Ten seconds later he was turning blue and foaming at the mouth . . . And that was the last we ever saw of him."

"I can hear you, Supersonic. It's not nice to talk about me like I'm not here," Viper's deceptively pleasant if not slightly muffled voice called over to them. She was, in fact, covered from head to toe in a layer of dark latex beneath her jumpsuit, with only two small air holes at her nostrils for breathing. "And I still hate that stupid nickname," she growled.

"Hey, don't be upset, Viper. I was just about to impress her with tales of your cold-blooded success the last five rounds in the Dome."

As the poisonous hybrid clucked her tongue in dis- taste, Supersonic shot Finn a wink and continued with her introductions.

"Next to her is her partner in ruthlessness, Rock."

"That's not my name and you damn well know it, Supersonic. And quit giving the newbie tips."

"I'll tell you what," Supersonic teased. "If you can catch me, I'll stop."

Finn's eyes sought out the young man sitting cross-legged in his cell. He was slender but lean, with dark-blue hair and olive skin. His face was somewhat obscured by his hands as he held it as though in pain. His hunched posture looked nothing short of miserable. A black box the size of Finn's fist sat in the corner, and it appeared to be connected to the young hybrid by several black wires affixed to his head and chest.

Supersonic blew him a kiss, undeterred.

"*Rock* is half-Kreetian," she told Finn as she pointed at the black box. "If that vibe cannon didn't emit constant ultralow frequencies to keep his brain fried, he'd harden his skin and break his way out of here. Isn't that right, Rocky?"

He could harden his skin?

"Shut up already," the blue-haired male moaned pitifully.

"One more and then I'm done," she called.

Supersonic motioned to the last cell on the left where a small man sat in an empty cell with his eyes closed. Despite his round cheeks and youthful appearance, a smattering of gray hair covered his large, slightly conical head. His skin was a sickly shade of gray as well.

"That's Gray Matter. He's been hush-hush so far about what he is and what he can do, but he's survived three rounds in the Dome without a scratch, so he must be doing something right."

The ashen hybrid lifted his head and opened his eyes in acknowledgement. He wasn't restrained in any way and his cell was empty of the lasers she'd glimpsed or any other safety devices.

He would seem utterly harmless were it not for an astute gleam in his eyes. If he'd survived three rounds in the Dome, he must be hiding something powerful behind his diminutive frame.

"So, what about you and the kid?" Supersonic questioned, eyeing the boxes covering Finn's hands.

"What about us?" Finn asked, feigning confusion.

Supersonic was sharp and didn't miss a beat, rolling her eyes before repeating,

"What can you and the kid do? Hopefully it's something good or you'll both be dead by sundown."

Apparently, they had even less time than she'd origi-
nally thought.

"Listen," she told the woman as she leaned closer, "we're
not here to hurt anyone. We're here to rescue all of you."

Supersonic's eyes went wide before she sputtered, her loud
belly laughs leaving Finn's ears ringing.

"I'm sorry," she gasped between chuckles, struggling to
regain her composure, "but could you be any more cliché?"
She held her stomach as she called over to the poisonous
hybrid, "Viper, did you hear the good news? The plucky lady
and her sidekick are here to save us."

Finn could practically hear the smile in Viper's voice as she
purred, "Then what are they doing in cages?"

"She's telling the truth!" AJ shouted from his cell.
Apparently, he'd woken sometime during their conversation.
"We rescue the blended. We come from a ship full of them."

"*Blended*? Sounds like how I order my favorite drink, *mutt*."
Supersonic chuckled as her wide eyes shot to the other cages.

"Wait, is this ship the one you were crying about last night?"
Viper's muffled voice sounded amused as she called to him
from her cell. "I don't think they can do much rescuing if the
Reliance knows where they are."

AJ's jaw clenched as he blindly twisted his head, searching
for the source of the sarcastic voice.

"They'll come for us!" he yelled defiantly into the air.

Finn's gut twisted, and her mouth went dry. Last night
she'd told AJ it would take more than a few Reliance soldiers
to get the best of his brothers. In the light of day, however,
she was finding it hard to hold on to that hope. Even if they'd
heard her warning yesterday, what were the odds it had given
them enough time to escape?

Enyo's face flashed in her mind, followed by Tiri, Conrad,
and lastly . . . Iliana.

After everything they'd been through together, was she
really never to see her sister again? Never to see any of them

again? How was she supposed to hold on to hope without Jax's annoying ribbing or Lex's constant chatter?

How could she do anything but grieve when the possibility was becoming more and more real that she'd never again feel Conrad's gentle touch?

The Solidarian shifted slightly in his cell, drawing her attention, and Finn caught his gaze. His red-tinged eyes peered into hers with alarming intensity, as though he could read her dark thoughts, before turning away abruptly.

Shaking off the strange moment, Finn felt determination surge through her. Despair was not an option. Even in her worst moments, no matter what, there was one thing she could always count on: she was a survivor.

She didn't know how to be anything else.

Finn called out to the room.

"Listen to me carefully. We don't want to hurt any of you. If we work together, we could all survive long enough to the get the hell out of here. No one has to die in the Dome . . . not anymore."

This time, both Supersonic and Viper cackled in amusement. Rock moaned from the floor of his cell and Gray Matter cocked his head to the side, an eerie smile lifting his pale lips.

"That's a very nice sentiment, *Brain-Dead*," Viper's condescending voice mused, "but you must be truly hollow in the head if you believe that."

"Brain-Dead!" Supersonic exclaimed on a laugh. "That's perfect! Welcome to the Imminent Death Club, Brain-Dead."

The speedy hybrid shot a wide smile to the room and Finn felt a muscle tick in her jaw as she struggled to maintain her composure.

"*The Imminent Death Club*?" she asked Supersonic impatiently.

"Well yeah, there are two ways to get out of the Dome. One: you die. Two: you get bought by some hoity-toity Reliance asshole and *then* you die."

"Speak for yourself," Viper interceded. "I'm far too valuable to be killed, and once I dispense of our new friends in the Dome, I'll be sold to the highest bidder. You can't imagine how desperate I am for a change of clothes."

Finn shook her head in frustrated disbelief. *The Imminent Death Club* seemed to be a morbidly appropriate name for the group. Soon, they would all be unleashed in the Dome and none of these hybrids seemed to have any issue killing one another off to keep themselves alive.

Finn had no intention of killing anyone, regardless of what the Reliance wanted for their twisted little games. She couldn't . . . not after Sophie. It had become a hard line in the mud, one she refused to cross ever again. She'd hoped she could get the group to cooperate with her plan, but they were proving to be difficult.

How was she supposed to keep herself and AJ alive with five powerful hybrids gunning for them?

As if on cue, a low hissing sounded in each of the cells as billows of white gas began to fill them.

"Time for the Dome," Supersonic whispered, her eyes glimmering with anticipation.

Finn's panicked gaze flew to AJ as the gas reached her. She dove lower to the ground, hoping to stem the gas's effects, but her head had already begun to spin, and her breaths had shallowed in her chest.

"I'll find you in the Dome," she promised him, her voice hoarse.

Finn could've sworn she saw him nod, mouth tight with fear, before the gas swallowed her.

THIRTY

Finn awoke to blackness to find she'd been moved from her cell. Thin streaks of light stole across the passageway through the tiny window of a steel door as a low roar of screaming and applause shook the ground beneath her. Somewhere outside, speakers blasted the Union of the Planets' six-note melody. She was still underground, but this time, she lay in a heap in an empty stone corridor. She was unsurprised to see a small intercom and the thin barrel of a laser gun affixed to the rocky wall above her.

She still had no shoes, but the boxes around her hands had been removed.

Thank the Gods for that.

Finn flexed her sore wrists as her eyes flitted around the space. When the Union of the Planets' anthem died down, an unfamiliar, slightly accented baritone echoed outside.

"Ladies and gentlemen of the Reliance, welcome to the Dome! Rest assured the games will begin shortly. We have eight talented half-breeds participating on this fine afternoon, ranging from half-Khaleerian to our fan favorite half-Solidarian. Remember, all half-breeds who survive the Dome will be available for viewing and purchase shortly after the games."

Finn heard a cry of excitement burst through the crowd at the pronouncement and struggled to hold on to some semblance of calm.

"Are you ready to meet your half-breed contenders?" Again, the roar of the crowd shook the ground with its enthusiasm. "Entering from door number one, let's hear some applause for one of our newest additions to the Dome: a half-Anunnaki! He might seem young and unassuming, but beneath that youthful façade lies the heart of a beast. With the twitch of an eye, this half-breed could convince you to shoot your own mother . . . or, even worse, . . . empty your safes."

Several scandalized gasps stole through the crowd before the arena erupted into applause and heavy bass music began to play.

Hold on, AJ.

"Entering from door number two . . . Oh this is exciting folks . . . we have our very first half-Teslan! As rare as they are dangerous, this half-breed can steal all your secrets with a touch, so keep your distance. Give it up, ladies and gentlemen!"

Finn just barely heard several mechanisms click over the din of the crowd and earsplitting music as the door in front of her began to open. The answering light was glaring, and Finn had to shield her eyes else risk being blinded. She held her ground inside the passageway, waiting for her vision to adjust.

Seconds later, the intercom on the wall to her right crackled and sounded. The laser gun whirred to life, rotating until it pointed at her head.

"Get out there," an impatient voice growled through the speaker.

Eyeing the gun, Finn forced her shaky legs to move through the doorway and out into the Dome.

Just as she'd seen in her mind when touching the walls and windows of Aquarii, the entire space was encased in a dome made entirely of hard-light projections separating the spectators from the games' participants. The projector itself appeared to be mounted to the Dome's peak.

She saw her face broadcasted on several giant holoscreens spread throughout the arena and swallowed hard at the fear she glimpsed in her own eyes. She drove herself to stand straighter and relaxed her features until her face was devoid of expression.

More laser guns were mounted several feet apart outside the Dome, their muzzles pointed at its center. There, she found what could only be described as an obstacle course of death.

The right side of the Dome nearest to her had been converted into a minefield of point-defense auto turrets. Enabled and powered by artificial intelligence, the guns were able to automatically target and fire in rotating intervals. Just past that, a huge wall with red-and-blue handholds zapped and crackled with electricity. On the other side of that wall, Finn could just barely make out a smattering of pedestals raised above some kind of boiling liquid.

Thousands of Reliance spectators surrounded her on all sides, their gazes hungry as they stomped and clapped in a sea of red and gold. Their cheers quieted as some of them began to gasp, their eyes focused on something near Finn.

Her head snapped to the left where she found AJ, free of his silicone bindings. His dark eyes swirled and sparked with color, and his chest heaved in furious breaths. His black hair was wet with sweat and his skin even more pale than usual. The boy had spent most of his life in captivity being tortured by the Reliance and she could only imagine how terrifying and triggering this must be for him.

"AJ!" she called to him sharply. His panicked face immediately flew to meet hers, the colors fading as they did. "We can do this, kid. We just need to stick together."

Blessedly, he had the presence of mind to hear her words. His face set with determination as he managed a sharp nod.

"Our next half-breed comes all the way from Xandar. She's fast, she's sassy, and you all know and love her. Please give it up for our half-Xandar!"

The crowd exploded in cheers as the door to Finn's left opened and a blur of burgundy streaked out into the Dome.

She was so fast Finn could barely track her movements as the half-breed did circles around them. Finally, she slowed to a stop in between Finn and AJ, throwing her fists over her head in a shameless bid to egg the crowd on. Her dark eyes glinted with amusement as a wide smile broke out on her face.

At her antics, the announcer released a soft chortle of amusement before continuing.

"Next, we have another new competitor and our youngest of the day, but don't let her age fool you, ladies and gentlemen. This half-Merlidian is as dangerous as she is small."

Another door opened into the Dome and several seconds passed before Carrow stumbled her way out, her little hands shielding her eyes from the brightness. The child's yellow curls fell in waves around her round, delicate face. Even from the distance, Finn could tell her eyes were the same unique shade of cerulean as Conrad's.

Despite the dramatic tone of the announcer's voice, the crowd appeared unimpressed with the newest addition to the games. Sporadic claps and cheers rang out, but for the most part, they seemed to have lost their excitement.

Finn shot AJ a look she hoped he understood and called out to the child.

"Stay close, Carrow. AJ and I are going to take care of you. You're going to be okay."

The little girl's blue eyes widened as she seemed to recognize Finn's voice. Her lips pulled up into a shaky smile and she nodded in understanding.

Taking advantage of the crowd's lapse in energy, the announcer's voice took on an impossibly deeper tone.

"The only thing harder than this next half-breed's skin . . . is his heart. That's right, folks, our next competitor has four kills in his short time in the Dome. From the stony cliffs of Kreet, say hello to our half-Kreetian!"

As the crowd once again let loose with raucous applause, Finn watched as one of the doors opened and Rock sauntered out. Freed of the wires causing him so much pain, the Kreetian cut an intimidating figure.

No longer hunched in agony, he stood to his full height of at least six feet six inches; his blue hair was mussed and his chest puffed out in pride. His face was set with determination, and as he looked over his fellow competitors, his blue eyes gleamed with hatred. His lips twisted in a cruel sneer as he met Finn's eyes.

She broke the stare when the announcer launched in again.

"Now, you can look at this next contestant all you want, folks, but do not touch. This poison princess comes all the way from our state-of-the-art labs on Arcturus. That's right, with the latest advances in Arcturian science and a little help from the Gods, our forefathers have created a half-Sandsaran. She hasn't been in the Dome long, but she has already established herself as a merciless contender. Get your gold ready, citizens, because this half-breed is in high demand!"

Finn was too shocked to focus on the rest of the man's words.

The Reliance is making half-breeds? How is that even possible?

Sandsarans were normally incapable of breeding with humans or any other species outside of their own due to their poisonous dermis. Apparently, the Arcturians had taken the laws of nature into their own hands. No wonder Viper was a ruthless, heartless competitor.

She'd been grown and raised in a lab.

Her dark thoughts were cut short by the screams and cheers of the crowd as their volume increased tenfold. Earning the loudest ovation yet, Viper sauntered into the Dome and waved webbed four-fingered hands at her adoring fans. Without the latex covering her body, Finn could finally see her fully. Her skin was covered from bald head to webbed toes in dark scales of varying shades of blue and green.

Viper's yellow, reptilian eyes scanned the space around them before they landed on Finn and narrowed. She stopped next to the half-Kreetian and whispered something to the tall hybrid that caused his sneer to widen.

"This next competitor is somewhat of a mystery. Despite some significant *prodding*, he has been mum on his parentage. The authorities upstairs tell me he is quite dangerous, but you'll have to decide for yourselves."

A hush of wonder fell over the crowd as a door opened and Gray Matter stepped into the Dome. He took casual, sure-footed strides until he came to stop in between AJ, Viper, and Rock. His curious gaze flitted through the Dome with mild disinterest.

Slowly, more and more members of the crowd began to giggle and whisper to one another about the strange-looking hybrid, but the subject of their interest seemed unaffected.

"This next half-breed needs no introduction. You love to watch him annihilate his opponents. His death count exceeds hundreds. Too dangerous to live, but too entertaining to kill, give it up for our half-Solidarian."

The Dome exploded in pandemonium. The roar of the crowd became deafening as the last door to the left opened and the Solidarian stepped into the light. At the sight of his massive, imposing frame, the crowd jumped to their feet and cheered even harder. The Solidarian's bored yellow eyes scanned over them, obviously accustomed to the display.

In the light of Aquarii's suns, he looked even bigger outside of his cell; his sheer mass rivaled that of Grim's.

Supersonic was a wild card, and Finn wasn't quite sure what to make of Gray Matter yet, but she knew she could handle them both. Viper and Rock had made no secret of the fact that they would be gunning for Finn once the games began, and based on what she knew, both could prove to be difficult.

Despite all of this, it was the Solidarian and his dead eyes that scared Finn the most.

"Our final half-breed of the day is a bit . . . unpredictable, which is why we saved him for last. I have a feeling some lucky member of the Reliance will be snatching him up soon. Give a big, warm welcome to our half-Khaleerian."

A loud boom turned Finn's attention to the final door yet to be opened. As she watched, the hybrid on the other side battered against the steel frame over and over until the steel began to push outward.

Slowly, and with some difficulty after being pummeled, it opened. Almost immediately, the giant Supersonic had aptly nicknamed Bedlam, came storming through. He'd grown several inches in mass and his musculature, which had increased to at least three times its normal size, now bulged and stretched beneath thick red skin.

He dragged one of his horns against the hard-light interior of the Dome to little effect, his ripped and frayed jumpsuit trailing behind him in certain places like the train of a gown. The audience abandoned their applause in light of the delightful display and instead erupted in a chorus of laughter and jeers. Bedlam's feet pounded against the ground as he beat his chest with giant red fists and roared.

"It looks like someone is ready to get the games started," the announcer joked nervously. "Today's obstacle course has our competitors facing three challenges."

Bedlam roared and pounded his fists against the underside of the Dome, snapping his jaws at the audience on the other side. The hard-light projection remained in place, and the riveted onlookers appeared to be terrified and thrilled in equal measure.

"I guess we better get a move on before he starts without us." The announcer chuckled. "First, our competitors must make it through the fan favorite, No Man's Land, a section of the Dome surrounded on all sides by autotracking lasers. The turrets are set to fire in random intervals. Those who make it through unscathed will have to face the Wall of Death. As you can see, this rock wall has blue and red holds for our half-breeds to use on their journey to the top. The red holds are on a timer, set to release one hundred and ten volts of direct-current electricity. Only the blue holds are safe to use, but as you can see there are a limited number of them. Our half-breed contenders will have to fight if they hope to make it over." The irritating voice paused for applause before continuing. "But the danger doesn't end there. The final challenge they must face is the Moat of Pain. As you can see, we have several small pedestals elevated above a vat of boiling water. The liquid maintains atmospheric pressure, keeping its temperature at two-hundred and fifty degrees Celsius. I pity the half-breed who falls into *that* hot water." The audience laughed in appreciation at the man's play on words. "They will need to make it across the moat to the levers on the other side. There are four levers in total which, when pushed, provide a speedy exit for four of our surviving half-breeds. I hope you're ready for a gruesome show because the games start in five . . . four . . . three . . . two . . ."

At the end of the macabre countdown, a piercing horn blared, leaving Finn's ears ringing as the crowd rose to their feet and the hybrids scattered around the Dome began to sprint to the first challenge. A cloud of dust and dirt kicked up by the race surrounded Finn on all sides.

Chaos.

Her mind raced as she squinted through the dust to find AJ and Carrow.

Finally, she spotted them and moved to their sides. They both watched her with eyes wide with dread.

"Stay close," she ordered.

THIRTY-ONE

Shots rang out in the distance, kicking up more dirt as lasers fired all around the Dome. Finn grabbed the sleeve of AJ's jumpsuit in one hand and the sleeve of Carrow's in the other, steering them toward the madness. When a few feet separated them from No Man's Land, Finn pulled them both to a halt.

Ahead of them, Rock and Viper had almost made it halfway through the endless rows of auto turrets.

Finn held AJ and Carrow steady at her sides and dropped down to a knee next to the base of the nearest turret. She didn't have the time to study the firing patterns firsthand. Hopefully, any information she could glean from the Dome using her abilities would be enough to get them through unscathed.

Without the faint scent of Conrad's oil, Finn worried her abilities wouldn't be of much use. Instead, she focused on the musty earth, letting the scent of dirt and stale air anchor her. Finn inhaled deeply.

As she touched the weapon, hazy images flashed through her mind.

A soldier checking the turrets for efficiency.

An assembly line of workers putting the turrets together piece by piece.

Nothing useful she needed to survive this.

"Finn, what do we do?" AJ's eyes darted around the Dome in fear before returning to her. Her mind raced with fear and adrenaline.

An idea hit her suddenly.

She had no clue if it would work but she had to try something.

Finn pressed her palm against the well-trodden dirt, doing her best to drown out the sounds of laser fire and the rowdy crowd. Her head throbbed as countless images of carnage swarmed behind her lids. Everywhere she looked, she found dead hybrids, their sightless eyes open in shock and terror.

She had to fight down nausea at the sight and urged herself to move past the images. It took a few seconds of searching, but she finally found one of No Man's Land, and focused on it.

"Finn," AJ yelled. "We need to do something soon!"

She squeezed her eyes shut even harder as she shouted back. "I'm working on it!"

Several hybrids sprint through the dirt past endless rows of artillery. As they pass, the first three rows on the right begin to fire, filling the closest hybrids with smoking holes. The remaining group keep running, zigzagging until one row of turrets on the right and one on the left fire simultaneously, trapping two more of them within the crossfire.

The final four hybrids maintain their speed. Some push others to gain a few inches lead. Less than a second passes before the next three rows of turrets on the left rain fire over them. Two more fall into bloody, smoking heaps. Finn counts seconds as she watches. When she makes it to five, the final row of artillery on the left and right fire in a chorus of death.

Finn stood up and locked eyes with first AJ, then Carrow.

"Stay behind me," she told them sharply.

There was every chance the information she'd just gleaned was outdated. For all Finn knew, the Reliance recalibrated the turrets after every game. She could be leading two children to their deaths, but if they didn't try, they were as good as dead anyway.

She watched the turrets carefully as she counted.

Finn felt Carrow grasp the material at the hem of her shirt and sent a silent prayer up to the Gods for their survival.

The smell of ozone filled the air as the lasers fired. The last row of turrets had just fired. If her vision was to be believed, they would need to wait for the ones at their right to fire before going forward.

"Get ready to run," she told them, as she swallowed down her anxiety.

Blessedly true to the images she'd gleaned, the first three rows of artillery to their right began to fire in front of them. As soon as the last laser let loose, Finn sprinted past them, stopping in the space before the next row of turrets. AJ and Carrow followed closely behind, halting when she did.

Before they could make another move, a swirl of motion zoomed past them, cutting them off and kicking dust up into their faces. Supersonic stopped running abruptly, pausing by the next row of artillery set to go off.

She shot Finn an alarmingly cheerful grin.

"Don't take it personally, Brain-Dead. Every half-breed for themselves," she called out the reminder.

Putting her weight behind her shoulders, Supersonic pushed the muzzle of one of the turrets until its barrel was aimed squarely at Finn.

Shit.

Ignoring the roars of approval from the crowd, Finn grabbed AJ and Carrow and pulled them to ground, rolling with them in the dirt just as the laser fired. She bit her cheek in anger and pulled the kids to their feet, sprinting to the next space between turrets. They were almost halfway there. Finn panted from exertion and her limbs shook with the rush of adrenaline.

Her eyes widened when she caught a glimpse of Gray Matter, casually making his way past the turrets with ease. He seemed to know exactly when the next gun would fire, easily avoiding being maimed by the waves of laser fire.

The ground beneath them began to shake and a primal bellow rang out through the air. Finn turned to see Bedlam, all seven and a half feet and four hundred pounds of him, heading straight for them.

His dark eyes were crazed as he took a laser to the shoulder, but it barely fazed him. Instead, it seemed to only enrage him further. He bellowed and uprooted the nearest turret from the ground, launching it to the other side of the Dome.

Finn remained frozen as she watched the Solidarian follow closely behind the raging Khaleerian, using him to clear a pathway. He shot Finn a look that almost appeared amused, before refocusing and diving past the next wave. Bedlam tore another gun from the ground and launched it. It continued to fire wildly as it flew through the air.

Finn grabbed AJ and Carrow and pulled them along past the next row of artillery, doing her best to stay out of the Khaleerian's way. Movement caught her attention as a shadow was cast over their trio. Belatedly, her eyes flicked up to track another turret flying through air and headed straight for them.

"Get down!" she yelled, pushing the kids out of the way as she dived in front of them. The turret landed on its side in the spot where they had just been standing. The barrel was pointed directly at Finn's face, inches from where she lay. Time seemed to move in slow motion as the gun fired. Finn's eyes closed of their own accord and she braced for the searing pain.

It never came.

Finn opened her eyes to see the laser bolt had curved to the right, avoiding her by several inches. On a deep exhale, she jumped to her feet and found Carrow staring at her, her blue eyes glowing brightly as she focused on angling the beam away from Finn.

Finn ran to her and AJ, grabbing them once again and pushing them forward.

"I owe you one," she told the little girl with a gentle squeeze and a grim smile.

From across the field, Supersonic pointed in their direction and yelled, "Check out Micro! *Sometimes* my speedy little ass!"

Finn bared her teeth and growled at the woman from across the field. Supersonic merely waved and blew them a kiss before disappearing in a whir of motion.

The Solidarian had stopped moving to watch their little trio with an inquisitive, red-eyed stare. Finn didn't have time to ponder the meaning behind the strange shift in the mysterious hybrid. Instead, she waited for the last row of guns to fire and pulled AJ and Carrow to safety.

Bedlam remained in No Man's Land, tearing up the earth in his rage. The audience ate it up, jeering and yelling.

Finn bent at the waist and panted, giving them all a second to catch their breath. AJ caught her gaze and she smiled at the boy.

"See? That wasn't so bad."

He shook his head and returned her smile with a weak one of his own.

"Maybe you really are Brain-Dead," he scoffed.

Finn chuckled and rolled her neck, tracking the Solidarian as he jogged past. He stopped a few feet away from them but said nothing.

If he tried anything, she would be ready.

Looking past him, Finn eyed the fifty-foot rock wall before them with unease.

One down, two to go, she thought darkly.

THIRTY-TWO

Viper and Rock were already suspended on the wall and doing their best to avoid the red handholds. Viper's webbed hands and feet seemed to be hindering her progress. Using her speed to her advantage, Supersonic had already made her way to the top. Gray Matter was just beginning his ascent, his small, ashen frame dwarfed by the sheer size of the wall. He used both red and blue holds indiscriminately, seemingly unperturbed at the idea of being barbequed should one of the red holds go off.

"I forgot to mention one little rule about the Wall of Death." The announcer's amused voice filled the stadium. "Our half-breeds are on a time limit. In five minutes, all handholds, blue and red alike, will become live, electrocuting anyone still holding on. And for those of you who still haven't made it to the wall yet," he continued, "you best make haste unless you'd like us to provide you with some incentive."

The crowd laughed and shouted their approval as the Dome's mounted laser guns turned to take aim.

They weren't even giving her time to use her abilities. She was going to have to make a break for it and hope for the best.

Finn turned to AJ and Carrow.

"We work together to get up. Only touch the blue handholds, steer clear of the red."

"How are we going to do that? There are three blue ones for every ten red ones," AJ barked, wringing his pale hands nervously.

"We only have five minutes," Carrow whimpered.

"Just stay close and do as I say," Finn ordered as she made her way to the wall.

Belatedly, she noticed the Solidarian had followed them and taken a place on the wall near Carrow. His red eyes watched them carefully. She gave the giant hybrid a look that promised pain should he try to sabotage the little girl, but the big man showed no reaction.

Carrow reached up to take a blue handhold just out of her grasp. Finn motioned for AJ to start climbing and ran over to give the little girl a boost.

"Hold tight," she told the child.

The Solidarian watched them as he began to climb, grabbing both blue and red holds as he did. She supposed with his abilities, electrocution didn't carry the same threat as it did for the rest of them.

Finn ignored the commotion within the crowd and found a blue hold a few feet away from Carrow and AJ. She began to climb, hoisting the weight of her body upward with as much speed as she could manage.

As she guided the children to the nearest blue holds, she had no choice but to grab any available red ones and hope for the best.

She narrowly escaped a few as they zapped to life just after she'd removed her hand.

So far so good.

"Three minutes left," the announcer proclaimed excitedly.

The spectators began to stomp in unison, their frantic beat providing a manic soundtrack to the hybrids' race against death. Above, Finn could see Gray Matter making his way over the top.

"We're halfway there," she told the kids. "Keep going as fast as you can."

"Finn!"

She turned to find AJ frantically pointing below her just as a high-pitched shriek rang out. Carrow hung a few feet below Rock, struggling to hold on and desperately looking for a blue hold as the tall, blue-haired hybrid kicked at her hands. One of the red holds next to the small child zapped with electricity.

Distracted by the struggle with the hybrid above her, the sound surprised the girl and she lost her grip, leaving her hanging one-handed from a single hold. Her frightened blue eyes bore into Finn's.

The crowd screamed in delight as Rock shot them a grin and hustled to follow Viper over the top of the wall.

Finn moved quickly, making her way down to the girl as fast as she could. She didn't pay attention to the holds she grabbed, too desperate to get to her.

"Hold on, Carrow!"

She lunged for the child's forearm just as Carrow's grip slipped and she began to fall. Finn's fingers dug into the hold above her as she struggled to bear the child's weight and maintain her balance. She ignored the flood of images flowing through her at the child's touch. Grimacing, she held on with every ounce of strength she possessed, fighting gravity and her growing fatigue.

Can't let her fall. Can't let her fall.

Finn repeated the words like a mantra as she struggled to hold on.

Out of the corner of her eye, she glimpsed a large black hand swoop down and grab the girl by her bicep, pulling her from Finn's hold. Carrow flew into the air with a surprised shriek, her yellow curls trailing behind her, and Finn watched in shock as the Solidarian pulled her onto his back with minimal effort. Not missing a beat, Carrow wrapped her arms tightly around the giant's neck and held on for dear life.

A hush had fallen over the crowd sometime during their struggle.

"Uh . . . uh . . . two minutes left." The announcer stumbled over his words.

A low rumble shook the ground and Finn heard Bedlam's primal roar as he threw his body at the holds. Ignoring the rest of them, the enraged hybrid scaled the wall in record time, taking only four swift jumps before he plummeted over the other side.

"Follow me," the Solidarian instructed in a low rumble.

Ignoring her surprise at hearing the man's voice for the first time, Finn rushed to follow closely behind. They made their way up with increasing speed, mimicking the Solidarian as he easily traversed the wall by lunging and jumping to find blue holds for the rest of them to grab. The other competitors stared down at them with wide eyes from their perch on top of the wall.

Supersonic pointed and yelled, "Do you see what I'm seeing?"

"I see four dead half-breeds, that's what I see," Rock sneered. He shot Finn one last hard glare before he, Viper, and Supersonic descended the other side of the wall.

Finn and her companions made it to the top shortly after and heaved themselves over. The sound of buzzing electricity filled the air mere seconds later. Finn's heart pounded in her chest and sweat soaked her burgundy pants and shirt. The Solidarian barely seemed winded as he gently put Carrow down next to Finn. AJ flopped to his knees at their side, trying to catch his breath.

"That was close," he huffed.

Finn's eyes slowly scanned the Dome around her where the entirety of the Reliance crowd in attendance remained uncharacteristically quiet.

The announcer coughed slightly before breaking the tense silence.

"Well, that was certainly an unusual display. I'm sure our next challenge will prove to be much more violent."

Scattered applause followed his pronouncement.

Finn and the others used the attached ropes to make their way down the Wall of Death. When their feet touched ground, she found Rock, Viper, and Gray Matter at the entrance to the third challenge.

Supersonic had already sprinted her way across the wobbly concrete pedestals and was in the process of pulling down on one of the four levers leading to freedom. She savored the moment, yelling in triumph and raising her hands over her head to incite the crowd.

Bedlam had already moved to the edge of the Dome to resume his double-fisted attack on the structure. With every violent, silent thud, the energy of the audience elevated as they gasped and thrilled at the controlled danger.

By the time she turned her attention back to the final obstacle, Gray Matter was almost halfway across, and Viper and Rock had jumped to their first pedestals.

"What's the plan?" AJ asked.

Finn studied the boiling, bubbling water simmering a few inches below the scattered pedestals. The structures floated above, secured by chains and moving slightly with the flow of water.

"Don't die," she told the boy.

"Works for me. Do we need to worry about him?" AJ motioned with his head toward the Solidarian.

The big hybrid met her stare for a moment before grunting and diving for the nearest pedestal. Once he'd landed and found his footing, his bald head turned toward Carrow and he extended his arms.

"Jump," he told her gruffly.

The child looked up at Finn as if waiting for permission.

The concrete pedestals were less than twelve inches wide, making it difficult to accommodate more than one. But Carrow was small for her age, and the Solidarian seemed confident she would make it.

Finn's mind swam. Did she trust him? He'd certainly shocked the hell out of her when he saved Carrow on the wall. If he had an insidious ulterior motive for aiding their trio, she was struggling to come up with what it might be.

Was it possible that the most brutal hybrid on the field wasn't as heartless as he'd been made out to be?

Either way, they were losing time for every second Finn hesitated. She made a split-second decision and nodded to the girl.

"It's okay. Do as he says."

Carrow turned and made a clumsy dive toward the first pedestal. The Solidarian caught her easily under the armpits and held her steady. Finn nudged AJ and they both took a deep breath.

In unison, they took a running leap to land on side-by-side pedestals a few feet away from the Solidarian and Carrow. The structure shook and wavered beneath Finn's weight and she fell to her knees in an effort to balance herself. She turned to find AJ had landed in much the same position. Steam hissed from the water below, causing sweat to drip from the boy's pale forehead in a steady stream.

The Solidarian jumped to the next pedestal, helping Carrow along once he'd gained his balance. Finn and AJ followed, struggling to jump the gaps from their stationary positions.

She was so focused on maintaining her balance and avoiding the scalding watery grave below, she didn't notice Rock staring at her from the next pedestal over.

When she finally found her footing enough to make the next jump, the hybrid's angry voice carried over to her.

"You're messing everything up! The Reliance wants a show, not this hand-holding peace rally you and your stupid friends have conjured up."

She caught Viper's wicked smile out of the corner of her eye and found her waving a webbed hand cheekily just as Rock leapt from his pedestal to Finn's.

The impact of Rock on the platform jostled them both and Finn fell to her back with her head hanging precariously over the water as the pedestal bobbed to the left then the right under their weight. Rock found his footing and immediately straddled her with his large body, throwing punches at her face and chest.

She rolled from side to side, desperately dodging each hit as she did. His fists were hard as stone, making each punch punishingly effective and Finn winced as each one slammed into the pedestal with a sickening *crack*.

"Finn!" AJ yelled. "Leave her alone, you bastard!"

She rolled her hips to the side, struggling to gain leverage and dislodge the angry hybrid. A crushing right hook clipped the side of her head and Finn saw stars. Had it fully connected, she would've been killed.

The apex of the Dome spun above her, and her body went slack from the force of the blow. She barely heard the rush of the crowd or AJ and Carrow's screams over the high-pitched ringing in her ears.

Still straddling her, Rock brought his fists together over his head and yelled in triumph, soaking up the audience's frenzy for violence. Finn fought to remain conscious.

She only had a small window of opportunity to escape. Unfortunately, she was having difficulty getting her leaden limbs to cooperate.

She'd been hit before—more times that she could count—but never by someone with diamond-hard fists like Rock's. The glancing blow had knocked her on her ass and rendered her stupid.

She also thought she'd been hit so hard she might be hallucinating. Through her bleary vision it almost looked like the cheering hybrid's head was smoking.

Finn squinted through the blood dripping from her forehead to get a better look, her eyes widening as she realized Rock's blue hair was indeed on fire. As if feeling the weight of her dumbfounded stare, he glared down at her.

"What are you looking at?"

The flames continued to grow, the scent of smoke and burning hair filling her nostrils.

Rock sniffed the air, confusion furrowing his brows as he looked for the source of the smell.

Viper cupped her blue, scaled hands and yelled from her pedestal, "Rock, you're on fire!"

"What are you talking about?" he called back.

Finally, the dots seemed to connect, and Rock's eyes shot heavenward as he patted and swatted at the flames on his head.

"She said, you're on fire, dumbass."

The Solidarian's deep rumble sounded next to Finn's right ear. She managed to turn enough to see him standing chest-deep in the boiling-hot water. His right hand was still suspended in the air and pointed at Rock. The dark skin of his palm was smoking.

Judging from his calm demeanor, the deathly hot water of the moat didn't seem to be having any effect on him whatsoever.

His eyes, red and gleaming, tightened as he locked eyes with Rock.

The Solidarian grabbed the half-Kreetian by the arm and pulled him off of Finn. Rock's smoldering body went careening as the Solidarian threw his weight easily in the opposite direction. The hybrid's upper half landed on a nearby pedestal with an "oomph" as his legs splashed helplessly in the scalding water below.

Rock screamed in agony while he desperately struggled to pull his body up onto the tilted pedestal. His pants had been burned off from the kneecaps down and the skin of his legs was covered in angry red blisters.

"Viper! Help me!" he cried as his body rolled in anguish onto the pedestal's surface.

The poisonous princess merely shrugged her shoulders and turned away from him, jumping down from the last pedestal to the ground below. Without a backward glance, she sauntered to one of the remaining levers and made a hasty exit. Gray Matter followed closely behind, leaving two final levers available for them to make their escape.

Finn felt a warm hand wrap around her bicep.

"Can you walk?" the Solidarian asked gruffly.

"That depends," she told him. "Is it just me or is this pedestal spinning?"

She thought she heard an answering chuckle but couldn't be sure. The Solidarian lifted her into his arms, carefully holding her above the water as he sloshed his way to the other side. There, AJ was in the process of helping Carrow jump from the last pedestal to the earth below.

The Solidarian's hand brushed Finn's as he readjusted her in his arms. She felt the telltale buzzing in her ears as images began to overtake her. In her weakened state and without her anchor scent to bind her to the present, Finn's mind careened into darkness.

Uh-oh.

She is standing next to an adolescent boy with inky black skin. He is staring at the ground intently, and his body is strung tight with tension as he bends over something she can't see.

Finn moves closer to his side to find his hands clenched in fists and fully engulfed in blue flames. The bodies of an older man and a young pregnant woman lie on the ground in front of him. Their vacant eyes stare skyward and blood pours from wounds in their chests and stomachs, causing Finn to stumble back in horror.

It takes a moment before she hears the screaming. As the images around her become clearer, she realizes they are surrounded by thick, black smoke and desperate screams . . . tortured screams. Everything within her line of sight is ablaze, including the soldiers' barracks nearly thirty feet away.

The screaming is coming from within.

Finn coughs and swats at the smoke as another scream of agony joins the rest.

She turns to see the boy throw his head back and pound his chest. Hot tears stream down his face and shine within his red eyes.

Finn snapped back into awareness as the Solidarian placed her feet on the ground next to Carrow and climbed up beside her. Steam wafted off of his strong body and the remnants of his burnt jumpsuit hung loosely from his large frame. The intimidating man was a far cry from the boy she'd glimpsed in her vision.

Finn's head pounded, but the Dome had blessedly stopped spinning and she found she was able to stand without much trouble.

"Are you okay, Finn?"

She found AJ watching her with worried eyes and gave him a thumbs-up.

"Thanks to him," she said, pointing at the Solidarian. "What do you say we get out of here?"

"Rock already got through and pulled one of the levers. There's only one left."

Rock managed to get through with his legs burned like that?

A barely perceptible shiver stole through Finn at the thought. She could only imagine the kind of determination— or anger—that had fueled him to accomplish such a feat.

It was safe to say she wasn't looking forward to seeing him again.

The Solidarian interrupted her dark thoughts as he stated, "We can all use the last exit. It has never been done, but there are no rules against it."

Finn looked around her small group of allies and smiled.

"What do you say we get out of here?"

AJ and Carrow returned her smile while the Solidarian remained characteristically stoic. They made their way to the lever and Finn let out a sigh of relief.

A low, guttural howl stopped the breath in her lungs and stalled her hand above the lever. Bedlam was still on the outskirts of the Dome, tearing up dirt and pounding on the projection.

She couldn't leave him behind.

Finn grasped the final lever and pulled down, turning to the others as an exit tunnel opened before them.

"Go! I'm right behind you!"

She watched as the Solidarian, AJ, and Carrow dove through the tunnel's opening to safety. Turning back around, Finn desperately yelled over to Bedlam.

"Come on, Bedlam! Over here!"

The enraged hybrid paid her no attention as he moved toward the final obstacle to tear up: the pedestals; he bellowed in pain as the water burned his red skin.

The half-Khaleerian was so lost to his rage, she doubted if he even heard her.

The door behind her let loose a groan as it slowly began to close.

"Please!" she screamed. "Come with us!"

She could have sworn the big beast's eyes flickered with awareness as he met hers. Before she could capitalize on the moment, however, strong arms wrapped around Finn's waist and dragged her into the tunnel.

She screamed frantically as she watched the laser guns affixed to the interior of the Dome turn and take aim at Bedlam.

"No!"

The door closed on Bedlam's pained cries as the guns fired.

THIRTY-THREE

H ot tears streamed down Finn's face and her chest rose and fell with heavy sobs. Something akin to compassion sparked in the Solidarian's eyes as he released her, but he said nothing.

Carrow wrapped her little arms around Finn's waist and squeezed. As soon as the doors fully closed, gas began to seep from the vents, coiling around their group like a snake.

Rather than fight to stay conscious, an overwhelmed Finn embraced the impending darkness.

When she next awoke, they had all been returned to their cells and their restraints had been replaced. The blood had been washed from Finn's face and her left eye and temple had begun to swell. The wound felt hot to the touch and Finn winced every time she turned her head too quickly.

A low moan sounded across the way and she caught sight of Rock's long body lying flat on the floor of his cell. His wires had been reattached and a fresh jumpsuit covered the burns and blisters on his legs.

"I'm going to kill you," he hissed to Finn. "As soon as we get out of here again, you're mine."

Before Finn could react to the threat, AJ blindly slammed his shoulder against the glass separating his cell from Rock's.

"You touch her and I'll kill you!"

Unimpressed, Rock groaned once again as the vibe cannon sent another ultralow frequency shooting through his body.

"Rock is right," Viper added. They had dressed her again in the latex suit. "Brain-Dead and her little kiddies are walking expiration dates. The Reliance wants a show and if you don't give it to them, you'll be dead either way. I can make it quick for you." She murmured to Finn, "One touch would hurt a lot less than letting Rock get his hands on you again."

Finn wasn't so sure she agreed.

"I'm sorry," Supersonic interrupted, "but are we just going to ignore the giant fire-breathing dragon in the room? The Solidarian actually helped them, and don't get me started on the badass haircut he gave Rock."

Rock turned to glower at Supersonic, revealing a singed bald spot on the back of his head. Watching them interact so casually caused something to shift in Finn's brain, the dim flame of despair igniting and searing a trail of rage straight to her chest.

"Bedlam is dead!" she cried, punching the glass with her fist. "Do any of you even care? He died for nothing. Nothing! So the Reliance could get their kicks, and you're all more than happy to give it to them. We should be helping each other get out of here. Instead you're acting like a bunch of Reliance dogs, sitting and playing fetch whenever master says so."

"Somebody better hose her down, she's having a fit," Viper called out cheerfully.

"Can it, Petri Dish," AJ growled.

"Look," Supersonic said softly, "we're not saying we like it." She paused to glance over at Viper and Rock before correcting herself. "Okay, I'm not saying *I* like it, but we call it the Imminent Death Club for a reason. It's just the way things are. And I don't know about you, but I'm kind of allergic to dying."

"Then stop worrying about killing each other and listen to me," Finn snapped against the glass. "Look around you. The Reliance has us in these cages because they're *scared*. But instead of using that fear, you're playing right into their hands. You're afraid of what they'll do to you if you don't play their sick games? If you'd cool it with the bloodlust for two seconds, you'd see that."

"That's easy to say after your first day in the Dome," Viper countered, examining a latex-covered hand. "Impassioned speeches are nice, but they only go so far. You think you're the first person to spout off about working together?" She scoffed and shook her head. "It never lasts. Eventually, you'll wind up just like the rest of us. Ask the Solidarian. He's seen it for the last fifteen cycles. He probably helped you today because seeing that glint of hope in your eyes is almost as entertaining as its going to be when the Dome squashes it out."

Finn's gaze shot over to the Solidarian automatically. She found him already watching her intently, his face giving nothing away as to the thoughts swirling underneath.

"Is that why you helped us?" she asked him quietly.

The big man's jaw clenched, but he said nothing.

"All of that emotion won't serve you well if you wish to accomplish your goals."

Finn's head followed the direction of the unfamiliar voice to find Gray Matter watching her intently. His back rested casually against the glass of his cell, giving the illusion of a man without a care in the world, but Finn could see the intelligence behind his gray eyes as he studied her.

"The Solidarian helped you because I told him you were genuine in your desire to save us," the small ashen hybrid revealed. "He also saw it for himself in the Dome, as we all did. I've been waiting for someone like you to arrive."

It didn't escape Finn's notice that the rest of the room had fallen silent as they all listened intently to Gray Matter's soft voice.

"What are you talking about?" she asked the strange hybrid.

"I know I might not look it"—he waved slender hands toward his cone-shaped head for emphasis—"but I was born with a unique gift. Some might call it foresight. I simply see it as the ability to gather the sensory data around me and predict the most probable outcome."

She supposed that explained why he'd done so well navigating the Dome's obstacles.

"Good for you. What does that have to do with us?" AJ asked sharply.

Gray Matter shifted slightly in his cell.

"Given my gifts, it is highly improbable that I would allow myself to be captured by Reliance soldiers and thrown into certain death, don't you think? Unless of course I wanted to."

Wait, what?

Finn couldn't imagine that anyone in their right mind would willingly participate in the Dome's games. Maybe Gray Matter was insane, it would certainly explain a lot.

"Are you saying you got yourself caught on purpose?" Finn asked in disbelief. "Because of me?"

"There is an undercurrent of change in the air. I can perhaps feel it better than most. The Disobedience is rising again and this time they will not be so easily defeated. I couldn't predict who I would find within this Dome, but I knew someone here would lead me to them."

The Disobedience?

"The Disobedience were wiped out when they lost the war against the Reliance and their Arcturians centuries ago. How could they be rising again?" Finn asked.

The Reliance had placed the survivors into the lowest castes and shipped them to the Outer Rings as a way to keep them and their offspring locked in poverty and servitude.

"Wait, you got yourself caught so you could be a part of some nonexistent resistance?" Viper snickered, interrupting. "I've been with the Reliance my entire life and they are stronger than ever. They *made* me for the Gods' sakes. If there was ever any danger of overthrowing them, I would know it."

Gray Matter ignored her snide comments, addressing the room as his spherical eyes held Finn's.

"If the Reliance knew what the Disobedience had up their sleeves, they would be quaking in their gold-plated boots."

Instantaneous fear gripped Finn in a cold vise. *Did he know about Tiri?*

It seemed impossible, but as she continued to hold his sharp gaze, her heart pounded.

Gray Matter seemed to sense her disquiet.

"Don't worry," he murmured. "I'm on your side."

She didn't know what to believe anymore. If this strange-looking hybrid could be believed, he'd gotten himself captured and placed in the Dome just for a chance to get close to the crew of *Independence*. She knew Grim had some kind of grand plan for the hybrids—an endgame for the mess he'd made of her life and everyone else's—but did he really think he could overthrow the Reliance?

Had he been putting together a new generation of disobedients right under her nose? None of it would matter if he'd been caught along with the others.

"And what about you," Finn asked the Solidarian. "Are you on our side?"

She didn't expect an answer from the typically silent hybrid. He surprised them all when his low, gruff voice uttered, "What's the worst that could happen? The Reliance decides to finally put me down? I've been waiting fifteen cycles for that. The brain says you might have a way to make those scum-suckers pay. I'll hitch my ship to yours if it means I get revenge."

As she'd thought earlier, the detached man in front of her with his red-tinged eyes hardly resembled the boy she'd glimpsed crying into the wind as tears streamed down his face. She supposed no one would be the same after all he'd been through.

Still, she couldn't help but wonder if there was more to his motivations than vengeance. She thought she'd glimpsed something more from him in the Dome, but given how wrong she'd been about so many things lately, she was starting to doubt herself.

She understood his desire for revenge in a way many others probably couldn't. She also knew how dangerous that desire made him. The good news, the thing that kept her holding on, was the fact that, at least for now, he was on their side.

An alarm sounded within the room and a door buzzed open as several armed Reliance soldiers ushered a small group of spectators inside. Men and women dressed in ostentatious garb spanning the spectrum of red and gold regarded the menagerie of imprisoned hybrids on display with wicked smiles of delight.

The soldiers spread out to take their places next to the cells while the gawking spectators milled about, pointing and speaking to one another in hushed tones.

Two large groups in various stages of inebriation gathered around to admire Supersonic and Viper respectively.

"Did you see how fast she was out there?" one of them exclaimed to the group. "Imagine all the housework she could get done in the span of a few hours."

Another one pointed at Viper.

"There's the one the Arcturians created in their lab. I can't decide what I could possibly need a poisonous half-breed for, but it would make for an interesting talking point at parties."

"I guarantee you you'd never have to worry about someone stealing the flatware with her around," the man next to her remarked.

While most of them ignored Rock, Gray Matter, and AJ, a group of ten or so had begun to gather several feet away from the Solidarian's cell, peering inside with equal parts fear and elation. A gaggle of women with gold-dusted skin, feathered hats, and matching capes dared to draw closer. They giggled crudely as they pointed, stared, and murmured to one another.

The Solidarian took it all in stride, ignoring the hullabaloo as though it happened every day.

Based on what she'd seen so far, it probably did.

"Disgusting," Finn muttered under her breath. Her comment drew a nearby soldier's attention and he tapped the glass of her cell with his stunner glove.

"Shut up and behave," he ordered.

Before Finn could so much as shoot him a defiant glare, an overexuberant voice called out to them.

"How much for the little one?"

The slurred question turned the soldier's attention away from Finn and toward an odd-looking man standing next to Carrow's cell. Instantly, she recognized his unique baritone as that of the games' announcer.

He was relatively small in stature, perhaps a few inches shorter than Finn, with petite features. A sparkling cherry-red top hat covered his bald head. His face sported full glittery golden cheeks and thick, spiky lashes framing bright purple eyes too vivid to be his natural shade. His stare was glassy, and he seemed to be swaying imperceptibly, indicating he was one of the many in the group who had perhaps imbibed a bit too much following the games.

His lips were shiny and golden with gaudy amounts of glitter, causing them to sparkle in the artificial lights. The same treatment had been applied to his eyelids and cheekbones. He wore a formfitting three-piece suit of red and gold plaid and a round gold watch hung from a chain tucked into his pocket.

He was so peculiar, it took a moment for his words to sink in. When they did, Finn jumped to her feet.

"She's not for sale."

The odd-looking announcer let out a drunken belch, followed closely by a hiccup that shook his entire body.

"My dear"—he lurched closer to her on unsteady feet—"*everything* is for sale."

"I won't tell you again. Keep your mouth shut, *mutt*!" The soldier hit the glass of Finn's cell with extra force, and he shot her a deadly glare before turning to the announcer. "For you, Mr. Green? The Dome will accept two pounds," he told the man.

Mr. Green rose to his tiptoes and let loose a drunken whistle.

"Two pounds of gold? Gods alive, what are the worlds coming to?" The soldier merely shrugged and continued to hold his stare. "Oh, all right, have it your way. I'll take her."

"No!" Finn yelled and slammed her hands against the glass. Some of the onlookers began to turn away from their studious ogling of the other hybrids at the sound of Finn's cry. At her distress, the Solidarian stood abruptly to his full height in his cell, earning gasps of trepidation from his fans.

"Now, don't go making a scene, dear." Mr. Green shot her a stern look of reprimand followed by another hiccup. The soldier nearest to Finn nodded to the others and they made their way to Carrow's cell. A low hissing sounded, and the cell walls sealed as it began to fill with gas.

"Finn?" Carrow coughed and struggled blindly, but her eyes and hands were bound, making her efforts useless. "Finn, what's happening?"

"Leave her alone!" Finn screamed and battered her body against the glass to no avail.

The soldiers ignored her, entering the child's cell to remove her limp, unconscious body. The rest of the onlookers scowled at Finn as though she were spoiling their fun and returned to their observations of the caged hybrids.

As the soldiers carried the tiny, unconscious girl away, Mr. Green swayed and tripped over his gold shoes. He fell against Finn's cell, the palm of his left hand slapping against it with a loud *thunk*.

Finn was so disgusted with his drunken display that it took a moment before she saw the small piece of paper smashed between his palm and her cell. As she watched in surprise, Mr. Green's hand pushed straight through the glass. It was as though the solid material had become liquid, allowing his appendage to slip through the space like one might dip a toe in water. It did so without a sound, without even the tiniest crack.

She blinked once, then twice, to make sure she wasn't hallucinating.

Mr. Green's hand released the paper in front of Finn and she managed to cover it with her foot when it floated down to the ground. The bizarre man then pulled his hand back through her cell as if nothing had happened. Finn studied the spot where it had just been and found no abnormalities or deformities in the glass.

Mr. Green nodded curtly for her to read the paper.

She moved her foot slightly, her dumbfounded stare falling to the scrap as she did.

On it, written in delicate lettering, she read:

The Disobedience is coming.

Finn's gaze flew up to the sozzled man to find his dazed eyes had cleared; an awareness and intelligent light filled them as the inebriation left his expression completely.

"Hold fast, young lady," he whispered through the cell. "Don't lose hope."

Then, as quickly as his face had transformed, it did so again, returning to his glassy-eyed, slack-jawed stare as a soldier came up behind him to help him gain his balance.

"Thank you, my boy," he garbled. Finn stared in amazement as he leaned heavily on the man, keeping the soldier's attention squarely on his awkward balancing act. "The damn room keeps spinning on me."

She placed her foot over the note once again and watched his departure with her mouth gaping open.

Slowly, the corners of her lips turned up in a hesitant smile.

THIRTY-FOUR

The sounds of gentle snoring and the light stirrings of slumbering hybrids filled Finn's ears. A bowl of untouched gray sludge the soldiers had slid through the slot on her cell sat untouched at Finn's side. With the steel boxes covering her hands, she couldn't eat it even if she wanted to.

Night had fallen long ago but she was having difficulty finding sleep. Her head throbbed from the altercation with Rock, and her heart ached with the hope and fear that waged war against each other there.

Carrow was gone.

If Mr. Green's note was to be believed, the child was safer with him than she would be sitting under the Dome and waiting for the next fight to the death.

If Mr. Green's note could be believed.

Finn struggled between the idea that help was indeed on its way and the notion that the note had merely been a cruel joke played on her by the peculiar announcer.

Until she knew for sure, the note would remain her secret to keep.

She wanted desperately to believe that the crew of *Independence* had survived their run-in with the Reliance. Could Conrad and Iliana be plotting her escape at this very moment?

Finn felt blindly for the note in the dimness. It was too dark to read it again, but the image of what was written there had already been burned into her brain.

The Disobedience is coming.

She struggled with the sock covering her foot, rolling her heel against the ground until she finally managed to slide the thing off. Feeling with her toes, Finn fumbled in the shadows until her foot brushed against Mr. Green's note. She'd never tried this before, but filled with desperation and without her hands to guide her, she was willing to give anything a shot.

Finn put her face to the ground and inhaled deeply, letting the smell and taste of the dirty, tiled floor wash over her.

She latched onto the paper with her toes and closed her eyes. It took longer, and the images were hazier, but as she continued to concentrate, they gradually began to come into sharper focus.

Mr. Green, adorned in a glittery red robe, is seated behind a gold-dusted marble vanity. Sheets of paper are stacked neatly on top, as well as several jeweled pens, jars of various creams, jewelry, makeup brushes, and other mysterious containers. He is alone, save for the fire roaring inside a massive stone fireplace behind him.

He hums a jaunty tune to himself as he dips two fingers in a jar and begins to smooth the glittery gold contents over his lips, eyelids, cheekbones, and around the top of his bald head.

"I need you to get a message inside the Dome, old friend."

Both Finn and a slightly startled Mr. Green turn at the same time, searching out the source of the strangely familiar female voice. Finn can't quite place it and the speaker stands in the doorway several feet away shrouded in shadows, making it impossible for her to be identified.

Mr. Green gently sets the jar down and smiles wryly.

"One of these days, darling, I'm going to stick a bell 'round your neck and save myself from an early death brought about by heart failure."

The female voice continued, undeterred.

"I need you to find a way to tell the Teslan that the Luminary is coming for her. For them all," *the woman says sternly, ignoring Mr. Green's jest. "Montgomery and his crew are rallying as we speak."*

Finn struggles to see the mysterious stranger, but she continues to remain stubbornly cloaked in darkness.

Mr. Green studies his reflection in the mirror and dips a dainty finger back into the jar of gold glitter.

"It looks like the pieces are finally starting to fall into motion. It's about bloody time," he muses as he blots his lips and shoots a devilish grin at his reflection. "Things were starting to get painfully boring around here."

The enigmatic woman sighs.

"Be safe, Redmond. Your talents are needed if we are to win this war."

Mr. Green scoffs as he blends the gold dust on his cheekbones with a large, fluffy brush.

"I'm always careful, darling."

Shaking, Finn dropped the paper and released a deep breath. Hot tears burned the back of her eyes.

They're alive. Despite Nova's betrayal, the crew of *Independence* was safe.

And they're coming.

She had no idea who the secretive woman was, but at least she knew with certainty that Mr. Green's note was in fact genuine. He'd risked a lot to get it to her, and though she wanted to keep it close, she knew she couldn't.

Rolling to her side, Finn placed her aching face near the paper. Doing her best to compartmentalize, she ignored the pain and bitter taste of dirt as she pulled the note between her lips and worked it into her mouth. She chewed hard for long minutes, swallowing back bile until it began to dissolve enough for her to swallow.

Relief surged through her body, causing her limbs to sag as exhaustion overtook her.

"You seem calmer than before."

The Solidarian's low voice startled Finn from her thoughts.

Her ears strained in the darkness. She listened for any activity in the other cells, but the rest of the hybrids remained asleep.

"Shouldn't you be sleeping?" she asked the big man.

He answered her question with one of his own.

"Something happened when I touched you out there in the Dome. You saw something, didn't you?"

"Yes." She answered him honestly, too tired to guard her response.

She heard movement from his cell as he shifted closer to the glass separating them.

"What did you see?"

Finn closed her eyes, remembering the vision of the boy with flaming hands and the tortured screams of soldiers as they burned alive.

"I saw what you did to the soldiers who killed your family. It was . . . brutal but impressive for a kid. They tell stories about you in the Farthers, you know?"

His sarcastic whisper carried over to her in the dark.

"Stories of my monstrous deeds, no doubt," he bit out.

"And your execution," she told him, tapping one of the steel boxes on her hands against the glass meaningfully. He chuckled in response, the deep sound much more pleasant than she expected it to be.

"Reliance propaganda," he scoffed, running a dark hand over his bald head.

They were quiet for several moments before she broke the silence with a question that surprised them both.

"What's your name?"

The silence stretched between them. She supposed their conversation was over. He may be her ally in the Dome for now, but that didn't make them friends. She supposed she'd just have to keep calling him the Solidarian.

Finn leaned her head back against her cell and closed her eyes. His soft murmur reached her a few moments later.

"No one has asked me that in a very long time. My name is Aedan."

Finn's lips quirked slightly.

"Nice to meet you, Aedan."

He didn't return the pleasantry. Instead, he asked her, "Are you still worried about the girl?"

She smiled into the night as she thought about shy little Carrow safe on *Independence*. She wondered if the child had made friends with Tiri yet, and the idea filled her with warmth.

"Not anymore."

Surprise colored his tone as his voice reached her once again.

"Care to tell me why?"

Finn's smile widened.

"Because the Disobedience is coming."

After several beats, Aedan released a soft exhalation, followed by low laughter. "So, the brain was right."

Finn let loose a soft sigh. For the first time since finding herself in the Dome, she willingly allowed her eyelids to flutter closed and fell into a deep sleep.

Help was coming, they just needed to keep themselves alive long enough for it to reach them.

THIRTY-FIVE

Using the chunky, gelatinous meal cubes in varying shades of gray they were served twice a day as a guidepost for the passage of time, Finn surmised that three days had come and gone since her first voyage into the Dome and the arrival of Mr. Green's strange note. She'd resorted to eating without her hands like a feral dog in order to keep up her strength.

Three days without any sign of rescue.

She hated to admit it to herself, but as each day passed in a blur of sticky gruel and the guards' stern glares, the spark of hope that had been lit inside of her began to dim.

How long before it was extinguished completely? What if something had happened to Shane and his crew? What if they weren't coming? Countless doubts plagued her as the buzz of fluorescent lights and jeers from Viper and Rock drove her slowly but surely deeper into madness.

"You okay, Finn?"

She gave AJ a concerned look through her prison of thick glass.

"She looks the usual amount of brain-dead to me." Viper chuckled. Her yellow eyes, the only thing visible behind her latex suit, smiled.

Finn ignored the deadly hybrid and offered AJ a half-hearted smile.

"Everything's fine, kid, I'm just going a little stir-crazy in here."

Her eyes flitted around their underground jail, finding it suspiciously empty of Reliance guards for the third day in a row.

"They're waiting for a new shipment," Supersonic called out, as though reading Finn's mind. "It's why we have such long breaks between Dome shows." She gestured at the other prisoners. "They've got to replace the merchandise."

Finn rolled her eyes and shot a glower in the fast-talking hybrid's direction.

Merchandise? She supposed it was true enough; they were nothing more than goods to be bought and sold by the Reliance.

"Don't worry," Viper purred to Finn, "you'll get your chance to die soon enough."

As if on cue, the outer doors buzzed and every hybrid's head, including Finn's, turned in unison.

Two lines of soldiers marched into the space, an array of staffs, pulse rifles, and stunner gloves drawn and ready for anything. Moving as one, they filled the cramped space and fanned out to stand in pairs by each cell. Behind them, more soldiers poured in, trailed by three midnight-blue boxes the size of Finn's shower stall on *Independence*.

A low hum sounded as the cubes hovered in the air, one following behind the other as they floated to a stop near three empty cells. One of the soldiers tapped away at a hol-opad and the boxes dropped to the ground with three simultaneous thuds. On a hiss, their side panels opened to reveal three bound and blindfolded bodies. They were limp and unmoving as the soldiers manhandled each one and threw them unceremoniously into the empty cells.

A deep, strangely familiar voice called through the opened doorway. "Keep an eye on the Chihiri halfling; she's feisty."

Recognition slammed into Finn like a falling meteor, and she began to shake. Goosebumps broke out over her arms and the back of her neck.

It's not possible.

And yet, somehow it was.

The chancellor entered through the doorway. He seemed shorter than she remembered, less imposing. Though what he lacked in stature, he made up for with intensity. His black eyes immediately sought out Finn's, a feral smile forming as they made eye contact. *That face!* The haunting visage of the worst possible ghost imaginable.

He's alive!

The last time she'd seen her captor and torturer he'd been bleeding out on the ground from a gunshot wound to the stomach. A gunshot fired by Finn.

A long black-and-gold cloak hung from his wide shoulders and the dark, thinning hair left on his head had been slicked back in his usual style. His shiny, pointed boots clicked against the floor with each stride that carried him over to her.

"Hello, *dove*." He hummed his nickname for her like a curse. Leaning in closer, his warm breath fanned against the glass, creating a sphere of fog in front of Finn's startled face. "Surprise," he whispered.

She took two clumsy steps back and away from the glass, feeling the blood drain from her face as she did. She began to shake uncontrollably.

As he watched her reaction, seeming to relish in it, his cold eyes gleamed with unbridled glee. The rest of the room surrounding them had gone deathly silent as their exchange continued. Every ear, hybrid and Reliance alike, was perked to hear what would happen next.

"It cost me two perfectly good Aquariian healers to undo the damage your little bullet caused," he spat, "and even then I still feel a twinge in my kidneys every time I take a piss."

The chancellor paused to look her over with an assessing gaze. "But here I am and"—his eyes took her in slowly from head to toe, his lips curling with disgust—"here *you* are."

His palm came up to press against the glass of her cell gently, and he released a sigh of regret.

"And I had such high hopes for you . . . such plans." Abruptly, his wistful air subsided and his eyes gleamed with pure hatred. "My guidance could have shaped you into the most powerful half-breed these worlds have ever seen."

"Guidance?" Though it was still shaky, Finn finally found her voice, and her eyes narrowed at the monster from her nightmares made flesh. "Is *that* what we're calling torture these days?"

His eyes narrowed at her display of defiance, as though sensing the anger slowly overpowering her fear.

"That *torture* as you call it, only made you stronger . . . forced your abilities to the forefront. Your potential was limitless. But no," he growled, "you had to go and get your feelings all twisted up over a useless *mutt*. What was her name again?"

A trembling murmur left Finn without her even realizing it until it was too late.

"Sophie."

"Ah, yes. *Sophie*," the chancellor breathed, sensing her weakness and pouncing on it as he leaned closer. "You never forget your first kill."

Sophie's anguished cries filled Finn's head as she stumbled backward, her back hitting the wall of her cell hard enough to knock the breath from her lungs. Without any escape, the cries grew louder, staining her vision with the image of the little girl's blood-soaked dress.

The chancellor smiled, his evil eyes crinkling at the corners.

"I must admit, I was disappointed by your debut performance in the Dome. It's a shame to see such a talented killer denying her true nature. No matter, you'll turn on them eventually. Perhaps we'll catch a glimpse of it tomorrow." He held his hand up to his face in a feigned whisper. "You seem to be fond of the Anunnaki boy. Maybe I'll add him to my collection."

Finn's body was so racked with tremors, she couldn't respond. Instead, she watched with tears streaming down her face as the chancellor turned his attention to the rest of the hybrid prisoners.

"I'm putting a price on this one's head."

Rock and Viper perked up in their cells.

"What kind of price?" Viper asked him boldly.

"Whichever of you kills her tomorrow in the Dome will not only be granted their freedom, but I will personally see to it you receive enough gold to live out your days peacefully and in comfort."

Finn tried to ignore the way the other prisoners' mouths dropped open in shocked hope. Viper and Rock looked at each other meaningfully before returning their gazes to the chancellor.

"What's the catch?" Rock growled.

"No catch." The chancellor waved his hand and clucked his tongue. He locked eyes with each prisoner before returning his stare to Finn. "All I ask is that you make it hurt."

She didn't dare look around at the rest of the group for fear of what she would see. As a sinking feeling of dread filled her chest, she knew what she'd find.

He'd just signed her death warrant.

"Good luck, my dove." With that final amused whisper hanging in the air between them, the chancellor strode past the cells, his cloak trailing behind him.

Finn shivered, cold dread spreading its way through her as her brain and body began to shut down. The sound of his receding footsteps hit her like gunshots. Dimly she recognized AJ calling out to her, but she barely heard him over the sound of her own heartbeat.

Once the chancellor had made it through the doors and she could no longer hear his retreating steps, Finn collapsed into a heap on the dirty floor.

THIRTY-SIX

"Finn, talk to me," AJ begged.

She lay on the floor of her cell, her back to the rest of them as her mind swam in an ocean of despair and confusion.

The chancellor was alive. She hadn't killed him.

"Oh look, the newbies are awake," Supersonic chirped somewhere in the distance. "Welcome to the Imminent Death Club, I'll make this quick. Do you see that half-Teslan on the ground over there with the red hair? All you really need to know is some bigwig Reliance guy promised a life of comfort and gold to the half-breed who kills her . . . painfully."

AJ growled angrily just as Viper cut in.

"What are you doing? They weren't even awake when he made the offer. We've got dibs."

"Fair is fair," Supersonic shot back.

"I don't understand," one of the newcomers moaned groggily. "Where am I?"

Supersonic sighed heavily and launched in with her introduction-to-the-Dome speech. When she reached the chancellor's proposition, Finn finally rolled over.

"You know he'll never follow through with that offer, don't you? The Reliance will never let you disappear with *their* gold and *your* freedom. Even if you kill me in the Dome, you'll never get what he promised."

The blindfolds had been removed from the newcomers' eyes, but their hands remained bound. They seemed completely unfazed by her impassioned speech. Their minds worked to process all of the new information they'd just been given, and all three studied Finn quietly as though tracking her movements and downloading them as data in preparation for the Dome's games.

Finn returned the favor, assessing the half-Chihiri. Her plumb-colored skin was covered in iridescent scales that glittered in the artificial light. The half-Saosin had his leathery, talon-tipped wings secured tightly behind his back by thick bands. What appeared to be a half-Goslan—judging by the translucent tentacles sprouting from his ribcage—was next to him.

The notion seemed ridiculous, given that no human in their right mind would ever breed with the deadly tentacle-clad alien, but after hearing of Viper's origins in a Reliance lab, she supposed it wasn't all that surprising.

The Saosin seemed harmless enough, though those deadly wings could prove problematic. The Goslan's tentacles would be a challenge, but Finn felt confident enough in her defensive maneuvers to consider him a nonthreat.

The Chihiri, however, was a wildcard.

A full-blooded Chihiri came equipped with a unique set of vocal cords. It allowed their voices to reach octaves beyond the normal realm of most alien and human hearing. The anomaly had varying effects on the galaxy's different races. She'd seen some become entranced by the odd notes and others repelled to the point of incapacitation.

"She's right," Aedan interrupted gruffly. "The chancellor is toying with all of you. In all my time here, I've never seen him make an offer like that."

"Wow, he must really hate you," Supersonic chimed in cheerfully.

"Someone has gotten real chatty all of a sudden," Viper sneered, her eyes narrowing on the Solidarian before turning Finn's way. "I think I'll take the risk, especially if it means putting Brain-Dead out of her misery."

"Get in line," Rock snarled. His scalp had done some healing in the days following the Dome, but it did nothing to improve his disposition or seething hatred for Finn.

If the gleam in his eye was any indication, it looked as though he'd spent the last three days plotting all the ways he planned to make her suffer.

"You touch her and I'll kill you!" AJ yelled.

"I'd love for you to try, whelp," Viper called to him in a singsong voice.

"Enough!" Finn yelled and rose to her feet. "If you want a future free from the Dome, you'll work *with* us instead of *against* us. I know the chancellor. He gets off on torturing our kind. This is just another one of his games."

"The chancellor is the biggest supplier of half-breeds to the Dome. Everyone knows that," Viper spat in Finn's direction. "He spends cycles honing their abilities through pain. He's a legend, and the Reliance gives him free rein. If he says he can get me out of here with the added bonus of making you bleed, I choose to take him at his word."

"Me too," Rock snapped.

Finn held onto the fleeting tether of hope still inside her. Her voice softened as she pleaded with them.

"Please. I know if we can just hold on a little longer, I can get us out of here."

Viper laughed, the sound rumbling from deep in her belly.

"Did you hear that, Rock? She still thinks she's going to break us out."

As the laughter continued, Finn's chest squeezed painfully.

There would be no reasoning with them. If Shane and his crew didn't show up soon, the other prisoners would gladly stain the Dome with Finn's blood.

She glanced over at AJ and winced at the fear and anger pulling his beautiful features into a harsh frown.

She gave him her best attempt at a reassuring nod before returning to sit in the dirt with her back against the cell.

All she could now was wait and plan.

Wait for help to arrive and plan for the worst

As the day bled into night and the lights above them dimmed, the hybrids grew quiet with anticipation, and Finn did her best to get some rest.

She dreamed of bloodied dresses and the chancellor's cruel voice.

THIRTY-SEVEN

They were awakened early the next morning by the telltale hissing within each cell as the prisoners were gassed. Finn sat on the ground and waited for unconsciousness to claim her.

Just as she had a few days ago, she awakened in a dark corridor; the low din of the crowd could be heard outside.

Finn pushed herself to her feet and waited. Eventually, the door before her opened and she was awash in blinding light. Rather than wait for her eyes to adjust, she moved quickly into the Dome as she sought out AJ. She found the boy standing nervously several feet away.

She hustled to join him as Mr. Green continued with his obnoxious introductions.

The three new hybrids were already inside, their bodies huddled close together as each one shifted on their feet and darted wide eyes around the Dome.

With the others occupied, she rushed to fill him in on the plan when she reached his side.

"They're all going to be gunning for me today. You need to stay close to Aedan and keep your distance. I can take care of myself but I can't be worried about you too."

"I'm not leaving you to fend for yourself," he argued. "Who's Aedan anyway?"

Finn rolled her eyes at his obstinance.

"He's the Solidarian and he's going to protect you."

He'd already promised Finn he would last night when they'd both spent the dark hours planning for the next day in the Dome.

"Finn, I can help you," AJ contended.

"AJ!" she yelled as urgency began to overtake her. Viper and Rock had just sauntered into the Dome, waving enthusiastically to their cheering fans. "I need you to trust me and do as I say. Got it?"

His eyes narrowed and his jaw clenched tightly, but he nodded once in agreement.

Aedan emerged next, his red-tinged eyes seeking out Finn's. The large hybrid made it over to them both in record time, stopping at her side as his eyes scanned the Dome.

"I hope you're ready for this," he told her as he watched the crowd with growing disgust. "I just want to reiterate that this is a terrible plan." Several meters away, Viper and Rock were watching her with cruel smiles playing at their lips. Their bloodthirsty gazes, alight with anticipation, remained locked on hers. Finn clenched and unclenched her fists as she returned her would-be murderers' stares.

She wasn't looking forward to the task ahead. Their goal was simple: kill Finn. They had no one to protect, no morals to uphold or honor.

Despite their obvious bloodlust, Finn refused to kill them, a fact that put her at a clear disadvantage. Aedan had tried to reason with her on that point last night, but she'd already made up her mind.

She would not be the killer the chancellor claimed she was.

As the final hybrid entered the Dome to uproarious applause, Finn's eyes scanned the crowd, only to stop short. Her heart began to pound in her ears. The chancellor sat in his own private section, surrounded by soldiers in the very front rows of the crowd. He studied her face with a malicious grin, as though he'd been waiting for her to notice him.

"Noted," she told Aedan, doing her best to hide the quaver in her voice the chancellor's presence caused. "Besides, what could go wrong?"

The Solidarian chuckled under his breath.

"At least you haven't lost your sense of humor."

"At least there's that," Finn muttered. She turned to face Aedan. "Take care of him," she pled, nodding in AJ's direction.

"You have my word," the Solidarian promised.

At that moment, the crowd began to hush and Mr. Green's voice filled the Dome.

"You may notice the Dome looks a tad empty. I've just been told that things will be a little different today, given the events during our last games. Our half-breed competitors will no longer be competing in one of our custom-built obstacle courses of death."

There was something wrong in Mr. Green's voice; a hint of trepidation she'd not heard before. Her heart started to sink.

Bystanders began to murmur to one another, their low buzz growing louder with each second that passed.

"What's he talking about?" Finn asked Aedan, the cold fingers of dread unfurling within the pit of her stomach.

"I don't know. This has never happened before."

"Yes indeed, ladies and gentlemen. Today you will see the Dome's most violent game yet. At the count of five, our half-breed contenders will be provided with an assortment of weapons. The last half-breed standing will be victorious and live to see another day in the Dome."

"Does that mean what I think it means?" AJ asked as Gray Matter made his way over to the trio.

"Yes," Gray Matter answered when he reached them. "It would appear as though our last foray into the Dome has resulted in some unforeseen consequences."

"They're going to kill us all," Finn whispered.

Horror began building inside of her as the truth sank in: Mr. Green's fear . . . the chancellor's presence . . . this new twist to the games. Help wouldn't be here in time to spare them from the bloodbath the Reliance had devised. They were on their own.

"The plan hasn't changed," she told others. "Keep each other safe and aim to incapacitate. I'll handle Rock and Viper."

They each nodded their assent as Mr. Green began his countdown.

"Five . . ."

"You might want to rethink your plan, Finn," Gray Matter whispered. "They won't show you any mercy, and lives will be lost whether you like it or not."

"Four . . ." The crowd began to stomp in unison.

"I'm not going to kill them," she said.

He sighed and nodded as though he already knew what her answer would be.

"They will come at you as one. Rock will attempt to incapacitate you. His anger will make him rash. Viper truly believes the chancellor's offer, and she will put on a show of making you suffer. Once you're dead they'll turn on each other."

"Three . . ." Rhythmic clapping joined the vigorous stomps.

"Why are you telling me this?" she asked him sharply.

His eyes held hers for a long moment.

"So you will see the truth you've been avoiding. Some of us will not make it out of this arena."

"Two . . . One!"

As the crowd erupted with maniacal cries of joy and anticipation, the ground shook beneath the hybrids and the earth opened up from the center of the Dome. A silver pedestal rose from the hole that had been revealed, elevating a pile of various blades and hardware onto the dirt.

"Go!" Mr. Green yelled.

The prisoners had been momentarily stuck, but at the sound of Mr. Green's shout, each of them burst into a sprint, racing to the mound of weapons at the center of the Dome.

Then, all hell broke loose.

THIRTY-EIGHT

Finn's feet pounded against the dirt as AJ, Aedan, and Gray Matter followed closely on her heels. The pedestal held a variety of blades from rusty daggers and throwing knives to longswords. Of course, the Reliance wouldn't provide them with guns or blasters to combat each other; where would the fun be in that? The games would be over far too soon, depriving the bloodthirsty crowd of their violent show.

Finn caught a glimpse of a large net trap with pitons meant to dig into the earth mixed in with the blades and winced when she saw Rock pick it up.

Moving quickly, she threw out her left leg and slid into the dirt to cut off the Saosin hybrid just as he reached the pile. She grabbed the sharpest-looking dagger and a short-handled sword with a blade the size of her forearm. Overall, it was light, and the large pommel made it easy to grip.

She stuck the dagger into the waistband of her pants and palmed the sword.

Finn heard a rush of air and dove to the side to avoid the Saosin's sharp wings. Apparently, he didn't appreciate being cut off. As she rolled away to her knees, something glinted in the light and caught her eye.

She smiled with recognition.

The other hybrids had passed up the object for more intimidating-looking weaponry, most likely not realizing what it was. Finn palmed the five metal rings banded together and slipped them over her fingers. A small projector the size of her fingertip rested against her knuckle, humming imperceptibly.

"Finn, look out!" AJ yelled somewhere behind her.

She heard a low whistle and turned toward the sound, raising her ringed hand in a fist just as a knife came hurtling at her face.

The projector hummed to life, creating a hard-light shield in front of her. The knife bounced off with a *zap* and Finn's shoulder stung slightly from the force of impact.

Long before their tech had been improved by time and the Arcturians, the Reliance Army had used these small rings to create hard-light projection shields that were impervious to harm.

Suddenly, the projector powered down and her shield disappeared. Finn dove to the left to avoid another blade as it came slashing down over her.

The shield design was flawed due to poor construction, the negative effects the shock absorption had on the user, and the shield's charge time between each use leaving the projector depleted and the wielder completely defenseless for short periods of time.

Finn jumped to a crouch and raised her sword just in time to clash against Viper's. The reptilian hybrid bared her teeth in a mock grin as she pushed against Finn's hold.

Aedan, pulling AJ behind him, flicked his fingers and sent a small ball of fire in their direction. The flames hit Viper squarely on her webbed sword hand and she let out a cry of pain as her weapon went crashing to the ground. Careful to avoid her skin, Finn launched a hard kick to the hybrid's midsection and sent her down with a grunt of pain into a crumpled heap.

"Thanks," she called to the Solidarian as she ducked to avoid the Saosin's talon-tipped wings.

The flying hybrid and the iridescent-scaled Chihiri had turned on one another and were currently engaged in a bloody battle. The Saosin dove from the air, his talons aimed squarely at the Chihiri's head. Just before impact, the

Chihiri's mouth opened and she released a low frequency cry. Finn couldn't hear it, but she could see the sound waves in the air where the shriek had left her lips. The force of it sent the Saosin careening backward until he hit the ground.

A blur of motion drew Finn's attention and she caught a glimpse of Supersonic running laps around the Dome. Did she plan to outrun them until they were all dead?

A blow to the shoulder caught Finn unawares and her ears rang from the impact. She felt a pop and then numbness from her bicep to her fingers. She teetered on her feet and turned to find Rock glaring down at her. She'd almost forgotten how much his hits hurt.

Almost.

The Kreetian interlaced his fists together and raised them above his head. He gritted his teeth as he brought them down over Finn. She raised her sword between them with her uninjured arm and his hands hit the blade with such force it broke in half.

"Shit," Finn muttered, tossing the weapon aside.

Rock smiled.

Fire sailed across the sky and someone screamed. Finn tried not to look, trusting that the Solidarian would protect AJ.

She backed away from the Kreetian, her eyes darting in search of something she could use against him. He barreled toward her, lowering his shoulder. Finn raised her ringed hand, holding the shield between his body and hers. Rock hit it with such force, he was knocked to the ground and Finn's injured shoulder was forced to absorb the shock. It popped once again with the impact as it fully dislocated.

Grimacing in pain as the shield powered down, Finn's arm hung awkwardly at her side. She doubted if she'd be able to hold the shield up again to withstand another hit like that.

Rock was already on his feet, his chest huffing with rage. He lowered his shoulders for round two. As if by some miracle sent from the Gods, he was quickly knocked aside by one of the Goslan's singed tentacles as the odd-looking hybrid attempted to land a strike on Aedan.

AJ had moved away from the Solidarian's protection, launching well-executed blows, while simultaneously dodging the Saosin as he dive-bombed the boy from above. Even as she cursed his rebellious streak, she couldn't help but feel a sting of pride.

Suddenly, he turned to her, his black eyes wide with alarm as he frantically pointed to something behind her.

She turned in time to see a short-handled axe hurtling toward her chest. This was it. There was no time to dodge.

Finn closed her eyes and prayed for a quick end.

Gods, please let AJ make it out of this alive.

THIRTY-NINE

S he waited for the blow to land but it never came.

"Godsdammit!" Viper yelled.

Finn opened her eyes to see Gray Matter standing motionless in front of her with the axe lodged in his small chest. The ashen hybrid's face paled even further as his dark eyes locked on Finn's. His body fell to the dirt in a heap and she sprinted to his side.

Viper let out another yell when Aedan, hands ablaze, came charging at her.

With Viper preoccupied, Finn focused on Gray Matter, applying pressure to his chest on either side of the axe in an attempt to stem the flow of blood.

"I thought you were supposed to be smart," she told him shakily. "Why would you go and do something so stupid?"

His spherical eyes blinked slowly and the air rattled in his chest as his breathing shallowed.

"It . . . was always . . . meant to be this way," he rasped. "I only wish . . . I could've seen . . . the Reliance . . . fall."

"Just hold on," she begged him desperately.

He placed a trembling gray hand over hers.

"I've done my job . . . Now it is time . . . for you to do yours." He paused to glance at the melee around them. "War is not . . . won without casualties."

His fingers squeezed hers lightly, and he took one last shuddering breath. As he released it, his eyes went blank and his body went slack.

"Let's make things interesting," Mr. Green suggested to the audience with a barely perceptible hint of reluctance.

The Dome's earth opened once again and another pedestal rose from the hole it revealed. A single stunner glove ascended into the fray.

Finn rose to her feet and gritted her teeth in anger. She lost sight of where the glove ended up as several of the remaining hybrids dove for it, stirring up a cloud of dirt around the skirmish.

"Still want to stick with the plan?" Aedan muttered angrily as he looked at Gray Matter's lifeless body.

War is not won without casualties.

Gray Matter's final words echoed in her head.

The dust settled around the scuffling hybrids, and when it did, Finn glimpsed the half-Goslan's bloodied body where he lay dead on the ground. The Saosin's wing had been struck through with a blade, and he struggled to take flight and escape.

Finn's eyes searched for the stunner glove but it was nowhere to be found.

"I don't see it," she told Aedan. "Where is it?"

"Sorry, Brain-Dead. No hard feelings."

Supersonic skidded to a stop several feet from their trio, her palm now covered in the sleek stunner glove. She raised her hand and closed it in a fist, wiggling her fingers to send a blast straight for them.

Finn engaged her shield, but the hybrid hadn't gotten the hand movements completely right and her aim was off. The blast missed Finn by a foot. She heard a grunt followed by a heavy thud and turned.

Though she'd been spared, Aedan hadn't. His big body now lay sprawled on the ground in an unconscious heap.

"No!" Finn screamed.

"Whoops." Supersonic blushed with embarrassment and launched herself into a dizzying sprint.

"What now?" AJ glanced around nervously.

"Stay out of the way and let me handle this," she told the boy. He looked like he wanted to argue, but was interrupted by a rush of air as the large net flew toward them.

Finn pushed AJ out of the way as the net collided with her, wrapping itself around her body and taking her to the ground. As soon as it hit earth, the pitons dug into the dirt and held her down.

"Finn!"

"Get back, AJ!" she yelled.

She watched helplessly as Viper came striding over, a long-sword grasped tightly in each hand.

"I'm disappointed," she cooed. "You made this way too easy."

"Viper!" AJ called out to the venomous hybrid from Finn's left. Viper turned to glare at AJ, only to stop short, her arms falling limply at her sides. "Leave her alone," he ordered.

"Leave her alone," Viper repeated.

Finn glanced up to find AJ's eyes swirling with an array of colors, his stare locked on Viper's.

"You want to let Finn out of the net now," the boy instructed.

"Yes," Viper replied flatly. She closed the distance between them and fell to her knees. Clumsily, her hands found the release on each piton, loosening the net and allowing Finn the breathing room to escape.

"I told you I could help," AJ boasted.

Finn watched a disoriented Viper take a seat in the dirt, her reptilian eyes blank.

"Not now, kid."

She shot AJ a frown.

"I don't think you can call me that anymore," he said, grinning widely.

Finn shook her head and sighed. At least he seemed to be enjoying himself.

As she began to lift the net from her body, she noticed the Dome had gone eerily quiet around them. She looked around to find Supersonic, the Saosin, and the Chihiri watching them closely.

Something was wrong. Where was Rock?

"Come on, Finn, hurry up."

"AJ . . ." Her panicked gaze shot over to him, ready to call out to him in warning. He saw the look on her face and his smile faltered.

The steady ruckus of the crowd hushed and AJ's eyes widened. Finn watched in horror as the tip of a blade shot through his sternum from behind, his blood spraying down over her.

A dull roar sounded inside Finn's mind as she watched AJ gurgle and gasp for air. The blade disappeared and the boy fell to the ground in a heap. His face landed mere inches from Finn's.

Behind him, Rock waved a bloody sword and raised his arms over his head in triumph.

AJ's sightless black eyes bored into Finn's soul, his frozen mouth parted in shock.

AJ was dead.

She released a rage-filled cry from somewhere deep within her belly, the sound of her grief causing even Rock to pause his celebrations to shoot her a nervous glance.

The crowd remained silent. Not even Mr. Green dared to speak.

War is not won without casualties.

Her mind screamed in denial.

Not AJ.

She was supposed to protect him.

She had failed.

Training with you is the only time I've ever really been happy.

Tears streamed down Finn's face as she remembered the boy's earnest expression and the shy blush of his cheeks when he'd admitted that fact to her.

A single clap sounded from somewhere in the audience and Finn tore her eyes from AJ's, seeking the source of the applause. She found the chancellor waiting for her, an amused smile tugging at the corners of his mouth as he slapped his hands together and broke the eerie silence. His dark eyes, alight with humor, taunted her from the distance.

As Finn watched the chancellor, something inside of her snapped irreparably. Her fractured mind conjured up an image of Sophie, her sad, sightless eyes staring skyward next to AJ as the circle of blood on her gown began to spread.

In a burst of speed, Finn shoved the net from her body and rose to her feet. Her chest heaved with angry breaths as she walked slowly in Rock's direction.

War is not won without casualties.

AJ was dead and for what? The entertainment of a bunch of rich barbarians? Refusing to kill the others had been a mistake . . . one that cost AJ his life.

Finn had been running from herself for most of her life, from a truth she knew deep down to her core: she was a killer. And now the Reliance wanted a show? Well, she would give it to them.

A calm stole over Finn as the screams in her mind quieted.

Her steady gait seemed to snap Rock out of his stupor and he brought the longsword in front of him and began to charge her. She didn't bother with the shield or her dagger, looking forward to the pain their collision would bring.

Rock picked up speed and slashed his sword at her on a yell. At the last second, Finn dove to her knees and leaned her head back, just narrowly dodging the blow. Coming to her feet, she turned and delivered a hard kick to the back of Rock's knees.

He staggered before righting himself. Throwing the sword to the ground, the Kreetian swung out a hardened arm and slammed her into the dirt, rattling her teeth from the impact.

His hand hardened around her throat, cutting off her supply of air. Rather than fight him, she welcomed the pain and embraced the fear.

She didn't just want to kill him, she wanted him to suffer.

Finn lifted a hand and slammed her palm against Rock's cheek. As she did, she conjured up every horrible thing she'd ever done, every horrible thing she'd ever seen.

The screams of agony, the memories of Sophie's lifeless body, her torture at the hands of the chancellor, AJ's unseeing eyes as the breath left his body for the last time.

Finn took the pain of every lashing and the horror of all she'd done and let them flow through her and into Rock.

His hold loosened and his eyes widened in alarm. Tiny droplets of blood streamed from his eyes like tears. She watched as his mouth opened in a silent scream of terror.

Finn lifted her ringed fist and shoved it into Rock's open mouth, engaging the shield.

"Do me a favor, Rock," she growled. "Choke on it."

The overpressure wave caused by the hard-light projection grew to the zenith of its specifications, forcing the contents of Rock's head to evacuate through his mouth, nose, and ears. Gore showered down over Finn in a macabre fountain of blood and gray matter.

She pushed what was left of Rock's body off her and got to her feet. In her tunnel vision, she missed the tiny armada of ships that had accumulated above the Dome.

Now that she was no longer under the spell of AJ's eyes, Viper had stood up and her confused expression turned to the Dome's peak and the ships raining firepower down on the Reliance soldiers surrounding the structure.

As she drew closer, Viper took in Finn's bloody visage.

"You were right," she told Finn in awe. "They came."

Finn closed the distance between them and drew her dagger from the waistband of her jumpsuit. As Viper's eyes widened in surprised confusion, Finn slashed the hybrid's throat. Her scaled hands went to the wound in a vain attempt to stem the steady flow of blood as she gurgled a pained cry.

As Finn watched, her eyes rolled back in her head and the *poison princess* collapsed in a heap.

Wisely, the three remaining competitors gave Finn a wide berth. Supersonic watched her with terrified eyes, ready to run if need be.

Screams began to sound within the Reliance audience and she finally noticed the war waging above the Dome. Soldiers fell left and right, their blasters and pulse guns no match for the airborne ships and their firepower.

One of the smaller salvage ships in the group, more heavily armored than the others, broke away from the fracas and aimed a laser at the Dome. The beam collided with the structure's projector, blowing it to smithereens. The hard-light projection around them flickered before disappearing completely.

They were free.

Shots fired around her from both sides, but Finn only had eyes for the chancellor. He stood near his seat, surrounded by a large group of soldiers protecting him. He yelled orders at them above the fray and darted panicked eyes around the arena.

Finn tightened her grip on the dagger and walked in his direction. She ignored the lasers and blasts firing all around her, waiting for the chancellor to spot her. A stray shot pierced her shoulder, but Finn barely flinched. She barely even felt it.

"Finn!"

She turned to see a small pod had landed several feet away, and found Conrad staring at her. His dreads were tied away from his face and his jaw was set with anger. His blue eyes scanned first the bloody dagger in her hand, then the blood and carnage covering her face and upper body. She watched, impassive, as his familiar azure gaze widened with horror.

Help had arrived.

FORTY

"You're too late," Finn muttered under her breath. She turned away from Conrad and continued walking.

As she reached the edge of the Dome, the chancellor finally noticed her and his eyes widened in alarm. She held his eyes as she bent to snag an axe in her free hand and broke into a sprint.

More shots pierced the air around her, but Finn merely ran through them, pumping her arms and legs as fast as they would carry her.

She darted through the chaotic crowd of terrified onlookers, dodging between shrieking Reliance ladies in their red-and-gold finery and the soldiers protectively positioned around them.

One of the guards surrounding the chancellor broke away as Finn neared and took aim with his blaster. No more than a meter separated them.

Finn raised the handle of the axe and sent it flying with a graceful flick of her wrist. It sailed through the air and landed with a sickening *thwack* in the soldier's chest.

She sprinted to his side and snatched the blaster from his lifeless hands.

"Kill her!" the chancellor shrieked. Several of his guards turned in her direction and Finn dropped to a knee, taking aim with the blaster and leaving smoking holes in each of their heads. A nearby soldier she'd failed to see punched her in the jaw with a gloved fist.

Finn spit blood, ducking the next punch as it came sailing toward her temple. Their tussle drew the rest of soldiers from their position around the chancellor.

Finn head-butted one as he charged her right side. Turning gracefully, she launched a hard kick at another's stomach. Yanking the blaster from around his shoulder, she shot four more guards in succession.

Her movements cleared a path between her and the chancellor, and Finn smiled coldly at the fear in his eyes as she palmed her dagger, still covered in Viper's blood. She grasped the clean, upper quarter of the blade and launched it at the chancellor. It sailed through the air past his head, leaving a small, clean cut on his cheek.

His hand shot up to the wound to wipe at the small line of blood dripping there and he smiled.

"You missed!" he called to her smugly.

"Not quite," she snarled back.

His smile faltered at the calm that had stolen over her features and his eyes widened in alarm. He gasped slightly as the veins in his face turned black, spreading out in a web around the torn flesh. Blood began to trickle from his nose as Viper's poisonous blood coursed its way through his body.

He stumbled before barely righting himself, a new wave of soldiers rushing to his side. Finn picked up a nearby blaster and moved to finish him off.

Before she could take two steps, strong arms wrapped around her waist and squeezed. She smelled the mint of Conrad's hair wax and let out a guttural scream.

"Let me go!"

It was too late. Conrad was already in the process of dragging her back through the Dome. Before long, the chancellor was swallowed by Reliance guards and she lost sight of him.

"No!" Finn screamed, launching an elbow into one of Conrad's ribs and dragging her feet through the dirt in a bid to slow him down. He groaned in pain but held tight.

Conrad turned their bodies as he made his way to the pod in the Dome's epicenter. Finn caught sight of Enyo's multi-hued hair and found her tearing her way through screaming soldiers with her deadly claws and fangs, while Axel slammed even more into the ground with brutal force. He'd puffed up to twice his normal size and his half-Khaleerian skin had darkened to a deep shade of red. At the pod's entrance, Grim watched their approach with eyes blackened by his rage; Aedan's large, limp form was slung over his shoulder. Behind him, Iliana's red hair clung to her dirt-streaked face as she took in the chaos with wide, horrified eyes.

In the distance, Shane cradled AJ's bloody body in his arms. Unabashed tears streamed down the captain's face.

"Don't touch him!" Finn shrieked and writhed in Conrad's hold. "Don't touch him!" Her arms and legs kicked wildly as she thrashed and bit at the air like a mad dog.

A sharp prick in her neck followed by a rush of cold stopped her movements short and the world around her went dark.

FORTY-ONE

Finn awoke sometime later to *find* herself in the sick bay aboard *Independence* with her wrists and ankles strapped to the bed in an inescapable hold.

She gave each a tug just to be sure and, as she suspected, they had no give.

"Shane thought the restraints might be safer for you."

Finn glanced over to find Conrad sitting quietly in a chair across from her bed. He sat hunched over with his elbows resting against his thighs. A mixture of dirt, blood, and sweat smeared the ebony skin of his face. His blue eyes looked weary, and he had a swollen lip and cuts on his face and arms.

"AJ's dead," she told him in a flat voice she barely recognized.

"I know," he said quietly, unshed tears pooling in his eyes.

"I didn't protect him," she whispered.

Conrad got up and moved to the side of her bed.

"It wasn't your fault," he soothed.

Finn felt cold. She searched for some emotion, something she could cling to but came up empty. It was as if everything had been shut off in the Dome, leaving her an empty shell.

"What about Viper and Rock?" she asked him. "Were they my fault?"

Conrad's eyes darkened with pain as if remembering what he'd seen on Aquarii.

The last tiny shred of the woman she'd been before the Dome died at the sight. She turned away from him and stared at the opposite wall.

"Exactly. *I'm* the one who was stupid enough to trust Nova. *I'm* the one who chose to bring AJ to Aquarii. And *I'm* the one who killed those people."

"Finn, you didn't have a choice."

Her fists clenched around the sheets at the half-hearted lie.

"I wanted to hurt them for what they did. I wanted them to suffer," Finn hissed.

When she turned back to Conrad, he was regarding her like a stranger.

Good.

At least his eyes were wide open to the truth now.

"Conrad, Shane needs you."

The deep voice drew Finn's gaze to the doorway and she found Grim standing there. His giant red body was clothed in his usual garb, albeit slightly torn and covered in dirt. His dark eyes remained on Finn. The tenderness she glimpsed there would have enraged her if she'd been capable of feeling anything.

Conrad got up and left without a backward glance. The old Finn would have ached at the sight, but whoever she was now couldn't force herself to care.

"I'm sorry we couldn't get to you sooner, Finn."

At the familiar feminine voice, she looked to Grim's left and felt a tiny glimmer of surprise to see Senator Califax's wife, the one who'd shown her a small kindness at the Unionization Ball on Cartan they'd attended weeks ago. Today, her stout frame wore a deep red jumpsuit with glittery gold feathers sprouting from the padded shoulders. Her brown hair had been tied up with gold ribbons.

What was *she* doing here?

Then it hit her; something oddly familiar about the woman's voice. Finn remembered her strange vision of Mr. Green and the mysterious woman who came to visit him in the night . . .

I need you to find a way to tell the Teslan that the Luminary is coming for her. For them all.

"You were the one who sent Mr. Green to me."

"Yes," the plump woman said as she shot Grim a knowing look. "The Luminary and I have been on the same side for many cycles now."

"And your husband? What side is he on?" Finn asked, remembering the revolting little man with the too-white teeth and wandering eyes.

"My husband wouldn't know right from wrong if they bit him in his gold-dusted arse. His position, however," she shared, smiling, "gives me access to the kinds of things our cause would be lost without." Her smile faltered as she regarded Finn sadly for a moment. "I'm just sorry they couldn't help us save AJ."

At the mention of his name, Finn's eyes flickered between Grim and Madam Califax before returning to their casual study of the wall.

"Get out," she told them.

She could practically hear Madam Califax's jaw hit the floor in shock at her rude dismissal. Regardless, the woman obeyed and the sound of her heels clacking against the floor announced her hasty exit as she retreated from the room.

"I meant both of you," Finn told Grim while keeping her eyes on the wall.

"*Dhala* . . . I—"

"Don't," she cut him off coldly. Unfazed, he merely cleared his throat and tried a different tactic.

"Can you tell me what happened when you touched the Kreetian? Iliana says she's never seen anything like it."

Finn remained silent, closing her eyes and patiently waiting for him to leave. After several tense minutes of silence, Grim swallowed hard and tried again.

"*Dhala*, I'm so sorry. I never wanted this for you."

She glanced in his direction and let out a quiet, humorless chuckle.

"I find that hard to believe." She turned to see Grim's dark eyes had widened at her tone, and he expelled a frustrated breath of air. She continued her thought in an almost robotic tone. "This is what you trained me for, isn't it?" she asked him. "You needed a competent assassin for your *bigger mission*. Well"—she bared her teeth in a mock grin—"I've got some good news for you: You wanted a killer? You got her, and she's ready to *play her part*."

"I never meant for *this* to happen. My hands were the only ones meant to get dirty."

"Wars aren't won without casualties," Finn told him flatly. "I know that now."

"*Dhala*, please . . ." His gruff voice wavered in a way she'd never heard before. "What can I do to make this better? What do you want? Anything in my power to give to you, I will."

"I want what you promised," she whispered impassively. "What you made me believe every time you read one of your books to me . . . stories about men with honor and happy endings where justice prevailed. You made me believe in it even though you knew it wasn't real."

"You were just a child then . . . with the weight of ten worlds sagging on your tiny shoulders. I wanted to give you something to believe in. I wanted to give you hope."

"That's just it, isn't it? You found a way to hurt me in a way even the chancellor wasn't cruel enough to do. You made me *hope*. You made me believe the worlds could be a just place . . . that doing good *mattered*. And then . . ."—Finn's gaze burned into his—"you sent me to steal from a courtesan and took all of it away."

She returned her stare to the bare, white wall so she wouldn't have to see the way the big warrior who'd never met a problem he couldn't fix with his fists trembled, his eyes glistening in the artificial light.

A few seconds passed before she heard the sound of his retreating boots and Finn was finally alone. She closed her eyes with a sense of relief.

She sensed when visitors stopped by, like Iliana and Isis, but she refused to acknowledge their presence or even open her eyes.

Eventually, the foot traffic through the sick bay ceased and Finn let her body go limp. It only took seconds for her to fall asleep.

For the first time in a long time, she didn't dream.

Two days had passed since their rescue from the Dome and AJ was finally getting a funeral. The *Independence* and her crew were on the run and had taken extra care to travel out of Reliance sight for the past forty-eight hours. Jax and Lex were leading them to their home planet, Tuathan. Finn knew little to nothing about the tiny planet in the farthest reaches of the Farthers, but Shane and Grim seemed convinced they would find both sanctuary and allies there.

In a few more days they would reach Tuathan and safety.

Only one task remained.

Finn watched on as a somber Isis placed a fat purple flower on the large steel cargo box holding AJ's body. Tears pooled in her silver eyes and tracked a pathway down her blue cheeks. She cast her stare downward and appeared to pray in a low whisper. A few seconds later, she moved out through the open door of the docking bay and pulled a quietly sobbing Tiri to her side. The little girl wore a black dress on her tiny lavender frame and her ringlets had been pulled away from her elfin face. Her green eyes remained locked on the box.

There hadn't been time to obtain a proper coffin and Finn could tell from the haggard look on Shane's face and the dark purple bruises under his eyes that the knowledge he'd be sending his brother off in a steel box meant for cargo burned deep. The captain ran hands over his stubble before placing them on the lid.

Conrad stood by his side in the bay, wraparounds covering his glowing eyes and his runic tattoos on full display. He placed a large hand on Shane's shoulder and squeezed.

Grim and Iliana stood in the hallway watching the proceedings in the bay through a large window while an unusually solemn Lex, Axel, and Jax held each other a few feet away. Both the horned Khaleerian and the courtesan maintained stoic expressions.

Finn stood quietly in the hallway and kept her distance from everyone. Carrow, Aedan, and the other rescued hybrids were not asked to the join the quiet ceremony.

Long minutes passed with Shane hunched over the box, his shoulders shaking as he cried for his little brother. Conrad wrapped his arm around the captain and bowed his head. They'd sacrificed everything to give their brother a decent life, only to watch him die before his fifteenth birthday.

And it was all Finn's fault.

She felt the familiar sting of guilt at the center of her chest and swallowed the lump rising in her throat. She couldn't do this. She couldn't watch them float AJ out of the hold into the cold darkness of space.

Not in that box.

Finn rubbed the pins and needles from her chest as she turned away from the group, her footsteps echoing down the hallway as she went.

I'm so sorry, kid.

Every time she closed her eyes, she saw the blood seeping from AJ's chest, saw the wide, dazed look of horror in his black eyes. She shook the image from her mind and quickened her steps.

She had her own endgame now.

Finn let a wave of numbness take over as she made her way through the ship to the training room.

She was coming for the Reliance . . . all of them.

ACKNOWLEDGMENTS

This book series has been a labor of love over the last decade. It started as the pipe dream of a little girl with a love of sci-fi and a desire to tell her own kind of story.

Seeing my writing in print has been my biggest dream come true, but it wouldn't have been possible without the help of some amazing people.

Firstly, I want to thank my husband, Jack, for your unending support. You came to me at a time when I needed you the most and helped to reinvigorate my desire and love for telling this story. Thank you for putting up with my crippling self-doubt and acting as my biggest cheerleader when I needed it most.

To Aaron, the supermodel, Kaija, the giver, Kaye and Karil, my fairy godmothers, and my parents; thank you for sticking with the book as it grew and changed. Your feedback and support have been integral in the evolution of this story.

Additionally, none of this would be possible without my editor and publisher at Endpapers Press. Andy, you believed in a debut author and have helped make a little girl's greatest wish a reality.

And lastly, to my daughter, River; you inspire me to be better and do better . . . every day. May you always have the courage to follow your dreams and the strength to see them through to the end.

www.ingramcontent.com/pod-product-compliance
Lightning Source LLC
Chambersburg PA
CBHW050354260626

47156CB00003B/726